QUILTERS of the
DOOR

A NOVEL BY
Ann Hazelwood

C&T PUBLISHING

Executive Book Editor: Elaine Brelsford
Copy Editor: Ann Hammel
Proofing: Hannah Alton
Graphic Design: Brittany Borden
Cover Design: Michael Buckingham

Published by C&T Publishing, Inc., P.O. Box 1456, Lafayette, CA 94549

This is a work of fiction. Names, characters, places, and incidents either are the product of the author's imagination or are used fictitiously, and any resemblance to actual persons, living or dead, businesses, companies, events, or locales is entirely coincidental.

We take great care to ensure that the information included in our products is accurate and presented in good faith, but no warranty is provided, nor are results guaranteed. Having no control over the choices of materials or procedures used, neither the author nor C&T Publishing, Inc., shall have any liability to any person or entity with respect to any loss or damage caused directly or indirectly by the information contained in this book. For your convenience, we post an up-to-date listing of corrections on our website (ctpub.com). If a correction is not already noted, please contact our customer service department at ctinfo@ctpub.com or P.O. Box 1456, Lafayette, CA 94549.

Trademark (™) and registered trademark (®) names are used throughout this book. Rather than use the symbols with every occurrence of a trademark or registered trademark name, we are using the names only in the editorial fashion and to the benefit of the owner, with no intention of infringement.

Library of Congress Control Number: 2020914954

Printed in the USA
10 9 8 7 6 5 4

Tributes and Dedication

After visiting Door County, Wisconsin, for over twenty years with my husband, Keith, my love and appreciation for the area has increased, thanks to the great hospitality industry there and the many locals who represent the peninsula so well.

Through my contacts and research, I met Barb Kinsey McKesson. Our lunches were extremely informative as we discussed the pulse of the local community and its history, politics, and current challenges. Barb is delightful and generously provided me with a wealth of information about Door County. Thank you, Barb!

As I began searching for my main character's home, I found a place that repeatedly drew my interest as I drove by. One fall day, I saw a woman raking leaves in the front yard. I stopped and introduced myself, communicating my interest in writing a fictional quilt series set in Door County. To my delight, I met Sara Bedore. She was more than happy to show me the interior of her family summer home and shared some of her family history with me. I fell in love with the cabin's charm and knew that it was perfect for Claire Stewart, my main character. I can't thank Sara and her family enough for letting me write about the seasons and fictional occurrences at this lovely place. Because of Sara's generous hospitality, I would like to dedicate this first novel of the Door County series to her. Thank you, Sara!

Ann Hazelwood

Introduction

Let me introduce you to my happy place. I am thrilled to have an opportunity through my publisher, C&T Publishing, to take you on a visit to Door County, Wisconsin, a place I have visited many times in the last twenty years. Many folks refer to Door County as the New England or Cape Cod of the Midwest.

Door County sits in the center of the upper Midwest's inland seas. Its shoreline comprises nearly 20% of Lake Michigan's 1600 miles of shoreline. Many of the county's 34 islands are accessible to the public. A year-round passenger ferry connects the northern part of the peninsula to Washington Island, its largest island with 700 permanent residents.

Here are a few statistics about this lovely area. There are 19 county parks, 11 historic lighthouses, more than a dozen marinas, over 100 art galleries and studios, 53 public swimming beaches, and 11 orchard markets. The county is a big producer of apples and cherries and is home to many yearly festivals. In 2019, Door County was voted Best Destination for Fall Foliage in *USA Today's 10 Best Readers' Choice Award* contest. Lest you think that it mimics the commercial feel of many vacation destinations, the vast majority of the county's land mass remains undeveloped, making it amenable to silent sports such as biking, hiking, birdwatching, and kayaking. This 70-mile-long peninsula packs a lot of punch for visitors looking for a unique vacation experience.

Throughout this series, I hope to engage you with much that the county has to offer. My research to write this series was done not only as a visitor, but also by getting to know the townspeople in their everyday lives. I am grateful for their generosity, frankness, and hospitality.

I want this series to be as real as being there yourself. I want you to taste the cherries, see the bright yellow maple trees, and smell the freshness of the Door County coffee made in the heart of the peninsula. As I have discovered, many of you have visited Door County, and when I announced that my new series would take you there, the response was "I love Door County!" I know that if you take this journey with me, you'll be telling your friends and family that you, too, have found your happy place. Visit www.doorcounty.com.

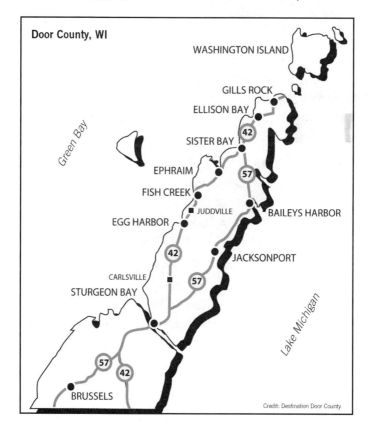

WHO ARE THE QUILTERS OF THE DOOR?

GRETA GREENSBURG is Swedish, in her sixties, and is one of the charter members of the club. As she leads the group, she holds firm in keeping to the tradition of only nine members who are diverse in their quilting styles. Greta makes quick and easy quilts and is one of the few members in the club who machine quilts.

MARTA BACHMAN is German. She's 57 and lives in Baileys Harbor. Her family owns a large orchard and dairy farm. Marta makes traditional quilts by hand. She typically has a large quilt frame set up in her home.

AVA MARIE CHANDLER is 54 and loves any kind of music. She served in the Army where she sang for anyone who would listen to her. She's blonde, vivacious and likes to make quilts that tell a story. She loves her alcohol, so no one knows when her flamboyant behavior will erupt. She lives in a Victorian house in Egg Harbor.

FRANCES McCRAKEN is the eldest member of the group at 78 years old. She regularly spends time in the local cemetery where her husband is buried. She lives in the historic Corner House in Sturgeon Bay and has a pristine antique quilt collection that she inherited. The quilts she makes use old blocks to make new designs.

LEE SUE CHAN is Filipina and is married to a cardiologist. They live in an ornate home in Ephraim. She is 48 years old and belongs to the Moravian Church, also in Ephraim. Lee is an art quilter who loves flowers and landscapes. She is an award-winning quilter who is known for her fine hand appliqué.

OLIVIA WILLIAMS is black and lives in an apartment over the Novel Bay Booksellers in Sturgeon Bay. She is 40, single and likes to tout the styles of the Gee's Bend quilts as well as quilts from the south. She is quiet in nature, but the quilts she makes are scrappy, bright, and bold.

RACHAEL MCCARTHY and her husband, Charlie, live on a farm between Egg Harbor and Fish Creek. She is 50 years old and has a part-time job bartending at the Bayside Tavern in Fish Creek. They have a successful barn quilt business and sell Christmas trees in season. Rachael makes their business unique by giving each customer a small wall quilt to match their purchased barn quilt.

GINGER GREENSBURG is a 39-year-old redhead who is Greta's niece. She and her husband own a shop in Sister Bay where they sell vintage and antique items. They reside upstairs and have two children. While she works in the shop, Ginger likes to make quilted crafts to sell and takes old quilt tops and repurposes them.

CLAIRE STEWART, 55, is single and is the main character of the series. She is the newest member of the quilting club because her friend Cher moved back to Missouri to take care of her mother. Claire was eager to leave Missouri and moved into Cher's cabin in Fish Creek. Greta and the club made a rare exception to let Claire replace Cher until Cher moved back to Door County. Claire, a blonde who is showing some gray streaks, is a quilter and watercolor artist who sells her artwork in galleries and on her website. Claire has a brother in Missouri who is a journalist and author, and her mother also lives in Missouri.

Chapter 1

"Claire Elizabeth Stewart," I said aloud as I drove along Interstate 55, "what are you doing?" I had so many thoughts going through my mind. Then I spotted a rest stop ahead. That just might provide me with a good place to turn around. I took a deep breath, activated my turn signal, and veered into the rest stop parking lot. I parked carefully since I was not accustomed to pulling a U-Haul. I got out of the car and looked at the container on wheels that carried the greater part of my most prized possessions. The air was chilly, so I rushed inside to get warm and to call Cher for some assurance. Thankfully, she answered quickly.

"Claire, what's up? Where are you now?" Cher asked.

"I'm at a rest stop off of Highway 55," I responded, feeling even more uneasy. "I think this just might be a crazy idea."

"Not again, for heaven's sake," Cher said, feigning an exasperated moan. "We've gone over everything a hundred times! It's normal for you to feel anxious. There are a lot of unknowns when moving to a new community, but it can be exciting, too!"

"Really?"

"Look, you already have a place to stay, and there's a new friend just waiting to meet you. I left some basic things for you until you can decide what to do permanently."

"I know, I know."

"You're arriving in Door County during the perfect season. I heard that the colors are at their peak. Fall was always my favorite time of year there." She paused. "What are you so worried about?"

"Well, leaving my mother, for starters, and to be honest, I'm not kidding myself about the fact that I'm running away from Austen, too."

"Your mother is fine. I'll check in on her. You know I will. Remember, she was all for you moving to Wisconsin. Forget Austen. He's obviously moved on, and so should you. The mere fact that he never came for you after you left is pretty telling, isn't it?"

"It is," I responded, feeling a familiar ache return. "I still can't believe I had the nerve to move out when he was at that medical conference, but if he had been anywhere around, I couldn't have done it."

"Look, Claire Bear, you'd better be on your way. Ericka will be looking for you. I gave you her cell number, so keep her informed if your plans change. You'll have everything you need when you get there."

"Yes, Cher Bear, I have everything," I lamented. "I have everything but confidence." I took a deep breath to calm myself. "How is your mom today?"

"She's pretty much out of it. Every day is different, but thanks for asking."

"You're a good daughter to have moved back to Perryville

to take care of her."

"And you're a good friend to take my place in Door County off my hands. It's perfect for an artist. You'll love it there, I promise."

"Okay, Cher Bear, if you say so. Remember, I can't promise that I'll buy your place until I've stayed there for a few months."

"I know. I'm not worried. You'd better be on your way now. I love you!"

"I love you, too!"

Cher and I had grown up together and attended the same schools. In elementary school, our fellow classmates called us Claire Bear and Cher Bear. As we grew older, we were the only ones who continued the tradition. It was a shared connection to our past. Cher and I had also attended art school together. When Cher married, she'd moved to Green Bay, Wisconsin. I missed her very much, but we texted or talked almost daily. Her marriage had fizzled after a couple of years, so she'd moved to Door County, a haven for artists up and down the peninsula. She'd pursued her art career much more than I had through the years. The thought of setting up my little studio where Cher had lived did seem exciting. From pictures she'd sent, the little village of Fish Creek appeared to be very charming.

I got a Diet Dr. Pepper out of a soda machine before I climbed back in my white Subaru. Cher had said that I had the perfect automobile for Wisconsin, so that was reassuring. As I got closer and closer to Wisconsin, I could see that it was going to be a beautiful state with charming barns and numerous signs urging me to buy cheese. I was blessed with light traffic on the journey, so it was easy for my eyes to wander across the landscape. All the while, I had many uncertainties running through my head. Would Austen ever know I had moved away? If so, would he care where?

Austen was Dr. Austen Page, a pediatrician in Perryville, Missouri. True and simple, he was idolized by many. When I'd met him, I hadn't known that he was a doctor. He enjoyed being with someone who had local connections. After knowing him for just a few months, I'd moved in with him. His home was lovely and provided me with a beautiful studio where I could make my painted wall quilts. I felt sure that I would never have that kind of opportunity again. In the beginning, it had been idyllic.

However, as time went on, it was evident that Austen did not want to get married. For the most part, I'd felt the same way, particularly at first. He seemed to really enjoy attending frequent social engagements with me and bragged about my abilities as an artist when we were out with others. I was fortunate in that many of his friends purchased my work.

My mother, Mary Elizabeth Stewart, was not happy about our relationship and never let me forget it. She would comment about how folks would talk, saying they would ask her point-blank if Austen and I were going to get married. I knew she wanted security for me. She often warned that my life would be incredibly challenging if I found I had to support myself in my mid-fifties. Mom was always nice to Austen, but he was perceptive enough to know how she felt about the marriage issue.

As the years progressed, I'd realized that I was spending more and more time alone. Austen and I socialized less and less. Our conversations became less and less frequent. I began to feel restless and unfulfilled in the relationship.

It was just undeniably clear that I needed to move on. Austen happened to be away at a four-day medical conference in Chicago. I knew it was the perfect time to move out without his interference.

Mom was pleased when I chose to move in with her. I waited and waited for Austen to call or come to talk with me, but he never did. I was hurt, but I knew it was the perfect way for us to end the relationship. After all that time together, there was nothing more to say, really. To her credit, Mom was kind enough not to say "I told you so."

In the midst of my deciding what to do next, Cher had announced that she was coming back to Perryville to take care of her mother, who was in the beginning stages of Alzheimer's disease. She also had a few other health issues, but Cher was adamant that she could provide the care her mother needed.

Even though I was the one to initiate the breakup with Austen, I still felt the sting of a failed relationship. Cher was the first to suggest that I move to Door County and take over her place. At first, I thought the idea was crazy, but I also thought it sounded perfect for my personal life as well as my little quilt business. I agreed to make the move even before telling Mom. I'd never forget the disappointed look on her face. After we talked, I assured her that Cher would be around if she needed help. Despite her own personal sadness at my decision, she was able to give me a hug and a smile of approval. Even now as I drove into unfamiliar territory, I remembered the warmth of her smile just as I entered Door County, Wisconsin.

Chapter 2

As soon as I crossed the bridge into an area that I would later learn was called Southern Door, the foliage became strikingly colorful. Sturgeon Bay, the largest town in Door County, was about to greet me. My destination of Fish Creek would take me on Route 42, which eventually snaked to the west side of the peninsula. I looked forward to exploring the east side in the future. To my left were the waters of Green Bay and to my right was Lake Michigan. The area was richly dotted with marinas. I slowed my speed, not wanting to miss a thing!

I loved seeing the many signs welcoming me to the charming "Door," as locals called it. When I saw a billboard for the Door County Coffee and Tea Company, I knew I had to stop. I was ready for a break, and I knew from Cher how popular their coffee was. Near Carlsville, I saw the beautiful white building on the left side of the road. I knew from the attractive fall blossoms and pumpkins that they used for decorations that I was in for a real treat.

As I entered, I recalled that the enterprise was a family-owned company and had been a Door County tradition since 1993. There was a café where I could order a cup of coffee and choose from a number of baked items showcased under a glass counter. There was no question that I had entered a world of cherries! There was cherry crumb coffee cake, cherry muffins, cherry nut cookies, cherry scones, and, of course, cherry pie. I asked the server to give me one of each! After all, what do we do when in Rome? When it came to coffee, I ordered cherry creme. Where else would I get such a unique coffee flavor?

While I waited for my order, I glanced towards a glass display wall that allowed me to see firsthand how the coffee was produced. I could have stood there all day! I watched the organized process with an odd sense of pride, somehow sensing that this new-to-me Door County would be my home.

After I paid for and collected my goodies, I ventured to the other side of the spacious store. Walls of packaged coffee and tea were displayed, enticing me to consider an additional purchase. As I took my first sip of the cherry creme coffee, I quickly picked up a package of it to enjoy in the cabin. I'd found my favorite coffee on my first trip to the store!

As I shopped around a bit, I saw that the store carried a variety of Door County souvenirs and a lovely array of shirts and clothing. I had always been a sucker for these types of items, but I tried to exercise some degree of restraint. After all, I hadn't even arrived at my destination yet, but the items certainly held my attention. There were cherries on so many of the selections. These items would be great to remember when it came time for Christmas shopping! Repeatedly, I had to remind myself that I was traveling and that I could not spend hours looking at everything.

As I stood in line to pay for my purchases, I noticed how it seemed as if every single person was so happy. The sales staff was pleasant, and the customers were excited to be there. I figured that this was the perfect place to stop as you entered the "Door," as well as the perfect place to stop before leaving the area. The only good thing about departing was that when I got in my car, the aromas of my purchases permeated the air. I inhaled deeply, keenly aware that my mood was improving greatly.

Driving on, I saw numerous signs for golf courses and wineries. The Door Peninsula Winery was straight ahead. I felt sure that many vacationers traveled home with a bottle of wine from there.

The next town I came to was Egg Harbor. What a precious name for a village! Traffic was a bit heavy as I made my way, but I was grateful for a closer look at what this little village had to offer. There were darling shops and restaurants, but when I saw Main Street Market, I remembered how Cher had told me that I would likely be doing my shopping there because they had such unique foods and produce. Perhaps a quick stop might be smart, since I knew there would not be a crumb of anything in Cher's cabin.

When I walked in the door, there was a coffee bar with treats to greet me as I got my cart. The neat and tidy place was very appealing. The beautiful array of produce caused my mouth to water. Of course, I had to have a bag of cherries, and the Honeycrisp apples were right in season. I also got my staple of bananas as I headed towards the expansive aisles of wine. Cherry wine? Why not? I wasn't a sweet wine person, but who wouldn't love cherry wine? My appetite was filling my grocery cart!

I could have stayed another half hour, but I reminded myself that I still wasn't home. The attendant at the checkout lane engaged me in pleasant conversation, and the elderly man bagging my groceries insisted on carrying them out for me. I decided that I could certainly get used to this friendly, easy lifestyle.

Chapter 3

As I drove to Fish Creek, I nibbled on the cherries, which were delightful. Passing a community called Juddville, I wondered how it had gotten such a name. I saw many tucked-away galleries amid the beautiful scenery. How quaint and inspirational to have a studio in this kind of creative environment. The road to my destination was up, down, and curvy as I drove down the final hill to enter Fish Creek. My excitement and curiosity grew knowing I was minutes away from a completely fresh start.

There was a four-way stop in the center of Fish Creek. Cher had said that there were no traffic lights in Door County. As I waited my turn, I noticed that the area was teeming with pedestrian tourists. I had to take care not to run into distracted people. I glanced at Cher's instructions, which told me to turn left, but my curiosity wanted me to turn right. Obediently, I turned left and drove slowly so I could observe the shops that lined both sides of the street. The bay was to my right. I could see it as I passed a couple of streets. Cher's place must have been closer to the water than

I'd realized. My GPS indicated that I should make another left on the corner where the Church of the Atonement was situated. The charming building was no bigger than most folks' living rooms and was nestled in a wood-like setting. I knew I'd have to check it out at some later date. I saw the Cottage Row street sign at the same time as my GPS announced that I had arrived at my destination. I looked straight ahead, and there was the small log cabin that Cher had described.

I pulled into the length of the grassy drive and saw an expansive front yard edged by tall cedar trees. I stayed in the car for a moment to take it in. Would and could this be my permanent home? I got out of the car and followed the steppingstones to the entrance of the cabin. The entire front porch was enclosed by glass and screens. Cher had filled it with wicker furniture that fit the space perfectly. I then noticed a car pulling in behind my U-Haul.

"Claire?" a voice called out. A woman stepped out of the vehicle and approached me.

"Yes?" I responded.

"I'm Ericka Hansen, Cher's friend."

"Oh, yes, of course. She told me you'd meet up with me when I arrived. It's nice to meet you."

Ericka gave me a welcoming hug. Her flurry of long reddish hair and pretty smile put me at ease. "You've just arrived?" she asked. "So, what do you think? It's pretty cute, isn't it?"

"Yes, it is," I said, looking it over. "It's small, but the setting is absolutely beautiful, and it's right in the heart of Fish Creek."

"Yes, and it's great for me as well because I always have

a place to park, which is a challenge around here during the tourist season. Hey, let's get you inside. I have my key if you don't have yours handy. George, my brother, will be over later to help you unload. He knows where to take the U-Haul when it's empty."

"That is so nice of him," I said. "Who lives in the gorgeous house next door?"

Ericka smiled. "Their last name is Bittner. Their landscaping is beautiful, isn't it? They're permanent residents but they are in Florida a lot. I think you'll like them. On second thought, before we go inside, perhaps I need to walk you around the house before it gets dark," she offered.

"Sure, let's do that."

Chapter 4

As we walked closer to the cabin, Ericka explained that the logs were Scandinavian-style flat logs that had been transported from Peninsula State Park to here in Fish Creek sometime in the 1940s. She then pointed out the carved numbers in some of the logs, showing the system for reconstruction when the structure had been relocated to Fish Creek.

"How very interesting!" I remarked. As we rounded the side of the house, I couldn't help but be surprised by the size of the backyard. "Oh! There's no yard to speak of."

"Not really. This high cliff has its good points and bad points. You can see where Cher added the bathroom, which comes close to the cliff. She's never had any problem with any debris coming down, though. It's pretty high up, isn't it?"

I nodded, looking up at the wooded cliff. "I'll bet it offers a bit of protection from wind. I see that there's no basement."

"No. They put these stone supports in when they had to do the plumbing for the addition. There's space under there, so don't get freaked out if you hear a critter or two running around."

I chuckled nervously. "Oh dear! We'll see how it goes if

that ever happens!" As we took more steps around the back of the house, I said, "These windows seem new and secure."

"Yes, and Cher painted a nice little red inner trim on them," Ericka commented. "Now, you know, there's no air conditioning," she explained as we rounded the house and returned to the front yard. "Not many people have it here because the season is so short. There's almost always a lovely breeze on this porch. Cher and I have spent many evenings sitting out here just enjoying the breeze."

"These huge cedar trees are amazing! They must provide some wonderful shade. I love the fire pit in the front yard."

Ericka smiled. "Yes, Cher has had so many nice gatherings around that fire pit. She left you two nice wooden lawn chairs, too, so enjoy!"

"Well, I guess we'd better go inside," I suggested, eager to see the interior of the cabin.

"I'll give George a call and ask him to come over with his friend to start unloading."

Entering the narrow porch, I knew immediately that this was where I would do my painting. In the daytime, the light would be perfect. The next room was the living room. It was a small area, but a beautiful, stately stone fireplace comprised the back wall. The mantel was filled with framed pictures, creating a homey feel. Beside the fireplace was a large copper container filled with firewood ready to burn, and along the wall was a comfy-looking couch that Cher had left behind.

"You have wood and a couch. What more could you want?" Ericka joked.

I laughed. "I love the hardwood floors."

"They're in every room. Here's the little kitchen. Pretty cute, if I do say so. I guess you could call it vintage decor."

I smiled. "Yes, perhaps 1950s from the looks of the sink. I love the cherry-print curtain, tablecloth, and accessories. That cabinet looks quite old."

"Yes, that holds most of the dishes, I think. It was probably too large for Cher to move."

"I really like this table for four right by the window that looks onto the porch. There's probably a nice breeze through here. Each antique chair is different. How charming."

"I hope you didn't bring a lot of furniture with you."

I shook my head. "I mostly brought things for my bedroom and studio. I just noticed the light fixtures. How clever and appropriate for a little log cabin." Cher's place was turning out to be a cozy little hideaway that would suit me just fine.

"So, here's the nicest room," Ericka said, leading me into a spacious bathroom. "This lengthy vanity, large tub, shower, and cabinetry are all new. They used the back of the stone fireplace for this wall."

"Yes, I love it," I commented. "I see that there's an old shed on this side of the house. I forgot to ask about it when we walked around outside. What's in there?"

"I couldn't tell you, but it's likely just storage. It looks as old as the cabin."

"An outhouse at one time, perhaps?"

Ericka laughed. "Cher says not. Let's go upstairs. The steps are narrow, so be careful."

"Oh dear! I hope my queen mattress will fit up these steps."

"Not to worry. I think Cher had a decent-sized bed up here. You have a room on each side."

"From Cher's photos, I thought one could be my office and the other could be where I sleep." We took a quick look at both rooms. "Why is there a little sink in each of the bedrooms?"

"It's weird, I know, but at some point, maybe it was the thing to do."

"Well, I won't have to go downstairs to brush my teeth or get a drink of water," I joked.

"There you go!"

Chapter 5

"Oh, I think I hear George arriving," Ericka said as she turned and went downstairs. I followed, eager to begin unloading my belongings. Ericka opened the door as two men approached.

"Come on in," she said, smiling. "Claire, this is my brother George and his friend Rob."

"Nice to meet you both," I said, shaking their hands. "Thanks so much for helping me out."

"Anything for Sis," George said, grinning. "Welcome to Door County. How do you like your new home?"

"I think so far, it's good," I said, but I could hear the hesitation in my own voice. My confidence began to waver once again. "I'm trying to take it all in. I sure hope we can find room for everything that I brought with me."

"No worries," George said as he and Rob turned to go back outside.

I followed them, wanting to feel assured that I was in good hands. When George opened the back of the U-Haul, he quickly assessed the contents.

"Glad to see a lot of what you have is organized," he said. "You ladies go back inside. As we bring things in, tell us what rooms to take it to."

"Are you sure?" I asked.

He nodded.

Ericka and I returned inside, and the process began. Thankfully, I had everything labeled. Soon, I was beginning to wonder if there was going to be any room left to walk! Eventually, George and Rob took a break and left for a bit. When they returned, they brought us food from Pelletier's.

"You'll be relying on that café," Ericka told me. "It's within walking distance from here. This is my treat, Claire," she said as she handed George some cash. She turned to me with a wide smile and said, "Welcome to Fish Creek!"

I returned her smile. "I should be the one treating," I protested.

Rob interrupted by saying, "Well, I suggest you keep your fingers crossed, because your mattress is the next thing to go up those stairs."

Everyone laughed except me. I looked nervously up the stairs and then back at George. They laughed again at my concerns as if the challenge were really of no consequence. Something about their comfortableness with one another soothed me. Cher must have developed good friendships here. "Did you guys know Cher very well?" I asked.

"Sure. This is a small community," George replied. "Ericka was really bummed about her leaving until she heard you were moving in."

I smiled and looked at Ericka.

"You should fit in just fine, being an artist and all," Rob added.

"I hope you're right. It feels odd to be somewhere where I don't know anyone," I admitted.

"You know us!" George corrected me. "Why don't we celebrate your arrival with a drink tonight down at the Bayside? You'll meet a lot of locals there."

"The Bayside?" I asked.

"It's the local bar on Main Street called Bayside Tavern," Ericka explained.

"I'm not sure I should do that," I said with a sigh. "I have a lot to do here."

"Ericka will talk you into it," George said with a grin. "What do you say we get this bed set up so you can sleep in it tonight?"

"Do you mind?" I asked, delighted that I would be able to sleep in my own bed on this first night.

"Let's go." George motioned to Rob.

They returned to the trailer and the process continued. I stayed on the porch and watched the activity. As I saw the joking and love between George and Ericka, I thought of my own brother. Michael and I never seemed that relaxed around one another. We were so different. He was a writer and I was a painter. Once he had secured his current job as the editor of a newspaper in Springfield, he'd seemed to be truly in his element. I thought that Michael viewed me as the little sister who was spoiled and flighty. We were generally friendly, but it was my impression that he always liked to think that the world revolved around him.

"So, what do you think about the welcome drink idea, Claire?" Ericka asked when the guys were outside. "The break would do you good."

"Okay, but just one drink," I answered. "I'm curious to

see what that place is like since the locals congregate there."

"Great," Ericka responded. "We'll go at about seven, and I promise to get you out of there after one drink."

"Deal!" I agreed.

"Okay, we're done!" George announced. "I'll return the U-Haul."

"What do I owe you guys?" I asked.

George and Rob exchanged glances and smiled conspiratorially. "I'd say a round of drinks ought to do it," George teased.

"Works for me," Rob added with a wink.

Chapter 6

After the guys left, Ericka and I sat on the porch. Although the men had done all the heavy lifting, I suddenly welcomed a moment to rest. "So much has happened so quickly," I stated with a sigh. "I don't know where to start."

"Take one step at a time, which means that we need to get linens on your bed. You have all winter to unpack."

"You're right about that," I agreed. "The thought of spending winters out here frightens me a bit. I hear it's brutal."

Ericka smiled. "Actually, it's kind of nice. All the tourists are gone, which means there's less traffic. You can get right in at your favorite restaurant, and there's a peacefulness about it that we all love."

"Hmmm," I answered, thinking about what she had said.

"There's plenty to do," Ericka continued. "Everyone looks forward to the Fish Creek Winter Festival. It's also snowmobiling and skiing season for those who love it. Your location is such that you can walk to many places right here in town, like the library."

"I'm disappointed that the cabin doesn't have a garage. I've always had one," I commented.

"You won't see many garages around here since lots of people leave during the winter. I agree that some of the snowdrifts are a problem, and they don't really start melting until April."

"April!" I exclaimed, my eyes widening. "Yikes!"

Ericka laughed and quickly stood up. "Let's get busy and get that bed made!"

Ericka helped me with the new flannel sheets I'd been dying to use. She agreed that they would come in handy. I was so lucky to have Ericka with me throughout this settling-in process. Our activities kept me busy enough to not realize that I had received text messages from both Mom and Cher.

Taking a breath, Ericka finally said, "I'll be back at seven so we can walk to Bayside together. It's a very casual place, so come as you are."

I nodded obediently and then warned, "One drink, remember?"

"One drink," she confirmed.

When Ericka left, I sat on the couch and called Mom.

"Oh, honey, I'm so glad you arrived safe and sound."

"I did, and Cher's friends have been extremely helpful. Everything is unloaded! It's a good thing I got a really early start this morning."

"Well, it sounds like you need a good night's sleep. I'll sleep better now that I've heard from you."

"Good. I'll call you tomorrow, okay?"

My mother would never understand why I had agreed to have a drink with my new Fish Creek friends. I even questioned my own decision. Telling her would only mean that she would worry about me unnecessarily. My next call was to Cher.

"Thank goodness! I was getting worried about you," Cher responded immediately.

"Did you think I had changed my mind and was heading home?"

She laughed.

"Ericka was here right away, and George and Rob got me unloaded."

"George is such a sweetheart, and he's easy on the eyes, I might add."

"Not to worry, Cher Bear. I came here to clear my head of such nonsense. I did agree to have a drink with the three of them at Bayside tonight as sort of a welcoming thing."

"Darn! I'm so jealous. I love that place. Rachael, one of the quilters you'll meet, sometimes bartends there on the weekends. She won't be there tonight."

"Well, I've got to freshen up, so I'd better go. I'll keep you informed. Right now, I'm just happy that my bed fit in the bedroom and it's all made up, ready for me to hop in. Oh, how's your mom?"

"She's good. Have fun! Love you, Claire Bear!"

"Love you, too!"

I quickly put on a clean sweatshirt and freshened up my makeup. I had to chuckle to myself; I had only been in town one day, and here I was, hitting the local pub!

Chapter 7

It was just after seven when Ericka knocked and then came directly through my unlocked door.

"Claire, I'm here," she called up the steps. "You didn't go to sleep on me, did you?"

"I'm ready," I replied, quickly making my way down the steps.

"It's getting colder, so button up."

I grabbed my sock cap and the heavier coat I'd brought.

Just down the road was the Bayside Tavern. Still observing the newness of the area, I took in what I could from the shops and restaurants we passed along the way. The coldness of the air produced steam from our breath. The Bayside Tavern appeared to be a small place from the street, but that was misleading. We walked into a crowded, noisy tavern, which we from the Midwest would call a sports bar. Multiple large screens were displayed around the room. Thank goodness that it was a smoke-free establishment.

"Oh, they're over here!" Ericka motioned as she walked to a table for four.

"I just told George that I thought you'd be a no-show," Rob teased.

I laughed as I removed my hat. "I intend to keep my promise and pay my workers," I quipped. I wasn't sure what to order until Ericka suggested I try a beer called the Spotted Cow. She said it was a Wisconsin thing — a cream-ale-style — that was extremely popular. I wasn't a beer drinker, but I hadn't been at all disappointed with any cherry-flavored treat I'd tested so far. It was worth a try, just to say that I'd had one.

Everyone was anxious for me to meet this person and that person, but the noise from the chatter and music was so intense that I wasn't sure I'd heard anyone's names. I felt very much like a stranger in this massive crowd. The guys were having their own fun, and it wasn't long before Ericka noticed that I was tired, even though I was trying my best to look like I was having fun. When she got close to my ear and suggested that we leave, I knew she "got" me. What a relief to feel like I had a good friend so soon after arriving here. We said our goodbyes, and the guys thanked me for paying for their drinks. We headed out into the cold, but it was refreshing after being in the claustrophobic room.

"I'll stop by in the morning to check on you," Ericka said. Then she added, "I have a surprise for you."

"Oh, that's nice. I love surprises," I said, wondering what it might be.

When Ericka dropped me off and left, I felt a sense of relief and was anxious to find my bed. Seeing my things crammed into the cabin was surreal. What would Austen say if he could see me now? I knew he would think I'd lost my mind, and it would confirm to him that I was indeed too eccentric for him. He'd liked to tease me about having an artist's mentality. Would I regret leaving him and the beautiful home I'd left behind? It was a bit too early to know. I was certain that I would continually be haunted by why I hadn't been important enough for him to come after me. I tried to picture his face when he'd walked into the house to find me gone, then tried to shake those thoughts out of my mind.

My mother had made a quilt for me, and it was one of the first things I had unpacked. Exhausted from the long drive and the events of the day, I dropped into bed and pulled the quilt up to my neck. It gave me both warmth and comfort. I had many things to think about. The next day would be a full day of unpacking. It would be fun to make that first fire in the fireplace and set up my studio on the porch. I checked my phone for any late messages. Still nothing from Austen.

I slept until around three, when I heard the wind howling around the little cabin. It sounded like tree branches were hitting the windows. I wrapped the quilt around me and decided to check downstairs. I flipped on every light switch I could find, then carefully descended down the stairs and headed for the kitchen to get a bottle of water. The kitchen boxes would have to be a priority when I unpacked; I had to squeeze between them to get to anything. I looked out each window. There was nothing but complete darkness. A good distance away, there was a streetlight. In time, I would get to know every sound here and would likely sleep through them all, but for now, I was exhausted. I looked at the comfy, worn couch and decided I'd camp there until morning. Mother's simple Nine-Patch quilt was warm enough as I snuggled to fit in the space. I pictured a fire before me and slipped into a deep Wisconsin sleep.

Chapter 8

The next morning, the sun came shining through the living room window to greet me. This would be my first official day living in Fish Creek. I was surprised at how comfortable the couch had been. I kept the quilt wrapped around me as I went to the kitchen to start my red Keurig coffee maker that was peeking out of one of the boxes. I placed it by the kitchen sink and prepared it for my usual Pike Place coffee from Starbucks, which I'd brought with me. When I looked out of the kitchen window through the porch, I saw an amazing sunrise. I would have to walk down to the marina early one morning to get a better view. I grabbed a banana to eat as I waited for each drip to enter my coffee cup. Every box staring at me in the kitchen would have to be addressed today. I had just taken the first sip of coffee when my cell phone rang. It was Ericka.

"Did I wake you?" she asked.

"No, not really. I'm having my first cup of coffee and staring at these boxes."

"Take your time. I'm sure you feel overwhelmed. I hope you slept okay."

"I did, thank you."

"I'm sorry to be calling so early, but I wanted to stop by your place to bring you something before I go to work."

"I have to warn you that I'm not dressed yet. Will you have time for a cup of coffee?"

"Perhaps. I'll see you in about fifteen minutes, okay?"

"Okay," I agreed, wondering why her gift couldn't wait. Knowing that I had a few minutes before Ericka arrived, I went upstairs to dress, putting on jeans and a sweatshirt. Would I ever be able to wear anything else while living here? By the time I finished dressing and combing my hair, I heard Ericka at the door. When I opened it, she was standing there with a fluffy golden cat in her arms.

"Well, good morning, you two," I said, laughing.

"Good morning! This is Puff."

I chuckled. "Okay, Puff. Is she related to Dick and Jane, by chance?"

Ericka laughed.

"Come on in. You didn't tell me you had a cat. Don't you leave her at home while you're at work?"

"Oh, she's not mine," Ericka said simply.

"Whose is she?"

"Yours."

"Oh, I don't think so," I said, confused.

"She lived here with Cher. Not to worry. I brought everything she needs, including her litter box."

She put Puff on the floor, and the cat immediately began exploring the surroundings.

I didn't know what to say as I watched Puff gingerly sniff my boxes. Finally, I managed to protest, "Cher never said anything about a cat."

"I was afraid of that," Ericka said apologetically. "Cats are no problem. I sneeze when she's around, so I know I have an allergic reaction to them, or else I would keep her. That's why Cher couldn't take her to her mother's house."

"This is crazy!"

"Look, she's no problem. I'd never even see her around when I came over here. She likes hiding places, like under the bed and couch. I'd see her perched on the chair on the porch occasionally, but she won't be under your feet, I promise."

"Oh, I don't think I can do this."

"Hey, give it a try. I have to run. Call me if you need anything and I'll stop by after work." Ericka got ready to depart.

"Ericka!" I said in dismay as I watched her leave. I looked at the cat staring up at me. "Okay, cat. This is the way it's going to be for now. There will be no messes in this house, including shedding. I hate cat hair. You will stay off my bed and use the litter box on the porch. And — I'll try to find you a new home." The cat gave a slight purr and went gallivanting up the stairs, oblivious to my plans. I went in the kitchen to take another sip of coffee as I called Cher. The call went to voicemail. Naturally. I waited for the beep and then said, "Okay, Cher Bear. We need to talk ASAP. It's about your cat. A cat was not part of the deal!"

Chapter 9

While in the kitchen, I began unpacking boxes. Empty boxes were going on the porch for the moment, as there was a light mist coming down outside. So much for the sunny day that had greeted me earlier. Cher had said that weather here could change on the hour, just like in Missouri. Cher had left some kitchen things behind, so I had duplicates of several items. That was not good, considering that there was only a small space for everything in the kitchen. Hours later, I had achieved a great deal. It was only then that I wondered where I would find Puff. I looked in the living room before I went upstairs. "Puff, where are you?" I called out. When I looked in the bedroom, I was shocked to see her sprawled on top of my quilt!

"Off! Off!" I commanded loudly as I gathered the quilt in my arms and shook it out. Puff dashed from the room and scampered down the steps. How could I keep that from happening again? Of all things, how had I unexpectedly inherited a cat? My cell phone rang. "Hi, Mom," I answered, still feeling frustrated.

"How did you sleep on your first night, sweetie?"

"I did fine, but it's quite different. I think I had fooled myself into thinking about this as a little vacation instead of my permanent residence."

"You always have a home here, remember."

"I know, but for some reason, I think I needed to make this move."

"I think so, too."

"I had an unexpected surprise this morning."

"You did?"

"Cher left her cat behind. Her friend Ericka was keeping it until I arrived. Ericka made it sound like it came with the place! Both Ericka and Cher gave allergies as reasons for not keeping it themselves."

Mom chuckled. "Well, how about that? I think it may be nice company for you. I remember when you used to beg for a pet. Now you finally have a cat. What kind is it?"

"I have no idea. She's golden with a lot of hair. Cher supposedly called her Puff, like in the Dick and Jane readers."

"Oh, how cute! Be happy that she's at home there — and she may remind you that you're the stranger."

"Oh, great," I moaned, thinking there may indeed be some truth to that. "Hey, I don't suppose you've run into Austen anywhere, have you?"

"No," Mom said flatly. "Now, you just forget about him. He's obviously forgotten about you."

"That hurts, Mom," I replied quietly.

"You're not a teenager anymore, Claire. Thank goodness the two of you didn't get married after all. By the way, I'm going to see Hilda tomorrow. I hope she'll recognize me."

"Tell her hello from me, and tell Cher that I hope her cat

survives with me."

"Claire, shame on you. You'd better get some unpacking done."

"Yes, you're probably right. Enjoy your visit with Hilda." I honestly thought I heard her chuckling as she hung up! I set the phone down and stared out the window. Why had I asked her about Austen? I wished I hadn't. She would surely have told me if she'd seen him or if he had called. He didn't use any social media because of his position, so I had no other way of knowing what he was up to. Mom was right. It was time to resume unpacking.

The very last box in the kitchen held my one and only cookbook. Mom said I should never be without it. Cher had left several others behind. One read *Cherry Cocktails and Appetizers*. Another read *All About Cherries,* and the other said *Cheery Cherry Bakes*. When in Door County, it was all about cherries, I guessed. The books did look appealing, and when I had time, I intended to look through them. I placed my cookbook on the shelf with the others. The day was passing quickly. Puff wasn't anywhere to be found, and at the moment, I didn't care. I was getting hungry and wondered whether to go out or not when I saw had a missed call on my phone. It was Ericka.

Chapter 10

"I'm just leaving work, and I thought I'd check on you."

"What you're really checking on is the cat — to see if she's still alive," I joked.

"Her name is Puff. Do you need anything? Did you get some things unpacked?"

"The kitchen is done. I put the boxes on the porch for now."

"Well, Monday is trash day, so break them down and put them in the blue trash can behind the house. Another thing you'll want to do soon is go to the post office and make sure they have your name associated with Cher's address. You do know that there is no mail delivery, don't you?"

"Oh?"

"You go to the post office not far from you. It's just down the street. It's also where the library is, so you'll want to visit that soon. The mail usually arrives between eleven and noon on an average day. It's actually a nice walk for you."

"Okay, I'll do that tomorrow. You've been extremely helpful, Ericka, with the exception of the cat, of course."

"The cat's name is Puff, and I think the two of you will be fine."

We hung up, and I knew I was lucky to have Ericka here in Fish Creek. Finally, a call came in from Cher.

"How could you?" I began in a huff. "A cat?"

"Calm down, Claire Bear. She's no trouble, and the cabin has been her home. How is everything else?"

"Okay, I guess," I mumbled.

"Don't forget that Saturday is your first quilt meeting. It's at the library at ten sharp, so don't be late. Most of the time, they're in the big meeting room there, if it's not booked. They're expecting you, so play nice. I had to jump through a few hoops to let them take you as my replacement. Like I told you, no one new typically joins until someone dies!"

"Gee, thanks! No pressure! Should I bring one of my wall quilts so they can know what kind of work I do?"

"Yes, that would be great. I tried to explain your work to them, but I'm not sure how much they understood. They will likely each introduce themselves. Greta has a strong personality and takes charge of the group most of the time. She has a heavy Swedish accent and a big personality, but don't let her scare you."

I chuckled. "I'm not sure I really need this group, but it's nice of you to suggest it."

"Yes, you do need this group! It will be a big asset for your business, and they'll help you get to know the Door community. Have you set up a place to work?"

"Not yet, but I love the porch, and especially all the light there for painting. I'll probably have to sew in the spare room upstairs."

"Just so you know, Puff occupies one of the chairs on the porch most of the time. The afternoon sun hits just right for her. In the winter, keep that little heater on out there. Hopefully it's still working."

"Well, evidently your cat seems to like to sleep at the end of your bed, too. I had to chase her off the quilt that Mom made for me."

Cher snickered. "Yes, that's where she likes to sleep at night. She won't bother you. All you have to do is feed her once a day and clean out her litter box."

"You make it sound so easy! How is your mom doing? Mom said she would be visiting her soon."

"Your mother has been so good about sending us food. She must think I don't cook — like you!"

We laughed together, but then I became serious. "I know it's difficult for you, Cher. Hang in there. I know your mom appreciates having you there."

"Some days, she doesn't even know who she's with. It's so sad. I just can't put her in a home, though. Plus, it's terribly expensive."

"I pray for both of you," I assured my good friend. "Well, I'm about to go out and find some hot chowder to eat for dinner. After all, it's one of the reasons I agreed to move here."

Cher chuckled. "If you walk straight out and turn left, the White Gull Inn's chowder is amazing. If you turn right, The Cookery is down the street. They're known for their whitefish chowder."

"Whitefish chowder it is. Thanks for checking on me."

"Give Puff a hug from me."

"In your dreams, Cher Bear."

"I still love you, Claire Bear."

"I love you, too." I shook my head and put on my coat, ready to head into the drizzle. It was an easy decision to drive instead of walk.

Chapter 11

The Cookery was easy to find, and I was lucky to find a parking space right in front. The two-story building had large windows so diners could see outdoors. The entrance was quite inviting, and I saw a counter of delicious goodies to purchase for takeout. I spotted cherry pies that looked like they'd just come out of the oven. They were extremely tempting.

Despite the nasty weather, it was a busy night at the restaurant. I was thankful that I got seated quickly. I ordered a fancy cherry cocktail, a bowl of whitefish chowder, and the slider appetizer. My appetite was growing. While I waited for the food, I observed who I presumed were mostly tourists. There were families with grandmas, retired couples, and young folks in love holding hands.

The meal did not disappoint. Everything was delicious. I knew I wanted this experience again, so when I got to the counter to pay, I ordered a pint of whitefish chowder and a whole cherry pie to go! Hey, when in Rome, remember?

When I returned home, it was dark. The house sat so

far back from the street that the little porch light could hardly be seen. When I opened the door, I heard a tiny meow. Puff jumped off her cushy porch chair and ran upstairs in a flash. I knew exactly what I would find when I went up.

As I got undressed for bed, Puff settled in comfortably on the quilt. I unpacked more clothes. Then I said, "Your time is up, Puff. I'm going to bed and I am not sharing it with you, remember?" I lifted the quilt, and she ran out of the room. I quickly shut the door, brushed off the quilt, and turned back the sheets for a good night's rest. Sleep came easier than the night before, which I took as a good sign.

The next morning, I told myself that I needed to scout out the library and a few other places in town. The foliage was still beautiful, so it would add to my experience. As I dressed, I wondered where Puff had spent the night.

To my surprise, as soon as I opened the bedroom door, there stood Puff, waiting for a chance to slip in. I quickly shut the door, leaving her at the top of the stairs while I made my way down. I knew she'd have to come down for her breakfast. I waited for the Keurig to make my first cup of coffee. I loved how the coffee maker matched the cherry-themed decor of the kitchen. I thought about heading to Pelletier's for breakfast; I knew they opened at seven thirty. I was surprised to get a text from Cher.

. . .Happy Fish Creek Fallfest! Wish I was there! How is Puff?

I sat down at the table and sighed. I'd had no idea about a Fallfest. Oh well.

> . . .*Thanks for the warning! Your cat is*
> *alive and well.*

. . .**Her name is Puff. Be nice! Enjoy the quilt
club tomorrow.**

I sent her a smiley face and proceeded to pour Puff's food into her dish. I called out to her, but no cat appeared. Walking to the porch, I observed the morning sun and looked for the best place to set up an easel. The porch certainly needed a good cleaning, as did the rest of the place. When I returned to the kitchen, Puff was eagerly eating her food. After I nibbled on the crust of the pie, I decided to don my jacket and take that morning walk. By the time I left, Puff was settled in her chair, content to watch me leave. I waved to her, surprising myself a bit with the action.

Chapter 12

As I left the driveway, I walked closer to look at the Church of the Atonement, which turned out to be an Episcopal church. I decided to attend a service there sometime. Across the street, the Community Church also looked inviting. To my left was the White Gull Inn. I'd heard that they were famous for their fish boils and candlelight dinners. Both sounded wonderful.

I decided to walk straight, which took me to the Alibi Marina. Water rushed against any obstacle, and it appeared that most of the boats were anchored down for the season. I observed the beautiful condos and cottages and wondered about the people who might inhabit them. I couldn't imagine having the luxury of a beautiful marina as a front yard; however, it occurred to me that this amazing setting was within walking distance from my new home. I turned around and went back up to Main Street. At this hour, most of the shops were not open. I did see a woman in a pickup truck pull up to various places on the street and replace mums that had finished blooming. How clever it was to keep the fall decor fresh for tourists.

I passed many colorful trees, and I took the time to photograph a number of them with my phone. So far, there was no sign of the library. I finally asked a woman going into The Cookery where it was, and she said it was close by and instructed me to keep walking. I did just that until I saw a sign for a coffee shop called the Blue Horse Beach Cafe. The sign read "Bites and brews in quaint warm digs." I had to go in.

I walked up the steps to enter and was immediately pleased by what I saw. A counter of yummy pastries and a large sign offering every kind of coffee I could imagine tempted me. Comfy chairs and tables were situated across from the counter, but I was interested in sitting in the glassed-in porch so I could look out onto the street. I ordered a pumpkin latte when I saw the fancy pumpkin design the barista could make on the top. How did she do that? I added an egg sandwich to eat in the restaurant and a couple of pastries to take with me. I joined the other customers on the porch when I saw a small table for two available. I knew instantly that this would be one of my preferred places to hang out.

While I enjoyed the sandwich, my attention was drawn to a man looking at his phone. He seemed to be deep in thought. The dark red scarf he wore complemented his dark hair. I loved watching people and always liked to try to imagine what their lives were like. Did he come here every day? I felt that he was a local person rather than a tourist. When the customers at the table next to me left, I took advantage of the quiet to check some emails on my phone. I looked up and caught the man with the scarf looking at me before returning my attention to the emails. Several other times, I felt his gaze on me. I started to feel uncomfortable. I decided to leave, glancing his way to make certain that I didn't know him. Confirming that, I gathered my things and made my way out of the restaurant.

I turned the corner to see a sign for the library. It appeared that the post office and library shared a space. Arriving at my destination, it felt good to come in from the chilly air. At the post office, the postal worker greeted and aided me as I worked to change my address. That little transaction didn't take long. Having completed it, I asked the worker if he could tell me the location of the room where the quilters met. He gave me a solemn gaze.

"I'm sorry, but that quilt group is not open to the public," he said rather flatly. "Did you know that?"

I nodded. "Yes, but I'm a new member — I'm replacing someone," I explained.

He looked at me as if he held me in suspicion. Then, with a change of demeanor, he relented and said, "Okay, just go down that hallway. On your left is a large meeting room. You know, they don't meet until tomorrow."

"Thank you!" I responded, relieved to receive the information and eager to move along. As I traveled down the hallway, I saw the tourist information office. I walked inside to see a large wall of brochures. The woman behind the desk greeted me and asked if I needed help. "I'm a new resident, and I just thought I'd see what you have here," I replied.

"Oh, well, then I suggest you pick up a copy of the *Door County Pulse*. It's stacked up there. It has a lot of local news."

"Oh, that's helpful. Thank you."

"Most people pick it up here when they come for their mail."

"I see. Well, thanks again."

Eventually, I located the room where the quilters would gather the next day. Now I knew where to go, had successfully changed my address, and had also happened across a newspaper that would help me find my way in these new surroundings. What a productive morning!

Chapter 13

Walking back home, I felt much more confident about my surroundings. There were so many crosswalks for tourists, which as a pedestrian, I was grateful for. Also, I noticed how willing drivers were to watch out for those walking. I purposely walked on the opposite side of the street going home so I could look closer at the businesses on that side. Many had placed end-of-season sale signs in their windows. As I passed Edgewater Cottages and Holiday Harbor Cottages, I noticed how their occupancy was filled in this busy season. They were in the center of Fish Creek, facing Main Street with their cottages backing up to the water. As I strolled, I happened across a restaurant called Juniper's. I looked up to see a second outdoor level for dining. It had a bar and a retail component as well. I looked forward to dining there someday. There was so much to explore in this small town!

I found it necessary to pick up my pace as I felt the air getting cooler. I was glad to get home and feel welcomed by the warmth of the cozy cabin. Puff was curled up on her wicker chair and raised her head to see who was coming in the door.

Was she expecting Cher? When she saw that it was me, she went back to sleep.

As I stepped around and over boxes, I was reminded that I still had a big task at hand. I removed my jacket and put away the goodies from the Blue Horse Beach Cafe. Was it too soon to make a fire? It sure would feel good on this chilly day. Maybe I should text Cher and ask about the fireplace. I retrieved my cell phone from my purse.

> **...It's a nice day for a fire. Are all signals go?**

. . .Don't forget to open the flue or you will suffocate! Have you ever opened a flue before?

> **...No.**

. . .Then wait for Ericka or George to do it.

> **...Okay, thanks!**

Well, so much for that idea. I needed to switch gears. I looked at numerous boxes of books and had to decide where to put them. There certainly wasn't enough shelving. My collection appeared to be quite diverse. It used to consist of all self-help books, but then I gravitated to feel-good books like *A Fine Romance: Falling in Love with the English Countryside* by Susan Branch. I had all of her books and had read them again and again.

I chose to take a break and settled into the comfortable couch. Before long, I dozed off, but later woke to something furry touching my nose. As I became more aware, the sensation startled me, and I discovered that Puff had made herself at home on my lap as I'd slept. "Oh no you don't!" I said, sitting up. "I am not your mom. Go back to your porch." Puff made her exit, giving me an even gaze as she made her way back to her chair.

As the evening settled into total darkness, I noticed the vast quietness. A sense of loneliness began to hover over me; I knew that it could develop into a consuming sensation. I certainly couldn't expect Ericka and her friends to entertain me on a regular basis. How would this solitude feel in the wintertime when I was snowed in? I decided that the best thing would be to get busy with a project. I stood, ready to shake off the feeling of dread before it took root!

I emptied the last box in the living room, feeling quite proud of myself. Buoyed by my accomplishment, I decided to rearrange the room to my taste. I picked up the old rug from the beautiful hardwood floor and dragged it to the porch to throw away, then rolled out the small one I'd brought with me. It had brighter colors and would perk up the space. I had a few throw pillows that matched the red, yellow, and navy blue in the rug. The activity forced me to do some cleaning as well. I wiped down the mantle and placed some of my personal pictures on it. I had left my framed picture of Austen behind, but I refused to let myself dwell on that. Each step I took made the little dwelling feel more like home.

At bedtime, I went upstairs, closing the door behind me. I had to decide what to wear for my big event the next morning. I had no idea how to dress for the quilt group. I wished I knew more about them. I also had to decide which one of my quilts to take for show and tell. I wanted it to show both my quilting and painting skills. Cher had tried to assure me that the group would like my work. She'd said they were all remarkably diverse in their quiltmaking. I wanted to believe that if they had approved of Cher's quilts, they would like mine as well.

Often, when I felt anxious, I would pray and ask the Almighty to comfort me. As I became more aware of my nervousness regarding going to this new quilt group, I turned to Him for support. He knew me so well, and my faith was the only thing I could really trust in my life. After spending some quiet time in prayer and contemplation, I felt confident that He would be with me in that room with the quilters the next day.

Chapter 14

I woke up early the next day so I would have ample time to get ready for my quilt club debut. I chose to wear a plain cashmere sweater paired with black slacks and leather boots. I scrutinized myself in the mirror and decided that I was appropriately dressed for the occasion.

Knowing Puff would likely be perched at the door, I opened it slowly and left only enough room to squeeze myself through. Puff's meow let me know that she disapproved of being an outcast from my bedroom. I went downstairs and fixed her breakfast. When she didn't appear, I assumed that she was pouting somewhere. I, however, enjoyed a cinnamon bun from the Blue Horse. I glanced at my phone and saw that I had just received a text from Cher.

...Good morning, Claire Bear! Good luck today. Tell them all hello for me and let them know that I miss them.

. . .Thanks, I will. I'll let you know how it goes.

I checked my watch and decided to drive rather than walk. I looked in my box of quilts and decided to take my wine country quilt. It was one of my better landscape pieces and showed both hand quilting and hand painting. I put it in a plastic bag and headed toward the door. Puff followed me as if I had invited her to go. "Behave yourself, Puff. I'll see you later." The cat turned her head in wonder as if she'd understood every word I'd said. I had to admit, that look was kind of cute.

It was nearly ten when I entered the building. I followed an African-American woman who appeared to have a quilt in her hand. When she saw me, she said good morning but walked right past me.

"Good morning!" another woman said as I entered the large room. "You must be Claire Stewart." She had a heavy Swedish accent, so I assumed that she must be Greta.

"Yes, I am," I acknowledged, reaching out my hand. "Thank you for letting me attend."

"Have a seat," she said after we had shaken hands. "There's coffee, so help yourself."

"Thanks," I answered as I decided where to sit.

"You're Claire?" another woman asked. "I'm Rachael. Come sit by me."

I smiled to myself as I made my way to where Rachael was sitting. Why had I wondered about what I should wear? Rachael wore denim overalls like she was heading straight to a hayride after the meeting! "Thanks, I will," I said, sitting down.

"Attention, everyone," Greta said, her voice raised. "It's ten o'clock. Does anyone know where Ava is?"

"Here she comes!" a younger woman with thick dark

hair declared.

"I'm here!" Ava said, making her entrance with a giggle.

Ava was hard to miss. She bounced in wearing a flashy rhinestone jacket. The bubbly blonde looked in my direction and sat down next to me. As I looked at each person around the table, I had to admit that Cher had been correct when she'd said the group was very diverse. I had even picked up on different accents before the meeting started. Now, when it was time to begin, all eyes were on Greta.

"Good morning," she began. "Claire Stewart has joined us today. As you may recall, she has moved into Cher's cabin in Fish Creek and will be attending our group until Cher returns."

When she paused, I said, "Thank you, Greta. I'm pleased to be here, and I really appreciate the opportunity to be a part of your group." I could feel everyone's eyes on me, and I wondered if I had spoken out of turn.

"I guess we should make a few introductions for Claire's benefit," Greta suggested. "Cher probably told you that we are a closed group. We have a long history together. When this group was started, the intent was to a have a truly diverse group of quilters who could share their talents. We are not competitive, and we strive to be respectful of everyone's tastes and techniques. We also have a rule that what happens at the club stays at the club." Greta smiled as she glanced at the members throughout the room, then turned to face me. "Cher explained that you incorporate paint into your quilting. Is that correct?"

"Yes, that's right," I replied. "I brought an example with me. I've been able to sell my quilts and will be looking for outlets in Door County, which I hope you can help me with."

"We'll have show and tell a little later," Greta informed me without replying to my request. "Let's begin our introductions, shall we?"

Chapter 15

"Should I start?" Ava inquired. Once Greta gave her a nod, Ava turned to me and said, "Welcome, Claire. I'm Ava Marie Chandler. We love Cher and are pleased that you've chosen to move to Door County."

I smiled at her, appreciative of her kind demeanor.

"I'm the wackiest quilter in the group," Ava said frankly. Some members stifled giggles while she continued, nonplussed by their behavior. "I like to use embellishments and tend to use bright colors. I never know where I'm going when I start a quilt," she said. She paused before adding, "My husband and I have an old Victorian house near Egg Harbor." Ava then turned to the woman sitting to the other side of her, indicating that her introduction was complete.

"I'm Marta Mae Bachman," the other woman said softly. "I'm probably the most traditional quilter in the group. I like making the same patterns that my family has made through the years. I live on a farm on Route 57 in Baileys Harbor. I have a big garden in the summer, so I don't have time to quilt until winter. My son and husband take care of our livestock.

Cher loved coming out to the farm every now and then. Sometimes she'd sit there and paint. You're invited to do the same if you'd like."

"Thanks, Marta. I would like that," I responded.

"I'm Frances McCraken," the next woman shared. Frances's hair had been grown out to an attractive natural gray. She clearly enjoyed accessories because she was adorned with a wide variety of jewels, from stacked bracelets to layered necklaces. "Don't call me Fran. I prefer to be called by my given name," she informed me as I smiled and nodded, memorizing her preferences. "I love antique furniture and quilts. I like to quilt old tops when I can get them, and I do them all by hand. I live in Sturgeon Bay in the same house I was born and raised in."

I smiled, sensing she would be quite a character. "How nice!" I responded.

"I'm Lee Sue Chan," the next woman said. "I'm originally from the Philippines and am married to Dr. Chan, who practices in Ephraim. Besides quilting, I love to garden. I add a lot of appliqué to my quilts, and I do everything by hand. I enjoy entering my quilts in competitions and have been fortunate enough to win a few nice awards." I had to listen carefully because her accent was very thick. She continued, "I look forward to seeing your work, Claire."

"Your work sounds most intriguing, Lee," I responded.

"My name is Olivia Williams," the African-American woman from earlier stated. "Many years ago, I lost my husband, and quilting has been a lifesaver for me."

"I'm sorry about the loss of your husband," I responded.

Olivia continued, "I live in an apartment in Sturgeon Bay above Novel Bay Booksellers. I'm looking for a different place, however. Frances and I sometimes ride together. Have you heard of the Gee's Bend quilters? I like to make quilts in that style. This group teases me about making mostly scrappy quilts in wild prints and colors. There's no piece of fabric too small, so remember me before you throw your scraps away," she advised with a smile.

As Olivia explained her quilting, I noticed several members exchanging glances and giving knowing smiles to one another. "I'll remember that," I replied, also giving Olivia a smile.

"Hi, Claire. I'm Ginger Greensburg," a younger woman said. "I'm Greta's niece. I feel fortunate to be a member of this group. My husband and I have a vintage resale store along Route 42. We live in the same building. Because of our business, I like to repurpose things, and that goes for quilts as well. When I'm not busy in the shop, I'm making potholders and small quilts to sell. We have two children, by the way." She turned to Rachael, indicating that her turn was complete.

"Hello again, Claire," Rachael said. "Some tease me by calling me Rachael Ray, like the celebrity chef. My husband Charlie and I live out in the country between Egg Harbor and Fish Creek. We also sell Christmas trees at Christmastime."

"Wonderful!" I responded.

"We take orders for barn quilts and make them for customers. What we do to set ourselves apart from others in similar businesses is that I make a wall-sized fabric block to match it. That one distinction has helped us in an extremely competitive market. Come out and visit us!"

"I will!" I answered enthusiastically. "I love barn quilts."

"Last but not least is me, I guess," Greta stated. "Greta

Greensburg is my name, and as you can tell, I never lost my Swedish accent." She smiled. "I used to have a quilt shop in Green Bay, years ago, before I moved to Sister Bay. If you go past The Pig – oh, I mean the Piggly Wiggly – we just live down the road. When I had my shop, I taught quick and easy quilts, so they're mostly what I make. I still have some of my shop supplies in the basement."

"She still has a lot, let me tell you," Ava laughed.

Chapter 16

"We'd like to hear a bit more from you, Claire," Greta stated. "Do you have family?"

"I do," I responded. "I left my widowed mother back in Missouri. As much as she hated to see me go, she thought it was a good move for me. I've never been married and have no children. I have a brother who lives in Springfield, Missouri. Cher and I grew up together, which she may have shared with you. I give her a lot of credit for moving home and taking care of her mother. I'm hoping she'll move back here one day."

"Yes, that's what she told us," Greta confirmed. "We hope so, too." She smiled and said, "Cher said her cabin would be a tremendous change for you."

"Yes, I've never lived in a cabin before. However, I can say that I think I was ready for a change. I'm finding Fish Creek and Door County quite charming and friendly. I'll feel better when I can get my studio supplies unpacked and can begin to quilt and paint."

"Does anyone have any questions for Claire?" Greta asked.

At this point, the gathering felt quite businesslike. Lee raised her hand. "Where do you plan to sell your work?" she asked.

"Right now, I don't know," I admitted. "I'd like to find a gallery that is familiar with mixed media and textiles. I have a social media base that keeps me busy. A couple of galleries in Missouri still carry my pieces. I'm inspired by my new surroundings – like those incredible cedar trees on Cottage Row."

"You'll have lots of new ideas!" Lee agreed.

"What's been your biggest challenge since you've moved here?" Olivia asked, curious.

"Puff."

"Puff?" Olivia repeated.

"Cher left her cat with me," I said flatly.

"So you've never had a cat before?" Olivia asked with a smile.

"No, and she assumes that she owns the place and is determined to do what she wants." I heard some muffled laughter in the room.

"I have a barn cat," Rachael said. "Cats are like that. You'll just have to figure out a compromise so she thinks she's still the boss." She paused before adding, "It's similar with husbands."

At that, everyone broke into laughter.

"Claire, we wish you well with Puff," Greta said. "Did you name her?"

"No. Cher calls her Puff, like in the Dick and Jane books, remember?"

"And you brought something to show us?" Greta asked, moving on in a businesslike manner.

"Oh, sure! I brought my wine country wall quilt that

showcases my techniques," I said as I got the quilt out of the bag and spread it out on the table. Everyone got up and gathered around.

"Oh, Claire, this is lovely," Ginger said.

"It really is," Rachael agreed.

"Show us where you applied paint," Lee requested.

"Was it difficult to hand quilt through the painted areas?" Olivia inquired.

"It depends how much paint there is," I responded, pointing to certain areas. "I try to keep that in mind when I plan the quilt."

"So why the wine country theme?" Frances asked.

"Missouri has lovely regions in the state that are hilly and perfect for growing grapes," I explained. "As a result, we have wonderful wineries and villages that blossom with tourists."

"Your shading on the grapes is spot on," Ginger observed. "You must have had great training. I'd love to see you in action."

"Well, as you all know, I'm a traditionalist in every sense of the word, but you've created something very real and tasteful," Marta said.

"Thank you so much!" I responded. "I have to admit that I don't always know where I'm going when I start something."

"You love what you do, don't you?" Ava asked. "That's what it's all about. I create what I love, not what others love."

"Good point, Ava," I said. "Cher said that you're the queen of embellishments."

She threw her head back and laughed like I had just given her the best compliment of all time. "I think you could say that," she proudly agreed.

Chapter 17

"There are no rules when it comes to creativity," I said. "No two pieces of art are alike, and it's the artist's interpretation that matters. If the viewer connects, it's a bonus. Sometimes, when I observe a connection like that, I'm compelled to give my work away."

"That's commendable," Ginger remarked. "Quilters need to observe that connection with their friends and family as it relates to the quilts that they make. Why would you give a quilt to a family member who doesn't get what you do and may even put it in harm's way when a neighbor or friend would cherish it?"

"My point!" I responded. "I'm glad you like this piece. I'll probably keep it for myself."

"If I remember Cher's cabin, you don't have a lot of storage space for quilts or fabric," Rachael noted.

"I'm afraid you're right," I replied.

"Well, ladies, we must adjourn," Greta stated. It almost sounded like she was looking for a motion. "Marta would like to invite everyone out to her farm next month before the heavy snows come. She insists on serving lunch, and we are not to bring a thing. Claire, you'll enjoy seeing her place. Let's hope the weather holds. Marta, thank you for the invitation," Greta said.

Marta blushed, and she said nothing in reply.

"That sounds great," I said to Rachael.

"Do you have time to get a quick lunch at the Blue Horse?" she asked as everyone got up to leave.

"Sure, I love that place." Before I left, I made sure I said goodbye to each one of the members and thanked them again for accepting me into the club. I especially thanked Greta, whose approval I felt I needed. "Do you go to the Blue Horse often?" I asked Rachael as we headed that way.

"Just when I'm in town. Sometimes I get a lunch to go after quilt club is over and take it back to Charlie. I'm a sucker for their caramel lattes."

"I feel so at home there. There seems to be a nice mix of locals and tourists, which I like."

Rachael smiled, and we walked the remainder of the way to the restaurant in silence. Once there, we placed our order at the counter, and then I looked for a table on the front porch. While we waited for the food to be brought to our table, I inquired as to why the quilt group didn't have a name.

"You mean you haven't given us a name yet?" she asked with a giggle.

"What do you mean by that?" I asked, puzzled by her question.

"I think we're so unique that we've decided we don't need an official name. Most folks refer to us as the quilters from the library, which is fine by me. As you saw today, each of us are artists, and honestly, we just prefer not to be labeled. Some think we're a secret society. We've been called many things."

I smiled and nodded, thinking about what she had just said. "What did Cher call us?"

I had to think. "I think she always said 'my friends at club.' I was impressed by everyone I met today. Do you always get along?" Rachael began to answer, but stopped when our food was brought to the table. After that, the food got our attention, and I thought I would just skip the question. "How's the barn quilt business?"

"Really good right now. The tourists see them on all the barns and decide that they want to take one home."

"I can see that," I said as I bit into my tuna sandwich.

"This BLT is delicious! It's one of my favorites here," Rachael exclaimed. "So, Claire, what do you do for fun besides your quilt work?"

"If you're asking if there is a man in my life, the answer is no. I had one for the last five years or so, and I broke it off before I moved here."

"Oh my goodness! Did you move here because of him?"

"No, but Cher's offer came at the perfect time. I really wanted to get out of that small community after the relationship ended. He's a doctor and is well known."

"This is interesting. Were you living together?"

I nodded. "Yes. I had a rather good life with a new house and a studio to die for. I try not to think about that part of the story."

"You've got guts, I'll say that! As an artist, I think you'll be inspired in a whole new way here."

Just then, in came the handsome man with the red scarf.

He placed his order quickly and settled in at the same table where I'd seen him last, making a quick glance towards Rachael and me.

Chapter 18

"Do you know that guy?" I immediately asked.

"Yes, he's Grayson Wills. He's a looker, but don't get any ideas. He's a widower. His wife died at least four years ago or more, and I've never seen him with another woman, ever! He comes to a few civic things like Rotary and the Chamber of Commerce, but I don't see him out socially."

"Wow, that's something. Did they have children?"

"One daughter, who may be a teenager by now." Rachael eyed me closely and said, "Now, I'm happy to keep an eye out for you, but you'd better forget about Grayson."

"No, no, trust me. I'm not on the lookout for anyone," I assured her.

"Never say never. With me working at the Bayside Tavern, I may find a prospect for you there."

"I can imagine that you run into some unique customers there," I said.

"I hear a lot working there, as you can imagine, but I tell myself that what I hear at the tavern stays at the tavern."

I laughed and agreed with her statement. "Oh, the time is

flying by. I need to get going," I said, looking at my watch.

"Me too! Charlie knows that once I'm out of the house, he never knows when I'll return. I'm the people part of the business and make the contacts. He's happy staying at the barn and working on products."

"That's a nice combination."

"It's not always easy working with your spouse every day," Rachael said.

As we were leaving, I happened to glance over at Grayson Wills' table and found him looking at me. I quickly looked away and followed Rachael out of the restaurant. We said our goodbyes, and I felt good about my first experience with the quilt club at the library.

When I got home, I was expecting to see Puff sitting in her favorite chair on the porch. I called her name, but there was no response. Perhaps she was napping, which was what I felt like doing. I took off my jacket and went upstairs to change. The bedroom door was closed, so I looked to see if Puff was in the office. To my horror, she was snuggled on a stack of quilts that I had not found a place for!

"No, you don't!" I said, pulling away the top quilt. "You are not going to get hair all over my quilts! You go out to the porch!" Puff flew down the steps to find a safe haven. I shook out the top quilt she had been stationed on and reminded myself that I needed to find a safe place to store the quilts. The older quilts I had were in pristine condition and had not come at an affordable price. The chest I'd brought for my sweaters and outerwear would have to be emptied, and my clothes would have to go elsewhere. That chest was perfect for my quilts.

After I emptied the chest, I lined it with a white cotton sheet. I refolded the quilts as I reacquainted myself with each one.

My love for pretty quilts like my Rose of Sharon came from my Grandmother Stewart. She'd made it as a wedding present for my mother and father. I didn't know if she'd had her own name for it, but I truly admired the detail of her perfect appliqué and fine hand quilting. Mom had wanted me to have this quilt and had given it to me many years ago. Every quilt that was at all similar tugged at my heart after that.

Each quilt fit perfectly in the chest. Now I had to find a place for my stack of sweaters, jackets, and vests. Perhaps George or someone could create a storage space under my bed.

It was five in the evening when Cher sent me a text. I was on my way downstairs, telling myself it was a wonderful time for a visit with my friend.

Chapter 19

...How did club go? Why haven't I heard
from you?

. . .No news is good news! I'll call you in a sec.

I wasn't surprised that Cher was on pins and needles
wondering what I'd thought of the group and if I'd been
accepted. We had a wonderful chat as I filled her in on the
details of the meeting. Afterwards, I called Ericka and asked
if she thought George or his friend could help me by checking
out the fireplace and maybe building something to solve my
sweater storage problem. I told her I also had problems with
the TV and Internet connections.

"Sure! I'll tell George to stop by after work tomorrow."

"Naturally, I'll pay him."

"George won't take money from someone he likes. He
actually doesn't need it, and he'll be glad to help."

"Great! The quilt club meeting went pretty well."

"Oh, good! Congrats!"

"Rachael asked me to lunch at the Blue Horse afterwards. I really like her."

"I like her, too! She's down to earth. Last year, she and her husband sold Christmas trees on their property. Their neighbor grows them, but it's the perfect retail spot to sell their barn quilts. They serve hot cider and hot chocolate. It's very cool."

"Oh, it sounds wonderful," I replied. "Ericka, did Cher have a Christmas tree? If she did, where on earth did she put it?"

"I think she had it on the porch. I remember being able to see it through the windows."

"Great idea. I love Christmas. I'm trying really hard to talk my mother into visiting me here this year."

"Good luck with that. How is Puff doing?"

"She got in trouble today."

"Oh no. Now what?"

"I found her resting on top of my antique quilts that I hadn't put away."

"So? What's wrong with that?" Ericka asked.

"Shedding on my quilts is unacceptable."

"She means no harm, and cats love quilts, just like we do."

"Do you know if Puff is a girl or a boy?" I asked innocently. "I've just been referring to her as a girl."

"She's a girl. There are more tabby males than females, I'm told, so that makes her a bit of a rarity."

"Interesting!" I replied. "Hey, thanks for contacting George for me." We finished our conversation, and I prepared a simple dinner, ate, and straightened up some of my unpacked possessions. I then headed to the bedroom. First, I needed to check on Puff before closing that door. I found her downstairs, curled up by the fireplace like she was waiting for the warmth that it could provide. Maybe that was another favorite spot of hers. I said goodnight to her and headed up to bed.

My flannel sheets felt better and better as fall turned to winter. It was only seconds after I finished my prayers that my mind wandered to Austen. What was he doing? Was he in bed? Was he seeing someone else? I could call some of our mutual friends to find out about him, but I didn't want any information getting back to him. Since I was the one who had moved out, I felt sure that our friends thought of me as the bad guy. I had such fond memories of Austen before we began living together. He'd wined and dined me like I had never experienced before. However, it seemed that once he'd known I'd be there at his home waiting for him, I was no longer a priority. I'd spent years trying to remind myself that it was okay because his job came first. It was a noble job, and I felt guilty for being jealous of the time he devoted to it. The fact was, I left because I was neglected. It also struck me as odd that Austen worked with children all day but never wanted any of his own. I never pressed him about it, but it did seem like a bit of a disconnect to me.

I looked at the clock. It was already one in the morning. Did thinking these thoughts about Austen mean that I missed him? I wondered if he ever missed me. What was he telling folks about our breakup? Stop. I had to stop running these same thoughts over and over in my mind. He had moved on, and so should I. I repositioned my pillow, felt the softness of the flannel, pulled the covers to my neck, and fell asleep.

Chapter 20

The next day, I knew my first stop had to be the Piggly Wiggly grocery store. I had no food in the house except for a few takeout items from restaurants. I looked forward to going to Sister Bay, where the famous Tannenbaum Christmas Shop was located. I couldn't wait to find festive decorations and lights for the cabin. Additional lights would also make me feel safer coming home after dark. I put on my coat and saw Puff settled in her chair. When I said goodbye, she lifted her head as if to give me a nod farewell. She was likely getting used to my ways by now.

I slowly drove down Main Street and noticed that not very many places were open at this hour. As I approached the Blue Horse, I decided to park and get a coffee to enjoy on my way to the grocery store. When I got inside, I spied a batch of cherry scones stacked on a cake stand, just waiting for me to add one to my order. I couldn't resist! As I opened the door to leave, Grayson Wills was coming in. He held the door as our shoulders lightly brushed against each other.

"Thanks," I said.

"You're welcome," he replied in a rich, deep voice.

Back in the car, I munched on the scone as I drove along a scenic road that turned left at the top of the hill. I passed a string of shops that I would have to check out at another time. I knew of a well-known watercolor artist who had a gallery there. Perhaps she could help me find a place to sell my quilts.

I passed Gibraltar High School. The YMCA was nearby, a place where I might meet new people. The English Inn and Alexander's of Door County were restaurants that Cher had suggested I try. When I saw a sign that said Door County Medical Center, I figured that must be where Ericka worked.

I was driving slowly when I saw a big house with "Vintage Resale" on the sign out front. I knew it had to be Ginger's place. Perhaps on the way home I could stop and see her. For now, I had to keep looking for the Piggly Wiggly store, which was supposed to have a sign on the right indicating where I should turn.

There it was! I had arrived at the Pig. Just thinking of the name made me chuckle. There was an attractive strip of shops along the short drive to the store's parking lot. I saw a bookstore and craft shop next to a cute little diner. Another stop for another time, but not today. I was feeling the excitement of places unknown.

I parked, and when I got inside, I remembered Cher telling me that the store had just expanded. I was impressed with how well it was stocked and noticed how most folks seemed to know everyone else in the store! Clusters of shoppers visited with each other. Twice, employees stopped and asked me if I needed help finding anything. When had that ever happened back home? I must have had "tourist" written across my forehead.

As I filled up my cart, I wondered where I would put everything. Did people stock up for the winter here? I hadn't grocery shopped in a long time, so it was fun to see new products. When I got to the checkout line, I listened to the cashier greet everyone by name.

"Someone will help you out with this," she stated before I could ask.

"Do you do that for everyone?"

She smiled and nodded.

After checking out, I got in my car and paid attention to the name of the bookstore nearby, The Peninsula Bookman. There was a second location not far from me in Fish Creek. How could anyone get bored here in the winter? I needed to keep moving north to accomplish my goals for the day.

I drove down the hill through Sister Bay to see wonderful shops like the On Deck Clothing Company and other intriguing stores. I couldn't wait to try some of the seafood restaurants along the bay. On my left, traffic suddenly slowed. The reason soon became clear. Everyone was peering at the goats on the roof at Al Johnson's Swedish Restaurant! It was quite a sight to see the line of people waiting to get inside. Everyone was taking photos, and I recalled that Cher had said the restaurant had a gift shop to die for. On the left side of the road, there was a marina where vacationers strolled, looking at the boats and admiring the water. This lifestyle could become addictive.

Chapter 21

I determined that my next stop would be the Tannenbaum Christmas Shop. It was in a former church, so I watched for the church steeple that was to be on my right. It was hard to miss. As I neared the location, traffic slowed due to the number of cars pulling into its parking lot. It was a sight to behold! A sidewalk full of multicolored mums and fall decor led to a set of double doors. People ahead of me were taking pictures. I knew I was headed for a special treat as I followed the throng of other customers into the shop.

A spectacular upside-down Christmas tree greeted us as we entered. The small entry area really showcased the tree. I had to stop and stare at the vast collection of ornaments and garlands, but knew I had to keep moving. It would be easy to stop and try to take in every little detail, but the glistening of color and lights drew me from one room to the next. Christmas music and the fragrance of the holiday told me that I was in a place that fed my soul.

I veered towards the left, where there was a large room of themed decor. Music boxes, baby's first Christmas items, and special collector's series were on display. A small offset room was full of nothing but ornaments. There was an ornament for seemingly every breed of dog as well as any character a customer might be searching for.

I took my time as I looked and eventually entered another large room where themed trees were on display. To my delight, there was one representing Door County and all its signature delights and locations. Tourists were gathered all around, trying to decide which ornaments they would take home. Oh, how special a tree like that would be in my new home! Perhaps Door Country ornaments could hang from a garland on the fireplace since my space was limited.

I continued to examine each tree. The Halloween tree was amazing. A nearby tree featured wine- and alcohol-related ornaments. There was another with only woodland animals. How fun it would be to have a themed tree in every room of the cabin!

As I walked around the corner of one aisle, I saw a wide staircase that was enticing and headed up. When I got to the top, I saw wreaths, lights, and even more Christmas home decor. I had to have some of these items, but where should I start? As I turned to go back down the stairs, the displays below created a breathtaking Christmas scene. I stopped for a moment to capture the beauty by taking a picture with my cell phone.

As I continued to marvel at the displays, it became obvious how friendly and helpful the staff was. There wasn't a question too silly or unimportant. As a customer, it was easy to feel overwhelmed by the sheer number of items to choose from. The sales associates seemed to be able to help shoppers focus and make their selections.

I found myself back at the music boxes. I kept hearing "I'll Be Home for Christmas," one of my favorite seasonal tunes. Perhaps this year more than ever, it would have special meaning. In one music box, a tree turned while snow fell gently around it. I knew I had to have it. If they had two of them, I would send one to my mother as well. When I carried it to the cashier, she was quickly able to find a second. After I checked out, numerous workers wished me a Merry Christmas. I walked to the car knowing that my next trip would be when I would make more specific purchases now that I was familiar with the shop's stock. I looked at my watch. I was hungry, and all I could think about was Al Johnson's restaurant. I simply could not be this close and fail to stop!

Miraculously, I found a parking spot on the street just as another car was leaving. I rushed in to find a crowd of hungry souls standing shoulder to shoulder, waiting for tables. When I gave my name to the hostess, who was wearing a Swedish costume, she said I should visit the butik while I waited. I was happy to do so!

The room was bustling with shoppers, who had armloads of Christmas goodies. If I headed to the right, there was a small section devoted to clothing and shoes. If I went to the left, Christmas gifts like stationery, candy, books, candles, ornaments, and an array of Swedish gifts filled the shelves. Should I just start piling up all the things I liked? I especially had my eye on the Swedish cookies, but that was probably because I was starved. The hostess called my name just in time! I couldn't get to my table fast enough!

The blonde Swedish waitress introduced herself and informed me that the restaurant was known for their Swedish pancakes. I had noticed a video depicting how they were made when I had first entered the waiting area. However, I realized that I was hungry for lunch, especially after the waitress told me about their famous meatballs. In the end, I took a more midwestern route and ordered a turkey melt with tomato bisque.

Chapter 22

As I waited, my mouth watered as I picked up the brochure sitting on the table. It said that each year on Al Johnson's birthday, "Wink" Larson would give him a live animal of some kind. It could be a burro, a baby pig, or a sheep. One year, it was a goat. It turned out that putting goats on the roof of a restaurant became a great tourist attraction. As I read on, I learned that the goats lived in a barn nearly a mile away and were brought in via pickup truck each morning. When the year's first snow was predicted for the area, the goats went to the barn for the rest of the winter. What a story!

When the food arrived, it was truly a gift from heaven. The homemade bread was amazing, and the soup was delicious beyond words. I ate like I hadn't eaten in years. I wanted cherry cobbler for dessert in the worst way, but my stomach rebelled at the thought. I got up to leave and knew I needed to head home for a good afternoon nap. I passed by Ginger's business, knowing I was not in the mood for shopping or chatter. Actually, she was close enough that I could visit her anytime. I did stop to get gas at the BP station near Gibraltar High School. Inside, it was good to see that the station had other necessities if I needed them. Before I drove off, it occurred to me that my phone had been exceptionally quiet. I got it out of my purse and saw it had been turned off. I had missed calls from Rachael and Mom.

As soon as I got home, I unloaded my groceries on the kitchen table. What had I done? Where would all of this go? I couldn't worry about that now, as I wanted to get back to Mom. I called her and said, "Hi, Mom! I'm sorry I missed your call. Is everything okay?"

"Sure. No problem. I just wanted to tell you that I got to visit with Cher and her mom. Cher is worried that you may not be adjusting very well to Door County."

"Oh, Door County is wonderful, but I'm still getting used to living in the cabin, and I sure didn't need a cat to take care of. I just got back from a wonderful drive and ate lunch at an interesting place. They have live goats on the roof, Mom! I can't wait to take you there when you visit."

She chuckled. "I'm not sure you have room for me!"

"I'll give you my bed and sleep on the couch, which is pretty comfortable. I really do hope you'll come for Christmas. It's not too soon to make a reservation."

"Are you sure you don't want to come home?"

"My home is supposed to be here now, remember? Everyone says it's a magical place in the wintertime."

"Those temperatures don't sound magical to me! I'm old! Michael is supposed to come home, you know."

"Michael can always come home. Are you going to see him on Thanksgiving?"

"Yes, and he mentioned that he may be bringing a girlfriend. I won't believe it until I see it."

"No hints about who she is?"

"Not really. Maybe you should call him. He still can't believe you left Austen to move up north."

"Well, he'd better believe it."

"Cher said she saw Austen in the hall at the hospital when she took Hilda in for some blood tests."

"Oh dear. What happened?"

"She said he ignored her completely."

"Sounds like him."

"I just don't understand him. Well, anyway, I hope you brought enough warm clothing for the winter."

I chuckled. "I'm fine. Let's talk tomorrow."

Mothers never stopped being mothers, and that was somehow comforting to me. I was thankful that I did not have to be a caregiver like Cher. I didn't take Mom's good health for granted. I was glad my dad had left her financially comfortable.

It dawned on me while stacking groceries in a small cabinet that I hadn't seen Puff since I'd arrived home. Why was I worrying about her? Cher would ask about her, that was why.

I passed on dinner since I was still full, but I did pour myself something to drink. I also had some famous Wisconsin cheese to nibble on. At eight, I heard a knock at the door, which startled me. I looked out and was relieved to see that it was George.

"George!"

"I hope I'm not dropping by too late, but I've been working so much lately. Ericka said you needed some things done. I can come back another time if you'd like."

"No, but George, you don't have to do anything for me.

You've already done so much." Even as I said that, I thought of my brief list of things that needed to be done.

"Well, perhaps I can take care of a few simple things while I'm here."

"To be honest, there are a few things. I don't have Internet, and I can't get anything on TV," I mentioned. "Would you like something to drink? It happens to be my dinner."

"Sure. While you're getting that, I'm going to check on your fireplace. It's a good night to start a fire, so I want to check your flue."

I went in the kitchen, got a drink for George, and made a platter of cheese and crackers. When I walked back into the living room, George was about to light a fire. I wanted to celebrate the moment. "A fire at last!"

"I happen to be pretty good at getting a fire going, so is that okay?"

"It is indeed. Here is your drink."

"Thanks, Claire."

We both were silent as we watched the beautiful flames erupt. The warmth made the cabin feel cozy. "Now it feels like home. Thank you."

"Any friend of Cher's is a friend of mine. Let me check a few hookups outdoors to see if I can figure out the TV reception and Internet connection."

As George went outside, Puff flew out from underneath the couch. Had she been napping there all this time? Was she afraid of the fire? She stood by the door as if waiting for George to return.

Chapter 23

"Okay, that should do it!" George announced as he came back inside. "Cher should have told you that she disconnected several things before she left."

"All that matters now is this beautiful fire," I said, raising my glass. "Here's to Cher!"

"Cher!" George said, clinking his glass against mine. "Now, is there anything else I can do tonight?"

"Nothing else for now. As winter sets in, I'm sure there will be more," I laughed. "I'm still getting used to life in a cabin."

"I believe the neighbors next door used to shovel snow from Cher's driveway. You might check with them about that."

"Oh, I will. I haven't had a chance to meet them yet."

When George sat down, Puff immediately jumped into his lap. He acted like they were old friends.

"I have a cat called Mitts. She probably smells her. I take it that the two of you haven't bonded?"

"I don't know what that means, exactly. I've never had a pet."

"She'll be great company for you."

"Hmmm, we'll see."

"So, Claire, what did you do for fun before you came here?"

"My pastime is painting. If you're asking if I do winter sports, I'd have to say no. If you're asking if I do summer sports, I'd still have to say no."

He chuckled. "Not even boating? You know, you're in Door County!"

"I do like being around water, but about five years ago, I got a bad case of vertigo, so movements like waves and sudden motions can trigger it."

"I've heard my sister talk about her vertigo."

"Well, I still manage to have fun, though."

"Ericka said you aren't seeing anyone right now," George said, quite out of the blue.

"She is correct."

"Does this mean that you would be open to me escorting you somewhere every now and then?"

I chuckled at his humor. "George, if you're asking me out, I have to turn you down. First, you're a tad young for me, and second, I'm not interested in having a man in my life right now. I just left someone back in Missouri, and I'm perfectly fine with not dating for now."

"That's what happens! Hey, I'm not looking for a wife either, but I think you would be a lot of fun to be with."

"Thanks, that's sweet of you to say." I paused and, uncomfortable with the silence, said, "How about some cheese?" Thankfully, our conversation then changed to Door County and how much I loved exploring the peninsula. After a while, George put a final log on the fire and announced that he needed to go. He refused any payment, and we said goodbye. Puff followed him to the door and meowed when he left.

As I waited for the fire to die down, I thought what a

compliment it was that George would be interested in me. There wasn't an ounce of attraction on my side, so I knew nothing would happen. What would Austen think if I had a man in my life? Perhaps he suspected that was the case since I had left town, but he may not have known that I'd gone to Door County. Who knew what he was thinking? I went to bed still thinking about him. Cher had reminded me that getting over this breakup would take time. I supposed I missed Austen more than I had anticipated.

Chapter 24

The next morning, I couldn't wait to start a fire on my own. First, I fed Puff, and then I ate the last of the cherry pie for breakfast. I wanted to be especially productive that day, so I could not ignore cleaning the front porch. Getting that done would enable me to set up my workspace. I could also set up my sewing machine in the office. My cell phone rang, and it was Rachael.

"Hey, good morning! I thought I'd give you an excuse to get out of the house tonight. I'm bartending at the Bayside if you want to stop by and have a drink on me."

"On you? Well, I can't refuse that. Can you do that?"

She laughed. "Yes, we have the freedom to make some of those choices with our favorite customers."

"So, you think I'm going to be a good customer, huh? George said you have great hamburgers there, so maybe I'll come by around six or so."

"Great! I have to go, so see you then."

I smiled knowing I had something to look forward to at the end of the day. As I began to maneuver around the front porch, I could see panic set in with Puff as she wondered where her chair would end up. It was rather comical to watch. "Not to worry, Puff. I think your chair will end up in about the same place after I clean the floor."

It had been a long time since I had done some real cleaning. Cher had left a limited amount of cleaning supplies, so I worked with what was available. As soon as I had shaken out the cushion on Puff's chair and moved it to clean under it, I put it back in the same place. Puff didn't waste a second before she jumped up to nestle into the spot. As soon as my easel was put in the proper position with the sunshine coming in, I assessed the room and decided I had accomplished what I'd set out to do. Moving the furniture to the other side of the porch had been a challenge, but I liked it there much better. I wasn't sure Cher would approve, but I did need to make the space work for me as I painted.

The day had flown by, and I went to take a shower in the spacious, updated bathroom. I loved looking at the back wall of the fireplace behind the sink. Who else would ever have this? As I dried my hair, I wondered if the Bayside was going to be part of my social life. I hoped not. I envisioned going to gallery openings every weekend and drinking champagne.

I put on clean jeans and a cable-knit sweater. I might not even be taking my jacket off since the air was so crisp. It was nearly six, so I decided to be on my way. Puff knew something was up as she followed me from room to room. When we got to the porch, I said goodbye and told her that she should be good. To my surprise, she meowed back. I didn't know if it was a positive response or a rebellious one, but it felt a bit like conversation, and it made me smile.

Rachael spotted me right away when I walked into the Bayside, which was crowded and noisy. She motioned for me to come to the other side, where she'd reserved a seat for me. On my way, I passed Ginger and her husband at the bar.

"Hey, Claire!" Ginger said as she reached for my arm. "Meet my husband, Allen. Allen, this is our new quilter, Claire."

"Nice to meet you!" I said, shaking Allen's hand.

"It's a date night for us," Ginger giggled, looking fondly at her husband. "Do you have a seat?"

"Yes, Rachael has one for me," I replied. "By the way, I passed your place recently but didn't have time to stop. Allen, are you in the shop as well?"

"No, I leave that mostly to Ginger, who works extremely hard at it. I work in Surgeon Bay."

"Well, good to see you both, but I have a hamburger on my mind right now," I said as I moved away from them and closer to my seat.

"So, what's your pleasure, girlfriend?' Rachael asked.

"Choose your best red wine for me," I requested. "Oh, and a hamburger with everything on it."

She grinned. "How do you want that cooked?" she asked. "Do you want fries or potato salad?"

"Medium-well and fries," I said, feeling guilty as the words left my lips.

"You do know that Bayside won best hamburger in Door County, don't you?"

"No, I didn't!' I laughed. "Bring it on!"

Chapter 25

"Hey, there," the man on the barstool next to me said in greeting. "I'm Fred, and this is Nettie, my wife."

"Hi, I'm Claire, and I'm a friend of Rachael's," I explained.

"We haven't seen you here before," Fred noted. "Are you new to the area?"

I nodded and smiled. "I hear this is the place to get a good hamburger," I said.

"You've got that right!" he chuckled. "We come quite often, and we think the world of Rachael. Where do you live?"

"On Cottage Row, right on the corner," I replied.

"One of those fancy places, huh?" Nettie said, teasing.

"No, not at all," I laughed. "It's a little log cabin that used to reside in Peninsula State Park."

"You don't say!" Fred exclaimed. "We're locals, and we probably know less than you newer folks!"

"I'm very new here, so I'm just getting settled," I explained.

"Nettie and I usually come here on Saturday nights because they have a band that we like that comes in around nine," Fred informed me.

"Thanks for the warning! I'll be long gone by then," I joked as my food was set before me. As I ate, I made small talk with Fred and Nettie. Unfortunately, Rachael was too busy to keep me entertained, but to my surprise, she put another glass of red wine in front of me.

"This is compliments of George," Rachael announced with a smile.

Across the bar, George and Rob lifted their glasses as if to offer a toast. I nodded, smiled, and took a sip of wine in response. All the while, I had some hesitation about encouraging friendships with the two of them in a bar. It just made me feel uncomfortable and was not something that I would typically do.

"Well, those young men seem to know you, Claire!" Nettie teased.

"It's just my friend Ericka's brother trying to be nice," I explained. "In fact, I need to be on my way. It sure was nice to meet the two of you."

"You too!" Fred said, rising to give me a hug like he'd known me forever. "I hope we see you again sometime."

On my way out, I slipped my coat on and waved a goodbye to Ginger and Allen, who appeared to be having an enjoyable time on their date night. I couldn't wait to get out into the fresh, chilly air. I was almost to my car when I heard someone calling my name.

"Claire! Claire!" George's voice carried across the parking lot as he rushed towards me. "What's your hurry?"

"Oh, George, I just came because Rachael invited me, and I wanted to try the hamburgers," I explained as I breathed in the chilly air. "I wanted to leave before the band started."

"Well, would you like to go somewhere quiet and have

a drink?"

I smiled and shook my head. "No, thanks. I just want to get home."

"Raincheck?" he inquired, tilting his head in a way that made his invitation more inviting.

"We'll see," I said quickly as I turned and got into my car. "Seriously?" I asked myself aloud as I drove off. "No way, José!"

I was glad to get into the house and see Puff, but I worried that George might stop by after he left the bar. I hoped not, especially after my rather abrupt refusal. I sighed and shook my head. I was feeling sleepy from the wine, so I went up to bed. Puff followed as if she might try to get into my room one more time. I was tired, but I wasn't tired enough to welcome Puff's cat hairs on my bed. I hardly remembered undressing as I curled up and fell fast asleep.

The next thing I knew, was there was bright sunshine on my face. I looked at the clock and saw that it was half past nine. I couldn't believe it! Puff must be starving. I pulled the quilt around me and headed down the stairs. The place was quite chilly. In the kitchen, Puff was awake and staring up at me in disgust. "I'm sorry, I'm sorry," I said, feeling bad. "You enjoy!" I said as I gave her some food. I fixed a cup of coffee and went to the couch to continue waking up. The phone rang, and I rose to get my purse and pull it out.

"Good morning!" Rachael's voice greeted me.

"I guess it's a good one. That wine you gave me really wiped me out."

She chuckled. "I am so sorry I couldn't visit with you more. We were really slammed."

"No problem. Nettie and Fred kept me company. They're the sweetest couple. For an older couple, they seem to still be madly in love with each other. It's so cute to hear them tease back and forth. Well, thanks for the drink. The hamburger was fantastic, by the way."

"Thanks. I'm glad you stopped by. I'm actually calling about another request. Tomorrow morning is our chamber of commerce meeting, and they're meeting at Pelletier's, right around the corner from you. I'd love for you to come as my guest. You don't have to join, but I think it would be good for you. It starts at eight, and Pelletier's serves a really delicious breakfast buffet."

"Well, why not? I actually had been thinking about joining the chamber at some point."

"Great! Since you're so close, I'll just meet you there. I'll try not to be late, so don't panic if you don't see me right away."

"Okay, my friend. Thanks for the invitation."

"Oh, I never asked, but does your business have a name?"

"Yes, The Quilted Palette by Claire."

"How clever! See you there!"

Chapter 26

I hung up feeling excited because I knew I would need more business contacts if I wanted to promote my business in Door County. My home business didn't look like it had before. There wasn't room for everything, but my sewing machine was plugged in, and things were out of the boxes, at least. When I went into the living room, I noticed that the quilt had fallen to the floor, and Puff was nestled right on top. "No, no, Puff. My mother would be furious it she found cat hair on this quilt." I looked down at Puff's tiny face and laughed. "If you like quilts so much, I'll try to find you one of your own, okay?" I picked her up and took her out to the porch, where her chair was waiting for her. I patted her on the head as she gave a disgruntled meow.

I went upstairs to get dressed and then began working in my office. Working from the desk I'd brought from home gave me some sense of familiarity. I'd left most of my fabric at Mom's house, just bringing what I would need for projects I'd already started. As I refolded and touched the fabric I had on hand, I could feel my sense of creativity returning. I only had one custom order to complete for a client. Hopefully, I could get to it soon and get it sent off. I was working from the client's photograph of a lovely beach scene. Touches of paint would bring it to life.

I had to build a clientele from here. I had noticed a gallery that advertised all-Door-County art. That let me know that there was a market here for tourists to buy art and take it home with them. Door County not only attracted artists and galleries, but was home to places like the Peninsula School of Art and The Clearing Folk School in Ellison Bay, which I'd heard so much about. I couldn't wait to check them out for myself.

By five, I surveyed my office, and it looked quite functional and even somewhat attractive. I hung a small plaque which had my favorite saying, "Do not worry. Say your prayers and be thankful." On another wall, I hung a small quilt that Cher had made for me.

My cell phone was ringing. It was Mom.

"How is your day going, honey?" she asked in her soft, sweet voice.

"Great! How about yours?"

"Very nice. I had lunch with Mr. Vogel. You remember him."

"Isn't he the lawyer that you and Dad always used?"

Mom giggled. "Well, he's been retired for quite some time, but he still gives me help and free advice when I need it."

"Nothing's wrong, is it?"

"Not at all. We just enjoy each other's company every now and then. He's looking for an assisted living place right now, so surprisingly, he's asking for my advice. He's been alone for such a long time."

"Well, I'm sure you each have many stories to share."

"Absolutely! We really have some good laughs sometimes. He has a good sense of humor," she informed me. "So, how's the unpacking coming along?"

"Better. I organized my office today. It was quite an undertaking, but I really like the way it turned out."

"How is Puff adjusting to the changes you're making?"

"She's adjusting. She loves the Nine-Patch quilt that you gave me. Every time I turn my back, she finds a way to snuggle up on it. When I move her off, she gives me an exasperated look and scampers away."

"Why would you want to do that?"

"Because she sheds all over it."

"For heaven's sake, let her enjoy it when you're not using it! I take it as a compliment, and it sounds like a good way for the two of you to bond."

"Are you serious?"

"She's not going to ruin it. It's totally washable; I've washed that quilt many times."

"I don't know. If I give in to her on that, she'll really feel like she rules the place."

Mom chuckled. "Now, be nice, Claire. By the way, I ran into Dr. Page when I went to the hospital's women's auxiliary breakfast on Wednesday."

"When did you start calling him Dr. Page instead of Austen?"

"When my daughter left his house," she said simply. "By the way, he didn't acknowledge me at all. I thought that was quite rude."

"Yes, it makes me sad that he's treating you and Cher that way."

Chapter 27

After a simple dinner, I settled in for a quiet night by the fire. I thought about my conversation with Mom. What should I make of her having lunch with Mr. Vogel? What should I make of Austen ignoring her at the breakfast? Perhaps he'd sensed all along that she'd never really liked him, even though she'd always treated him nicely.

I pulled the quilt up to my neck and felt something move near my feet. It was Puff curling up to the edge of the quilt. I was about to give her a nudge with my foot when I remembered what Mom had said about sharing the quilt with her. Okay, maybe just this once. The room was chilly, and we were both enjoying the fire. I tried not to move so as not to disturb her.

I woke up the next morning still on the couch. I looked at my watch and sat up quickly as I noted the time. I had to get to the chamber breakfast. When I pulled the quilt back, Puff took off for the porch. I showered and then dressed in a simple pantsuit. After I fixed Puff's food, I checked to see if I had business cards in my purse. It was nice to know I could walk to the meeting.

When I arrived, some folks were visiting outside the restaurant. When I got inside, there was a reception table where I could purchase my ticket, write my name on a tag, and pick up promotional materials.

"Hello, I'm a guest of Rachael's and a new resident of Fish Creek. I'm assuming Rachael called in an RSVP for us," I stated to a chamber employee.

"Are you Claire Stewart?" she asked.

"That's me."

"Welcome! Your breakfast has been paid for," she informed me. "Please fill out a nametag. Our president, Marvin Chandler, is standing to my left. He's from the Door Peninsula Winery. Feel free to go over and say hello."

"That won't be necessary," Rachael's voice said from behind me. "I'll introduce her."

"Good morning, Rachael," the chamber employee said.

At that moment, Mr. Chandler came our way, and Rachael introduced us. "Welcome, Claire," he said, shaking my hand. "We have a short business meeting today because our gathering today is more about networking. I'll be happy to introduce you to everyone. Help yourself to breakfast."

"Thanks! I'm pleased to be here." I followed Rachael to the food line. As we waited, I was surprised to see the man in the red scarf had also arrived. He was talking to someone. When he got his food, he had to walk by me to get to a table. He looked up and saw me, and his expression was one of surprise. "Hi, I'm Claire Stewart," I said. "If I look familiar, it's because I've seen you at the Blue Horse several times." He nodded and paused, not saying anything, so I continued. "I came as a guest of Rachael, whom I think you know."

"Well, not officially," Rachael said, appearing a bit embarrassed.

"I'm Grayson Wills with Sails Again in Ephraim," he said.

"I just moved here from Missouri and live in Fish Creek," I explained.

"Well, it's nice to meet you ladies, but you'll have to excuse me. I'm meeting with someone during breakfast."

"Well, it was nice to meet you," I said as he walked away.

"Well, I'll be!" Rachael teased. "That was a pretty aggressive move on your part. I think you had a purpose in mind there."

"Not really, but we've been looking at each other for some time now," I disclosed. "I don't know if he's shy or stuck on himself."

Rachael chuckled. "Well, he won't ignore you now, quilt sister," she teased.

"Quilt sister?" I laughed.

Chapter 28

The breakfast buffet was delicious. I ate with Rachael, and sitting near us were two women who owned a coffee shop in Sister Bay. They were very friendly and said they were located near the Tannenbaum Christmas Shop.

Occasionally, Mr. Wills and I exchanged looks, but each time, he would quickly glance away. The more I analyzed his behavior, the more I became convinced that he was shy and leery of a new face. "Now that I've thrown myself in front of Mr. Wills, would you find out if he's involved with someone?" I asked Rachael with a smile on my face.

"I will!" she responded confidently. "I know just who I'll ask. My friend Mark runs the Alibi Marina here in Fish Creek. I would bet that Mr. Wills keeps a boat there."

"Thanks!" I replied, giving her a thumbs up for enthusiastically accepting the challenge.

Mr. Chandler got everyone's attention and proceeded to give updates on events and committee meetings. He also announced that the next meeting would be at a restaurant called Chives, located in Baileys Harbor, and mentioned he was trying to get a speaker from the Green Bay Chamber of Commerce. After he reminded everyone that there was an election coming up, he took the opportunity to introduce me.

"Some of you may have already met Rachael's guest today. Her name is Claire Stewart, and she just moved here from Missouri. It sounds like she'll be contributing to our art community. Her business is called The Quilted Palette by Claire. Claire, we welcome you and hope you'll join the organization. There are many committees that could use your expertise."

"Thank you!" I responded with a nod and smile.

"Mr. Wills was giving you a pretty hard stare, by the way," Rachael whispered. "I have a feeling you're going to hear from him in the future."

"I'm probably not his type, but I love an interesting challenge!"

Rachael burst into giggles. "Let me know if you want to go to the next meeting," she offered. "Chives has great food."

"Let me think about that," I said. "I want my focus to be on art-related organizations if I can find them."

As I prepared to leave, several people introduced themselves. I lost track of Mr. Grayson Wills, which didn't surprise me. Rachael and I parted ways, and I began walking home. I was about to go in the house when I noticed that the woman next door was cutting back the spent blooms on her mums, so I walked towards her. She stopped and looked up at me.

"Good morning!" I greeted her with a smile. "We haven't

had a chance to meet. I'm Claire Stewart. Cher and I are friends, so she talked me into moving here from Missouri when she went home to take care of her mother."

"Oh, I know. I was so sorry to hear about her having to leave. My name is Cotsy. Dan, my husband, is at the store now. I saw activity at the cabin. Are you getting settled?"

"Pretty much. Things are a lot different here. I heard that you spend a lot of time in Florida."

"We do, but we'll be here until after Christmas this year. We actually love it here in the wintertime. It's beautiful! Our son and grandchildren live in Jacksonville, so we try to go there as often as we can."

"I don't blame you. I have to admit, I'm dreading the winter months here, which are much worse than in Missouri."

"Well, you'll find this location very convenient when you don't want to drive. So, are you employed?"

"I work out of my house, like Cher. We're both art quilters."

"Oh, how nice. I saw some of her quilts, and they were amazing. I don't know how you do it. I tried some scrapbooking recently, but even that takes patience, which I don't think I have much of."

"I'm trying to find a place to sell my work here in the county."

"With all the galleries and shops, you shouldn't have a problem."

"I've been admiring your beautiful landscaping and flowers. I'll bet you hate to see them die out."

"Yes, not to mention all the leaves we get here. We have

a short season, but I love gardening. Listen, if you should need anything while we're still here, just let us know. We want to have a little gathering of some kind during the Christmas holidays, so we'll be sure to include you."

"That would be great. Please drop in on me. You're welcome anytime."

"I'll do that!" she said as we parted ways. Where on earth had she gotten a name like Cotsy?

Chapter 29

Another week passed, filled with unpacking and trying to get familiar with Fish Creek. Puff seemed to appreciate that I let her use the quilt on occasion. The tone of her meows had seemed to soften. The next day would be my second meeting with the quilters, with the bonus that it would be at Marta's farm in Baileys Harbor.

November's weather was getting colder and windier. I was now in the habit of making a fire almost every night. Some evenings, I would sit near the fire and stare into it, just enjoying the warmth and beauty it offered. I was glad to have finished the commissioned piece that I had brought with me when I moved. I felt I had also made a big step by starting a painting of Cottage Row's narrow road, which was overshadowed by cedar trees on each side. In my painting, it was a challenge to capture the pale blue light coming through the trees. It was definitely a work in progress.

My cell phone rang at about ten just as I was thinking of turning in. I was pleased to see Cher's name appear.

"Are you in bed?" she quickly asked.

"No, but I was thinking about it."

"You're too young to be turning in this early, my friend. Don't you ever go out at night?"

"Not much. It gets dark so early now. I'm pretty content just staying here by the fire."

"Oh dear! My cabin is not a retirement home! Now, you may not need this reminder, but tomorrow is quilt club."

"Yes, Mama, I remembered," I joked. "Does that surprise you?"

"You're going, right?"

"I am, and Rachael is picking me up so we can go out to Marta's farm for lunch."

"Oh, you'll love it. She is such a good cook. I'll bet you'll have chicken and dumplings and some fresh apple pie from Marta's orchard."

"I hope so! That sounds great."

"It sounds like you and Rachael are really hitting it off."

"Yes, she's been so good to me. She brought me as a guest to the Chamber of Commerce breakfast."

"Oh, you didn't tell me about that."

"Cher, does the name Grayson Wills sound familiar to you?"

"I'm not sure," she said slowly. "Why?"

"He's a chamber member and owns a boat repair business," I shared.

"Not sounding familiar. Is he someone that you're interested in?"

"Not really, but he's gotten my attention. Rachael said she felt sure her husband would be happy to fix me up if I felt ready to go out."

"Well, his friends may be a little rough around the edges for you, so just be aware."

"Thanks. What about you? Have you been out?"

"A little. Carole and Linda from high school came over last week. They asked me to go to Cape and have lunch with them. We also did a little shopping. It was nice to get out."

"Wonderful! How are they doing?"

"Well, they had a million questions about you, of course. They wondered if you'd heard from Austen. I think they would love to hear from you."

"I know. I feel bad, but I really don't want to talk about all of that just yet."

"You can't run from life, no matter how far away you go."

I hung up, sensing that Cher had just given me some sound advice. I had run away from Austen rather than having a major confrontation. I still thought I'd done the right thing by moving out of that relationship and starting over. Interestingly, it made me happy that Cher and I were essentially exchanging friends, something that was keeping us from feeling so alone in our new situations.

Chapter 30

I was totally excited when Rachael picked me up to head out to Marta's farm. With fall colors mostly intact, the drive along Route 57 was beautiful.

"This may be the last weekend before our first snowfall," Rachael warned. "We could easily have a dusting before Thanksgiving. By the way, do you have plans for the holiday?"

"No, but I'm not concerned about that. I should check to make sure Cher has a snow shovel in that shed of hers."

"Well, you're invited to join us at our place. We typically draw a pretty large crowd, so we have Thanksgiving in the barn. We're going to try to have Christmas lights and decorations up by then, because our tree deliveries start around that time."

"It sounds fun!"

"It gets crazy. Charlie fries one turkey and bakes the other. He loves all the food preparation, and folks bring foods that we share. I don't know if you'd like all of that, to be honest."

"I'll keep your offer in mind. I may not want to miss it."

Rachael smiled.

We were a half hour out of Fish Creek, and I was really enjoying the drive.

"Marta is such a dear to have everyone over to her house each year," Rachael said.

"She seems so warm and loving. You said she's been in the club for a long time?"

Rachael nodded.

We turned off of Route 57 onto a small, narrow road lined with trees. Soon a freshly painted white fence appeared, which Rachael explained was part of Marta's farm. Next, we came to a large white frame farmhouse with a big red barn.

"This is a huge place," I observed.

"Oscar and Marta are big dairy farmers and have an enormous apple orchard."

Frances and Olivia pulled in next to us as we parked. Marta came out of the house to greet us. She wore a large bibbed apron that was tied around her hips, much like my mother had used to wear. She had a welcoming smile as we approached.

"Marta's wearing her hair in a bun today," I noted.

"Yes, she has really long hair that she mostly braids into some kind of style."

"Welcome! Welcome!" Marta's jolly voice greeted us.

"Marta, your farm is spectacular!" I exclaimed.

She beamed. "Come on in. Oscar has built a nice fire if you want to warm up."

Oscar joined us for a moment. He was wearing bib overalls with a red-and-black checked jacket that covered his robust body. He would make a great Santa! "Have fun, ladies!" he said as he left us and headed outdoors.

We all gathered in a spacious paneled room that had a large stone fireplace with a blazing fire. Marta introduced us to her eleven-year-old grandson, Billy, who took our coats. We were told to help ourselves to some hot cider that was waiting for us. The table with the cider was in a corner of the room and was topped with a red checkered tablecloth. I took a cup of cider and walked around to take in my surroundings. Before long, Marta asked us to move into the dining room. That room was occupied by a long wooden harvest table that was covered with table settings, glasses, and a fall centerpiece. Something told me this that this table was filled frequently.

Before we sat down, Marta said she wanted to show us the quilt she was working on. We followed her into the living room, where she had set up an old-fashioned quilting frame. I was reminded of my grandmother. The frame held a striking red-and-blue Log Cabin quilt that Marta had only started quilting.

"It's beautiful, Marta!" I exclaimed.

"Thanks." She blushed. "The blue fabrics are mostly from old shirts. The quilt is for Billy, and those are the colors he chose. I told him that he has to put in a few of his own stitches to make it his own."

Everyone chuckled, thinking of Billy learning and applying his first hand quilting skills. Some of the quilters remarked that they had never quilted at a frame like that. As they chatted, my attention was drawn to the shelves around the room, which displayed many, many family photos. The home gave me the feeling that many generations of Marta's family had enjoyed these same rooms through the years.

"Soup's on!" Marta announced as the group moved back

toward the dining room. "I hope you're hungry and don't mind having my dumplings again."

Everyone's response led me to believe that I was in for a treat! Two large soup tureens were placed in the middle of the long table, both filled to brim with chicken and dumplings. Two baskets of homemade sliced bread and a large bowl of orange Jell-O salad with celery and carrots were also passed around.

"Marta churns her own butter," Rachael said as she passed it to me. "Wait until you taste it."

I loaded my plate like it was going to be my last meal. Everyone seemed to enjoy every bite as we continued our conversations. It was fun to see this quilt group in an informal setting instead of in the more somber atmosphere of the library.

Chapter 31

"Save room for pie!" Marta advised as she busied herself in the kitchen. When she brought two hot apple pies to the table, I had to admit that I was full, but it was impossible to say no. Billy walked around the table putting scoops of vanilla ice cream on everyone's pie while Marta filled our coffee cups.

"Thanks so much for this delicious meal, Marta," Greta said.

"Thank you. I love to cook," Marta responded. "We did another apple picking before the first frost, so I have a small bag of Honeycrisp apples for each of you."

I couldn't believe her generosity. Billy was standing by the door, stacking the bags for us to take home following the business part of the meeting.

"We'll be back at the library for our next meeting," Greta announced loudly. "We have a woman coming to talk about Quilts of Valor. She's coming from Sturgeon Bay and is likely looking for help. Also, I want to remind you that the library is collecting coats for the needy," she added. Then she asked, "Do we have any show-and-tell projects today besides Marta's beautiful Log Cabin?"

"I do!" Frances responded.

We watched as she pulled a black quilt from a bag. Olivia proceeded to help her hold it up. The black fabric she had chosen for the background really set off the collection of adornments on the quilt. Frances wore a considerable amount of jewelry, and the quilt was constructed in a similarly layered style.

"I made this after my Aunt Lizzy passed. The blocks have some of her doilies, dress fabrics, and buttons in them. Making this out of things that meant something to her made me feel so much closer to her. It really reflects who she was and what she enjoyed collecting and wearing. I'm going to give it to her daughter for Christmas."

"Frances, that is really sweet of you," Greta replied. "We can tell that you put a lot of thought and time into it."

"Indeed!" I agreed.

Under the table, Rachael nudged my leg, and I was uncertain as to what she was trying to communicate to me.

"Any other show-and-tell items?" Greta asked as she looked around the table.

"I brought a baby quilt that I've just finished," Ginger said. "It's from a panel, but I did spend a lot of time embroidering family names on it. I worked on it in the shop when I wasn't busy. My sister-in-law is due any day now." The quilt was a darling ABC panel that Ginger had turned into a masterpiece.

"Very nice, Ginger," Greta complimented her. "If no one else brought anything, we should probably be on our way. We certainly thank Marta and Billy for the wonderful meal. I hope you all have a wonderful Thanksgiving!"

It was nice to see another side of Greta on this occasion. As Billy brought out our coats, we wished one another a good Thanksgiving holiday and thanked Billy as he handed us our bags of apples.

"That was a wonderful experience," I said to Rachael when we got in the car.

"Seeing that awful black quilt sure was an experience!" Rachael responded sarcastically.

"Rachael!"

"I'm telling you, that Frances is spooky. Ever since her husband died, she hangs out at the cemetery."

I chuckled. "Well, she's a quilter who happens to be a little different, that's all. I frankly love black in a quilt, but that was kind of morbid, I have to admit."

"Olivia tolerates her, and I know it isn't easy sometimes. Olivia can get weird sometimes, too, when she goes overboard with the Gees Bend quilts."

"Really?"

Rachael nodded. "I bought a small quilt made by one of them at an auction. I support their efforts, but sometimes, it's all Olivia wants to talk about."

"Well, there are a lot of injustices going on in the world, and many quilters depict them in their quilts. As an artist, I have no problem with that."

Rachael shrugged her shoulders.

It was late afternoon before I got home. I threw myself onto the couch, hoping for a nap. Puff walked by to see if there might be a quilt to sleep on. I decided I needed to report to Cher, so I gave her a call.

"How did it go today?" she asked.

"It was wonderful and interesting!"

"Dumplings and apple pie?"

"Yes, and a big bag of Honeycrisp apples to take home." I continued to tell her every detail about the lunch and Frances' black quilt. However, as we talked about the quilt, I noticed that there was something different in Cher's tone.

Chapter 32

"What's wrong?" I asked.

"Mom is really bad today. There's something else going on with her, I think. I'm taking her to the doctor this afternoon."

"Cher, I feel so bad for you."

"It's scary enough when I have to worry about her turning on something she shouldn't, like the stove or the water in the bathtub. I can watch for those things, but I can tell that she doesn't feel well. That's upsetting in a different way."

"I don't know how you handle any of it."

"I find myself wanting to scold her, and I absolutely cannot let myself do that."

"Can you take her anywhere?"

"I used to, but now I'm more cautious. She's unpredictable." Cher sighed. "She does seem to have a decent appetite most of the time, so that's good."

"Well, be thankful for the good moments."

"I try to remember that. Honestly, though, I feel like she's passing away before my very eyes."

"Oh, Cher Bear, I'll continue to pray for both of you. I

love you."

"Thanks, Claire Bear."

I hung up feeling terrible for Cher and somewhat guilty that I still had a healthy mother. I leaned back on the couch and let the tears roll down my cheeks. Eventually, I did take a short nap, until I felt the movement of Puff near my feet. I got up to make a fire. I planned to skip dinner since I'd had a big meal at Marta's. I turned on the local TV station and overheard a report that Julie's Park Cafe and Motel had been broken into. They said it was the sixth break-in in the area. Julie's wasn't that far from me here in Fish Creek.

A copy of the Door County Pulse was sitting on the table, so I scanned through it to see if any previous reports had showed up in there. The date on the newspaper was from two weeks ago, but I couldn't find anything. Feeling a little on edge from the news about the café, I picked up the phone and called Ericka.

"Hi, Claire," she answered.

"Can you talk now?"

"Sure. I'm just paying bills. What's going on?"

"I just heard about the break-in at Julie's. It's the sixth in the area. Do you know about any of the others?"

"I didn't hear about Julie's, but I know one of the clothing shops had a break-in last week."

"Do they have any clues?"

"The thieves seem to be interested in targeting businesses, so I wouldn't worry about it."

"Ericka, I'm sitting here in a very dark corner of Door County. I live alone and would be an easy mark."

"Do what you feel you need to do, but security systems aren't cheap. Maybe when you put up your Christmas tree lights, they'll help light your place. Naturally, if you need George's help to do anything, give him or me a call."

"Thanks, but if you hear any more about these break-ins, will you let me know?"

"Sure."

Not feeling much better as I hung up, I began to do some research on security companies in Door County. I wrote down a couple of phone numbers so I could get some estimates. Picking up my quilting helped me get my mind off the feeling that I was in danger. Thankfully, I passed the remainder of the evening in peace. When I glanced at the time, it was eleven, and I decided that it was time for bed.

Upstairs, Puff stood at the door, waiting for me to close it on her. I sighed. I had to give her credit for being tenacious! I picked her up and placed her on a corner of the bed. "Stay only on this corner," I instructed. She looked up at me in wonder. I crawled into bed and turned out the lamp on the bedside table. I waited for Puff to make a move, but felt nothing. Maybe she really did understand what I had said to her. I tried to convince myself that she was there to protect me, but I wasn't sure how that could actually be possible.

Chapter 33

When I awoke the next morning, I quickly sat up to find Puff still curled up on the corner of the quilt. I smiled to myself, pleased at her good behavior. I headed downstairs to fix her breakfast, and she quickly followed. My cell rang as I was opening the can. "Good morning!" I answered.

"It's me, Ericka. Are you out of bed?"

"Yes, I was just feeding Puff."

"Oh, good. I was going to ask if she was still alive."

"Funny."

"I want to drop off a petition that I'd like you to sign. It's about a development that I'm opposed to. I forgot to tell you about it last night when you called."

"Okay, I'll take a look at it," I agreed. "I'm still trying to figure out what to do about how dark it is back here. I think I must make some changes. Maybe it didn't bother Cher, but hearing about the break-ins makes me nervous."

"You mean like adding lights?"

"Yes. I was thinking about putting at least one where the shed is in the back. I'm also going to check on a security system."

"You're really serious."

"You mentioned George last night. Do you really think that's something he could help me with?"

"I don't know now. I spoke to him this morning, and he's working overtime at his job these days. Rob has done some things for me that required electrical work, so I could ask him."

"That would be great. I don't mind calling him if you would bring his number with you."

"Sure. See you soon. I've got a meeting at work this morning, so I can't stay long."

I hung up and fixed a cup of coffee, thinking that I was beginning to get hooked on Door County coffee. I wondered what kind of petition Ericka wanted me to sign. I didn't particularly want to get involved in anything controversial, being so new to the area. I got dressed quickly, and it wasn't long before Ericka was at my door. "Come in! Got time for a cup of coffee?"

"No, but here's the petition. This development affects all of us."

"What on earth is it?"

"It's a proposed development for low-income housing to be built on an exceptionally beautiful piece of property not far from here. We must protect this lovely county, because tourism is our number one economic source. The petition will explain the situation if you read it. I need you to sign it."

"Sure. I'll let you know what I think."

She gave me an odd look, clearly disappointed that I hadn't rushed to sign the document. Then she continued, "Oh, I talked to Rob, and he said for you to give him a call." She handed me a piece of paper with his number on it. "Your place is looking nice, by the way. I see that you're making some changes here and there."

"Thanks. Little by little, I'm figuring things out. I can't wait to decorate this place for Christmas."

"Christmas? We need to get through Thanksgiving first! Do you have plans?"

"No, but Rachael said I could join her. I'm not sure that I need to go anywhere, frankly."

"You and Cher are so much alike. Okay, I've got to run. Bye, Puff!"

Puff eagerly followed Ericka to the door as if there was hope of her being rescued, but Ericka was careful to keep her from escaping outside. I put the papers on the kitchen table. I would look at them later. My priority was to call Rob and get him booked to help me with an outside light. I got my phone and called the number Ericka had given me.

"Rob, it's Claire Stewart. Is this a good time to talk?"

"What's up? Ericka said you needed some lighting done, right?"

"Yes, I would like an outdoor light installed in the back by the shed. Can you do that?"

"Sure. I'll come by around three and see what I can do. I just need to know exactly where you want it."

"Thanks so much. I'll see you later." I hung up, feeling a sense of relief that I was doing the right thing. I then looked at my list of security companies and saw that there seemed to be only one in Sturgeon Bay. I called and had to leave a message for them to call me back. I felt comforted knowing that I had taken two steps to make myself feel more secure in my little cabin.

Chapter 34

I started reading the material Ericka had brought by, and as she said, it was about the city wanting to purchase land for low-income housing. They had first option from the landowner, who wanted to sell some acreage close to the Bluffs at Cottage Row that was now undeveloped. I was interrupted when Rachael called.

"Hey, what's happening there?" she asked.

"Oh, Ericka has me reading a petition regarding some proposed development here in Fish Creek."

"I see. She's getting you involved in the community, then."

"Well, it's interesting to hear about. I feel like I'm too new to have an opinion at this point."

"Well, I'm calling with a proposal of my own," Rachael said, sounding hesitant.

"Name it."

"I may have shared with you that we're starting the Christmas tree portion of our business this week. We just had our part-time employee quit unexpectedly. I usually help Charlie outside when the tree sales pick up, and the employee

116

handles the barn quilt sales inside the barn. Is there any chance that you could help us out every now and then before Christmas? I think you would enjoy it."

"Rachael, I have a job, and I'm not even totally settled in here yet."

"Can I at least show you around when you come? I wouldn't need you every day. You would meet folks, and there's nothing like being around Christmas trees during the holiday season! How about coming out tomorrow?"

"Tomorrow?"

"Yes, tomorrow. I'm still hoping that you'll join us here for Thanksgiving."

"Your Thanksgiving celebration does sound like fun. I'll think about it, and I guess I could come out for a while tomorrow."

"Claire, you're a dear. I promise that you won't regret it."

When I hung up, I wondered what I had gotten myself into. Even though I had grave reservations about taking time out of my own work schedule, being involved with a Christmas tree farm and barn quilt business sounded surprisingly perfect for the season.

I returned to reading the petition. There didn't seem to be a winning solution for this problem. Low-cost housing was needed for individuals working in the tourism sector. However, that piece of land was in a prime location, and surrounding homeowners were understandably pushing back. I didn't feel like I could sign the petition. I knew Ericka would be disappointed.

At three, I was pleased to see Rob pull in the driveway. I let him in from the cold so we could discuss my idea.

"So, you want an outdoor light installed. Do you want to come out and show me where you'd like it?"

I got my coat, we went behind the house, and I showed him the location where I thought he could attach the new light. I wanted it to shine brightly enough to illuminate the area around the shed. Rob told me to go back inside and that he'd check out the wiring and see what else he needed for the job.

"I'll take a cup of hot tea when I get done here," he suggested with a wink.

I poured the tea and began to think of other odd jobs that he might do for me. About fifteen minutes went by before he came back in.

"Mission accomplished. I know what I need and will be back to finish it. Man, that fire feels good. I guess winter has begun. Thanks for the tea."

"You're welcome. Do I owe you anything now, or would you like me to write you a check when you return?"

"Don't worry. We have time to settle up."

"Well, I have some other things when you're not busy."

"Like what?" Rob asked as he sipped his hot tea.

"I need shelves upstairs and something under my bed for storage."

"Show me the way," he said, setting his cup on the table. "Say, your place is really shaping up."

Chapter 35

I began by showing Rob the tubs filled with things that I still needed to unpack. He shook his head in disbelief. I showed him where I thought some shelves could be added for books. "I did bring this small safe with me that I keep my jewelry and some keepsakes in. Poor George carried it in. I didn't want to leave it with Mom."

"Well, that's all fine and good, but if you're afraid of being robbed, thieves can carry it out the same way. The last place you want to put this is in your bedroom. That's the first place anyone would look for such a thing."

"I suppose you're right. Where would you suggest that I put it?"

He thought for a bit. "What about that coat closet downstairs? Would it fit in there? You'd have to cover it with something."

"I think that could work, but that clever suggestion means that you'd have to carry it downstairs!"

We both burst into laughter.

"Okay, let's get 'er done," Rob said, trying to lift the safe. "This had better work, because I'm not going to carry it back up!" With significant effort, he got the safe wedged in the corner of the small closet downstairs. I told him I would think of a way to cover it. Before he left, I thought of the Christmas lights and asked if he could help with that as well.

"I'd better leave before I have a full-time job here," he joked.

Rob left, and I felt like I had taken a couple of productive steps to keep myself feeling secure while living in the cabin. I sat in front of the warm fire and started a Christmas to-do list, which included the gifts that I needed to buy. I needed to send a few Christmas cards, but then that would let a lot of folks know where I lived. Austen probably knew by now anyway. Perhaps one of the art galleries would have some nice cards with Door County scenes on them.

The day had passed quickly. I warmed some soup and returned to my place in front of the fire. Puff kept walking back and forth, looking for any sign of a quilt appearing on the couch. I felt like I was getting rather good at reading her mind. She was likely waiting to see if Cher would show up one day. My phone was sitting nearby, so I took a photo of Puff to send to Cher.

...Puff is still waiting for your return.

There was no response. Even though Cher had teased me about going to bed so early, I guessed that she was fast asleep in our little hometown. My thoughts returned to Rachael's offer of a part-time job. I needed to stay focused on my work as an artist. It would be easy to get caught up in a job that I had no intention of taking. Thinking about it was making me tired. Puff was camped at the bottom of the stairs, waiting for me to go up. I gave in to the early bedtime, and Puff followed. As soon as I arranged the quilt, Puff knew her place and got comfortable. If Cher could see this, she would never believe it! Puff and I fell fast asleep, each enjoying the warmth and comfort the quilt provided. The next morning, I was barely out of bed when my phone rang. It was Ericka.

"If it's alright, I'll stop by before work and pick up the petition."

"Sure. I just woke up, but come on over. I just couldn't sign it, Ericka. I'm sorry."

"What?"

"I'm still so new to the area, and to be honest, I can see both sides of the issue. I could easily be one of those low-income residents who can't find a place to live. Luckily, I have a nest egg to help me."

"Oh, brother! Claire, if the area keeps developing in the ways outlined by this proposal, Door County won't maintain its charm. Without that draw, tourists won't choose to come here, and they're our number-one means of economic development."

"You make a good point, and I commend you for fighting for what you believe. Until I get to know this county better, I have to stay silent."

"Okay, okay," she acquiesced. "How did it work out with Rob?"

"He's amazing. He'll be back to finish up some things. The light will make me feel safer. He may be back as early as tomorrow to get that installed, even if I'm not here."

"Good. I'll see you shortly, then."

Within minutes, Ericka stopped by with a look of disappointment on her face. However, she was pleased when I told her I was going to consider helping Rachael with the barn quilts. She had heard about their employee leaving and knew that they could really use the help.

Chapter 36

It felt like it could snow today. On the way to Rachael's house, I drove slowly to make sure I didn't miss my exit to turn off Route 42. Rachael had said there would be a sign advertising the Mistletoe Holiday House. I easily spotted the sign and turned right. Her business would be about a mile down the road.

There it was, a big red barn with a barn quilt prominently displayed on the front. Next to it was a small white building adorned with more barn quilts, lots of greenery, and Christmas trees. The whole scene could have been the front of a Christmas card.

I pulled into the spacious parking lot, where only a few vehicles were parked. Behind the barn was a modest ranch-style house that I assumed was Rachael's residence. Out of the barn came a man who must have been Charlie. He was a robust individual with a short beard and a big smile. He wore a red plaid shirt and denim jacket. To top off his outfit, his head was adorned with a Santa hat.

"Welcome, Claire! I'm Charlie. Rachael's feeding the

goats out back. She'll be with you shortly. We sure appreciate you helping us out here."

"Nice to meet you! Are you on Christmas tree duty today?"

"Well, I'm doing a little bit of everything until you and Rachael get settled inside the barn. Let's go inside where it's warm, and I'll show you around."

"Now, Charlie, I can't promise a whole lot. I want to see what's involved first." He nodded but held my gaze for a moment. I could see he was really hoping that I would be able to help.

It was good to get inside and see the large, colorful structure lined with barn quilts and hanging greenery. Charlie began to explain how some things worked. "We keep this woodstove going for folks to warm up by. We have a small one in the white house, too, since we have plenty of wood to burn around here."

"Charlie, you have quite a place here! Is that corner where you construct the barn quilts?"

"Yes, and that's the messiest area, too!" he chuckled. "We have things in various stages of completion."

"How many years have you been doing this?"

"I think we're coming up on six years now. This was my dad's dairy farm until he passed. He was barely surviving at farming, so we slowly started changing things. Rachael always had these quilt patterns around, and that led to making barn quilts. Our neighbor lets us use his property next door to grow the trees, and the two businesses make a nice combination during the Christmas season. In the off season, Rachael gets anxious to be around people, so she picked up the part-time job bartending at the Bayside. She loves it and makes fairly generous tips."

"Hey, Claire!" Rachael called as she came towards us. "I see you've met the boss!"

"Now, she's got that backwards!" Charlie claimed with a laugh.

"Your place is fabulous!" I remarked.

"Ladies, I'll leave you alone now," Charlie interrupted. "I have to get back outside."

"Thanks, Charlie," I said as he left.

Rachael immediately started walking me around as if I had already been put on the payroll. Everything was priced, and she even had a time chart to refer to when customers placed specific barn quilt orders.

"How about a cup of coffee or some hot chocolate?" Rachael offered. "We keep them both going all day long for folks. Most of the tree buyers come inside to warm up and sometimes go out with a barn quilt in their hands."

"That's great!" I replied. "I still don't know whether I should be doing this, Rachael. I'm not totally settled, and I need to get my business going here in Door County."

"You have the rest of the winter to do that," Rachael argued. "Remember, we have a late spring here compared to Missouri."

"You have a point there. Please don't be upset with me if I decide that this is not for me," I pleaded.

"I promise! Why don't you look around a bit? I need to finish up a package for the FedEx driver who will be coming soon. You'll want to check out the white house as well."

"Good idea!" After taking in the barn quilt store, I put on my gloves and headed outdoors.

Chapter 37

Charlie was unloading some greenery that had just been delivered.

"Can I give you a hand with that?"

"Well, sure! The wreaths go over on that wagon. I'll get this garland."

I had to admit, working with the aroma of greenery was well worth the chill I was experiencing. When I finished, I went into the white Santa house, where a woodstove was putting out some nice heat. The wingback chair sitting near it caused me to wonder if Charlie had taken a nap in it a time or two. A nearby radio was playing Christmas music, and a small wooden counter provided a place for people to pay. A live wreath was attached to the bottom of the counter, placed there by Rachael, no doubt. Santa Claus would like to live there!

Charlie came inside with a customer who was buying a tree. He cut some rope from a big reel and handed it to the man while he paid. They then discussed how to secure the tree onto the customer's vehicle as they went out the door.

When Charlie came back inside, I asked him if many people bought their Christmas trees before Thanksgiving.

"Well, like anything, they get picked over as time goes on. The cut trees can stand outside a customer's house just as well as here on the lot. It's when they bring them into a warm house that they begin to dry out."

"I see. Well, this may be the first time since my childhood that I'll have a real tree."

"You'll never go back, I guarantee you!" Charlie said with a chuckle.

I noticed another car pull up, so I went back to the barn to help Rachael.

"I've got a Crock-Pot of chili going, Claire, so help yourself when you get hungry."

"Oh, it smells so good! I surely will!"

"I hope you can help us on Saturday morning, because I have to help Charlie outside with tree sales."

"Okay, I suppose I can as long as you'll be close by for me to ask questions."

"Absolutely! Wear something red that is also warm. When that door opens, everything gets cold."

"I can do that!"

I didn't waste any time tasting some of Rachael's chili before I went back home. Rachael said I should take some over to Charlie in Santa's house on my way, so I did just that. The more I got to know Rachael, the more I could see why she and Cher were such good friends.

Charlie's eyes lit up when he saw the chili. He was cutting rope into different lengths. "Thanks so much, Claire. By the way, how is Cher doing? I kind of miss her showing up around here."

"She's pretty tied down with her mother. I think she'll move back here someday. She loves Door County."

"That's good to hear."

I left the farm full of love and with a full tummy. If that place didn't put you in the Christmas spirit, nothing would. As I drove along, I remembered the Mistletoe Holiday House. I decided to stop and check it out. Thankfully, the shop was still open. An elderly woman greeted me as I walked inside. I immediately saw that it was much smaller than the Tannenbaum Christmas Shop. It was inviting, and there was something about it that reminded me of my childhood. A garland of red cherries caught my eye, and I thought how appropriate it would be on my Door County tree. It would be perfect with a popcorn garland if I had the time to make one. I decided that three packages would be plenty. I wished the clerk a merry Christmas and went on my way. Once again, I was reminded how friendly everyone was here in the county.

It was getting dark when I arrived home. The good news was that there was a light shining in the backyard. I got a text notification, and it was Rob.

> **...Sorry I can't get by to do more. I'll be in touch. Rob**

. . .It's fine. Come when you can. Thanks!

Puff jumped off her chair when I came through the door. Maybe she was thinking that I had brought her something. She was becoming more and more communicative as time went on.

Chapter 38

For some reason, that evening, Cher and her mother were on my mind. After I built a fire, I decided to call Cher. It took her a while to answer.

"Oh, Claire, how did you know?" Cher said when she answered.

"Know what?"

"Mom is in intensive care. She had a stroke this morning."

"Oh, Cher, I'm so sorry to hear that. I didn't know. I was just calling because you were on my mind."

"I found her on the floor in the bedroom when I checked on her this morning. She can't seem to speak, so she may have tried to call out for me. They have her stabilized, thank goodness. They said that sometimes speech can return." Cher began to sob.

I didn't know what to say. As Cher's sobs continued, I asked, "What can I do?"

"I called your mom right away, and she met me at the hospital. I can't tell you how comforting it was to have her here with me for a while."

"Oh, I'm glad. I can only imagine how upset she must be as well."

"I thought she had called you."

"She hasn't, but I've been out all day at Rachael's. What are they telling you?"

"Not much. The doctor will see her again during evening rounds. It can't be good."

"Oh, Cher Bear, I wish I could be there to give you a hug. I will pray for both of you. Don't give up!"

"I'm so glad that you called. It means so much."

"You know I would be sitting there next to you if I could."

"I know. I'll call you as soon as I learn more. I love you."

"I love you, too."

When I hung up, I was thankful to not be facing what Cher was. I felt so helpless. Puff kept pacing in front of me as if she knew something was wrong. She finally jumped onto the couch and cuddled next to me. I didn't know what to make of it. "You probably sense that your mama is hurting right now. I wish she had you to comfort her." I patted Puff's head absently as she purred. I felt consumed by Cher's situation. Needless to say, I spent the rest of the night on the couch. I cried myself to sleep, and to Puff's credit, she stayed right there as if her purpose were to stand by me.

The next morning, I heard from Mom. She said she hadn't wanted to call until they'd had an update on Hilda and knew how she had done through the night. "I'm afraid this will take her from us," Mom said, weeping. "They're concerned about her heart. I'm going over to the hospital this afternoon. It's hard to watch." She paused a long time before asking, "So, have you made any Thanksgiving plans?"

"No. I do have some options, but I haven't committed to any one of them. I've agreed to help Rachael out at her place. It's quite unique. They sell barn quilts and Christmas trees. They're shorthanded, and she's done so much for me since I've been here."

"It's nice of you to help. Being there would be perfect for the Christmas season," Mom said. Then she returned to the subject at hand. "You know, you're welcome to fly home."

"You know I'll be there if Hilda passes, so don't worry about that. Right now, I need to be here."

"I understand. I love you, honey."

"I love you too, Mom. Please take care, and remember that I'm praying for all of you."

"I know."

As I hung up, I felt so bad for the pain my mother was experiencing. Hilda and my mom had been friends for as long as I could remember. I fed Puff and began planning my day around cleaning and laundry. I now had a part-time job to work around. It would be very different from working at home.

As I began to clean, I learned that Puff didn't take kindly to my vacuum cleaner. She crawled under the couch, which was actually helpful, but I hated the fact that she was scared. When I moved my cleaning operation to the porch, I noticed some snowflakes coming down. This was my first snow in Door County.

I went to check the forecast on my phone. It said there would not be much accumulation, which was somewhat of a relief. When I started cleaning upstairs, I wished again for shelves to help with my storage issues. I decided to call Rob. He barely let me speak before he began to talk.

"I know, Claire. I'm sorry I can't get there to help you. I promised to help George with some things that he's working on."

"So when do you think you can come back?"

"I'll have to let you know. Everyone in the county panics in the late fall trying to get everything done before the first snowstorm."

"I understand," I said, but my understanding didn't diminish my disappointment. I took down Rob's address and slipped his payment into an envelope.

Chapter 39

Frustrated, I had to make myself think of something more pleasant. I walked to the porch and decided where I would like the Christmas tree to be set up. I had a wide space for one, so it would light up the whole front of the house.

Glancing at Rob's envelope, it struck me that I had not been to the post office to retrieve any mail for some time. The idea of picking up my mail at the post office was something new to me. I hadn't been for three days, and the light snow flurries were a bit of a concern.

I dressed in warm clothes and went on my way. A latte at the Blue Horse sounded like a nice reward for going out. When I got to the café, I looked around for Grayson, but no luck. He was likely an early morning customer. I got my coffee to go and moved on to the post office. There, I saw Lee, who was about to leave.

"Nice to see you, Claire," she greeted me in her Filipino accent. "I thought about giving you a call to see if you had a place to go for Thanksgiving."

"How nice of you to think of me," I replied. "I've received

some invitations, thank you."

"That's good. I think you'll make friends easily here. Sometimes we host a holiday party, and perhaps you'll be free to come."

"I would like that. I've driven past your home, and it's so beautiful!"

"Thanks. We do love it. I'm off to Sturgeon Bay to go to Barn Door Quilts. Have you been there?"

"No, but I need to. There's so much to be done first, and then Christmas is around the corner."

"I love the bookstore down the street from there, too. That's where Olivia's upstairs apartment is located."

"Yes, she said she loves living downtown."

"Well, Claire, I need to be on my way. I'll be in touch."

"I have to go as well. Good to see you!"

I stopped at Fish Creek Market while I was out. I needed bread and ended up buying some turkey slices from their deli as well. They had a wide selection of items for such a small store. Once home, I was so tired that I decided an early trip to bed wouldn't hurt. I had a big day in the morning as I started my new job. Although I was tired, my mind was drawn to Hilda fighting for her life and how her struggle was affecting Mom and Cher. I wondered if they would run into Austen at the hospital. He knew Hilda and would surely find out that she was there. Perry County Memorial Hospital wasn't that large.

I had been in bed for a while when I suddenly heard noises outside that I had not heard before. Was it the wind picking up, or was I just being paranoid about the recent break-ins? When the noise didn't stop, I sat up in bed, feeling alert and a bit alarmed. I decided to get up and look out the window.

I gently slid out of the heavy, warm covers so as not to wake Puff, who was sound asleep. I couldn't see anything from my bedroom window, so I decided to check downstairs.

I went to the top of the stairs and listened before I started down. Everything was quiet. The noise had stopped. I walked onto the porch and saw nothing unusual, but did hear a slight wind blowing through the cedar trees. I went to the back of the house but couldn't see the entire backyard. At least the light made me feel more secure. I would check for footprints in the snow in the morning. Seeing nothing unusual, I decided that I was fine and convinced myself that I had imagined the noises. I went into the kitchen for some water. Surely that would let any intruder know that I was awake and aware. I felt a bit frustrated that I was this easily unnerved. I went back upstairs and crawled under the covers. Puff sensed that was something going on and looked up at me. "Go back to sleep, Puff," I whispered.

I managed a couple of hours of sleep before my cell phone rang on the bedside table. I looked at the clock. It was only five in the morning! Who would be calling at this hour? I fumbled through the covers and reached for the phone. It was Cher.

"Mama's gone, Claire! She's gone forever!" Cher exclaimed through sobs.

"Cher, I am so, so sorry," I said in disbelief. "When did she die?"

"Around three this morning. I didn't want to disturb you." Little did she know that at that time, I had been walking around the house. "I knew you had to be the first to know so you could help your mom through this."

"Have you told Mom?" I asked.

"I'm going to call her next."

"What can I do besides come home and be with you?"

"Don't make any plans until I talk with the rest of my family."

"Sure. Wouldn't you know, Thanksgiving will be in the middle of all of this."

"Yes, and Mom loved that holiday so much."

"Keep your chin up, Cher Bear. I love you and will share your tears. You did everything you could to be there for her. I can't imagine how much she appreciated you doing that for her. You've been a gold-star daughter, and don't forget it. I love you."

"I love you, too."

Chapter 40

Later that morning, I was totally drained from crying. I finally got up and showered. I knew Mom would be calling soon, and I wanted to be strong for her. She would advise me as to when to come home. For now, I had to honor my commitment to Rachael and show up to help her. As I prepared Puff's food, she sensed that something was wrong. She kept turning her head as if she were asking me questions. Maybe she was feeling sorry for me! I wished I could know her thoughts.

I dressed in layers, knowing I could be outdoors some of the time. As I left the cabin, I saw some large footprints in the snow. I followed them to the back of the house, where they traced the circumference of the structure. How odd was that? I took a photo of the footprints on my phone. I followed the prints back out to the driveway, but they didn't go into the street. They went up towards the Bluffs at Cottage Row condominiums. I tried hard not to let my imagination run away with me. After all, I was safe now.

When I arrived at Rachael's, the parking lot was empty because of the early hour. I walked inside and felt the heat of the woodstove envelop me.

"Good morning!" Rachael and Charlie greeted me at the same time.

"Good morning to both of you!" I responded. "Are you surprised that I showed up?"

They laughed. "Help yourself to hot coffee. Come lunchtime, I have vegetable soup in the Crock-Pot," Rachael offered.

"Great!" I responded, inhaling the aroma of both.

"I've got to get over to Santa's house," Charlie noted as he put his gloves on. "Rachael, I'll need you out there when the Carters show up."

"Yes, sir!" she answered in mock obedience.

"I like your Santa hat, Charlie," I teased. "I'll bet it's really warm."

"It's in the spirit of the season," Charlie laughed. "Ho, ho, ho!" With a quick turn, he was off.

"Claire, I need to explain that two barn quilts will be picked up today. One is for Brunswick and the other is for Wills." Rachael gave me a wink.

I tried to extinguish the smile that appeared on my face and shook my head. While I hated to dampen the mood, I needed to tell Rachael about Cher's mother passing before customers began to arrive.

"Oh no! Poor Cher!" she said after I told her. "I had no idea she was that ill. I thought it was just the dementia."

"She had a stroke. That made everything worse. She also lost her ability to talk, which was really hard for Cher to take."

"I'll call Greta right away so the club can send flowers."

"That would mean a lot to Cher."

"I'll go to the office and do that before Charlie needs me outside. Just look around the shop and get familiar with things.

There's a feather duster if you see a need to dust anything off. We get pine needles everywhere from the trees, too, so it's almost always time to sweep up." With that, Rachael left to call Greta.

A couple walked in just as I began dusting. I asked if I could help, but they said they were just looking around while Charlie tied a Christmas tree to their car. They seemed to be fascinated with the barn quilts displayed all around the space. A bell rang from behind the counter, which made me jump. Rachael quickly came from the back room and got her coat.

"What's happening with the bell?" I asked, curious.

"It's Charlie letting me know that he needs help. I'll be right back. If you need me before then, you ring the bell and I'll return right away." I nodded and chuckled at their unique form of communication. As she left, in came the person I was curious about. Grayson Wills was wearing a denim jacket with a red plaid woolen scarf. He was even more attractive in casual wear.

"Mr. Wills."

He gave me a second look.

Chapter 41

"Ms. Stewart?" Grayson asked.

"You can call me Claire," I said with a smile.

"What are you doing out here?"

"I came to help Rachael today," I explained. "She and Charlie are short one helper, so I agreed to fill in. I thought it might be fun."

"So, are you having fun yet?" he asked, smiling.

"I just got here, but I'm sure I will," I replied. "Rachael said there's a barn quilt with your name on it waiting to be picked up. Do you have a barn?"

He shook his head. "No, but my mother does. She always gets excited when she sees a barn quilt, so I thought it would make a great Christmas gift."

"That's so sweet. Does she like quilts?"

"Oh, yes. She's quite a quilter. I have many that she's made."

"I hope you approve of this one. I can even wrap it for you if you like."

He picked it up and examined it. "I would appreciate that. This is very nice!"

"Did you know that this pattern is called Ohio Star?"

"Yes, that's why I chose it. My mother grew up in Columbus."

He walked around the room while I quickly wrapped the 30"x30" quilt.

"Here you go," I said as I placed it in his hands. "Is it satisfactory?"

"It looks great. It should be marked paid, as I gave Charlie and Rachael my credit card."

"Yes, you're good to go!"

"Well, Claire, have a great Christmas."

"You too. Maybe I'll see you at the Blue Horse before then."

"You've got me pegged, don't you? It's a regular habit of mine."

"It could easily become habit of mine as well."

"Are you going back to Missouri for Christmas?"

I was surprised he'd remembered where I was from. "No. I plan to have my first Christmas here in Door County."

"Well, I hope it's a merry one."

"Thanks!"

Grayson gave me a wave as he left the store. As I returned to dusting, I couldn't help but think about what a nice guy he seemed to be.

"Well, how did it go with Grayson?" Rachael asked as she came in.

"Mr. Wills was very happy with the barn quilt."

"That's it?"

"Yes, he just said that he got it for his mother, who grew up in Ohio."

"No personal conversation?"

"He was very nice and polite. That's it."

"Well, you sure were more aggressive at the chamber meeting."

"What did you expect me to say to him?"

"Well, you could have asked him a lot of questions about Door County so he could offer to show you around!"

I chuckled. "Seriously? I think we're both happy with the status quo."

"Okay, okay. So, have you heard back about any funeral plans for Cher's mother?"

"No. I plan to call her when I get home. You know, I have to go to Missouri for the funeral, and I'll stay a day or so since it will probably fall during Thanksgiving."

"Of course, that's fine. We can call one of Charlie's brothers to help."

"Good. Rachael, if you're going to be in here a while, I'd like to go out and select a tree."

"Sure! Charlie can drop it off later if you like."

"That would be awesome."

Charlie was helping someone else as I started looking at all the shapes and sizes of trees. The tree I picked couldn't be too big or too small for my back porch. It had to be just right.

"You see that tree by the white fence there?" I asked Charlie when he came my way. "That's the one I want."

"Okay! It's on us for helping, and I can get it to you this evening."

Just then, Grayson exited the white house with two wreaths in his hands. I'd thought he had left.

"I see you chose a Douglas fir," he noted. "It looks good! I chose a noble fir because they're supposed to have the strongest branches. Isn't that right, Charlie?"

Charlie grinned. "Yes, but most folks just go by the height and shape."

"Well, then I need one of those noble firs. Do you have one

similar to the tree I had chosen?" I asked Charlie. He turned, and Grayson and I followed him down another row of trees.

"Here's one, and it has a really good scent to it," Charlie pointed out.

"I like it. That's the one!"

Charlie and Grayson looked at each other in disbelief.

"Yes, that's the one!" I assured them.

They looked at each other again and chuckled.

"Here, Charlie, let me give you a hand with that," Grayson offered.

"Thanks!" Charlie responded, grateful for the help.

Chapter 42

I watched Grayson and Charlie load the tree onto Charlie's truck, then grabbed a live wreath for my door and threw it on top.

"What do I owe you?" I asked Charlie. "I can't let you guys give me this and even deliver it for free!"

"Yes, you can," Charlie stated firmly. "It's very kind of you to help us out on such short notice."

"I really appreciate this," I said. "I'll bet you hear a lot of delightful stories and meet interesting people through this job."

"We sure do," he agreed. "Grayson, I'll bet you'd enjoy a little part-time job like this. This is probably a slow season for you, right?"

"Actually, it's our busiest," Grayson replied. "Customers count on us to repair their boats in the winter so they're ready in the summer."

"Well, that makes sense," Charlie admitted. "Claire, I'll get this over to your house later this evening."

"That would be great. I'll be leaving town any day now, so I'd like to have it at the house and ready to decorate when

I return."

"I'll bet you'll need a watering feed of some kind, so I'll throw that on the truck as well. You've got to keep this watered as soon as it goes inside."

"Thanks, Charlie," I said, grateful for his expertise.

"Heading back to Missouri for Thanksgiving?" Grayson asked.

"Well, actually, I'm waiting to hear the details of some funeral arrangements," I explained. "My best friend's mother died. She was also my mom's best friend."

"Sorry to hear about Cher's mother," Charlie commented. "Give her my sympathy."

"So you know this person too?" Grayson asked him.

"I sure do. Cher, the daughter of the deceased, was in the same quilt club as Rachael. Of course, now Claire has filled her shoes."

"Thanks, but I could never adequately fill Cher's shoes, Charlie," I replied. "But Rachael reached out to welcome me into the group, and we became fast friends."

"That has to mean a lot," Grayson commented. "Well, I've got to get going and get this greenery delivered. You both have a nice Thanksgiving. Claire, I'm sorry for your loss."

"Thanks for your help, Grayson," Charlie said.

"Thanks for your tree advice," I called out to Grayson as he headed to his car. He turned around and smiled.

"Now there's a nice, single, local fella for you, Claire," Charlie teased with a wink.

"Is that so, Charlie? I'd better get back inside. I saw a couple walk in. I might get fired if I stay out here too long!"

Charlie chuckled and returned to work. When I got back to the barn, I could see that my help was needed. I did have knowledge about quilt patterns, and that seemed to be the question customers would ask most frequently. I also didn't mind talking to strangers.

At five, I checked my phone. I had missed a text from Cher that outlined the funeral arrangements. I could take a flight out of Green Bay, attend the funeral, and spend Thanksgiving with Mom. Luckily, it could all happen without me running into Austen. He had to know about Hilda's death by now. After all, it was a pretty small town.

"Thanks for your help today, Claire," Rachael said as I got my coat. "I hope you enjoyed it."

"I really did! Thanks again for the Christmas tree. It looks like I can be with my mom for Thanksgiving, but thanks for your kind invitation."

"You're welcome. Give Cher a hug from me. By the way, I saw you and Charlie having a conversation with Grayson. Is there anything that you want to report?"

I chuckled and shook my head. "Grayson advised me to get a noble fir because the branches are stronger. How about that?"

"Well, it's a start!" Rachael laughed.

Chapter 43

When I returned home, I felt I'd had a full, productive day. Puff was happy to see me. She jumped off her chair and followed every step I took. I had been home for around half an hour when Charlie arrived with my tree. I ran out to help him, but he insisted that he was fine.

"This isn't my first rodeo, Claire. This is what keeps me so muscular," he bragged as he flexed his muscles and laughed.

I laughed along with him as I held the door open and did what I could to make his task as easy as possible. The smell was heavenly, and I knew it would spread throughout the house. "Oh, it's even prettier than I'd imagined," I said when Charlie stood the tree up straight.

"It's nice to see where these trees end up after they leave the farm. I don't always get to see their destination. Again, I must remind you to check the water often. The trees soak it up quickly. By the way, have you given instructions to this kitty walking around that she is to stay out of the tree?"

"Goodness, I hadn't thought of that. Puff, did you hear that?" I said as Puff looked at me inquisitively.

"I don't know how much you plan to decorate, but cats love anything that dangles."

"Right now, all I have are lights. I'll keep your warning in mind as I purchase more things."

"Well, I'd better get back. Rachael had a nice roast cooking when I left, so I don't want to miss out on a good meal."

"No, you don't! Thank you so much for everything!"

"Happy Thanksgiving, Claire!" he said, walking back to his truck.

Charlie had some rough edges, but he was just a big teddy bear. I sensed that he and Rachael were quite happy together.

I stood and stared at the large, living thing on the porch and watched Puff prance around it like she was sizing up the situation. "You heard what Charlie said, Puff. You're not allowed to touch that tree, or you'll spend some time out in the cold." Puff looked at me like I was talking to the wind.

I did have to worry about her, especially when I left to go out of town. She had somehow claimed the front porch because of her wicker throne in the corner. She followed me into the kitchen as I made my flight reservations. Afterwards, I called Ericka to see if anyone could give me a ride to the airport in Green Bay.

"I can't help you, Claire. My vacation time is up. George may take you up on it since he'd like that time alone with you."

"I'm not in any way interested in George, sweet as he is, Ericka. I don't want to give him the wrong impression."

She snickered, indicating that she had been teasing and that I had taken her too seriously. Then she said, "I'll check around and call you back."

"Thanks!" We chatted for just a few minutes and then

hung up, then I went to the porch to put water under the tree. Puff watched, curious, but chose to stay in her chair. "Good girl, Puff. You'll like it when this is all lit up." My cell rang, and it was Ericka calling back.

"Sorry, my friend, no one is available."

"That's okay. I'll take my car. That will probably be best anyway."

"Please give Cher my love. Have a nice Thanksgiving with your mom in spite of the circumstances that brought you there."

"I will. I have to come back right after the funeral since I'm helping Rachael and Charlie."

"I still can't believe you committed to doing that."

"Hey, I actually enjoy it, and even got a free Christmas tree delivered for my front porch! You have to come over and see it after I get it decorated."

"I will. Have a good trip and a happy Thanksgiving."

Before I left the next day, I made sure the litter box was clean and that Puff had enough food and water for a few days. I thought of the tree. What could make it so that Puff wouldn't swing from the branches in my absence? I put two chairs right in front of it as if to protect it, even though I knew that might be wishful thinking.

I called Mom as I left the house. I almost called Michael to pick me up at the airport in St. Louis but decided it would be best to have my own rental car. That way, I would be free to get around while I was in town. Mom had mentioned how grief-stricken Cher was, but at least she didn't have to feel guilty about not being there for her mother anymore.

As I drove along, it was cloudy, cold, and windy and looked like it might snow. The weather would be warmer in

Missouri. When I arrived at the airport, I was pleased to see that I was scheduled to leave on time. If all went well, I could have dinner with Mom.

It had been a few years since I'd been on an airplane. The last time had been when Austen and I had flown to Las Vegas for a weekend. It was extreme, but very fun for him to get away where no one knew him. I wasn't into gambling, but he was intrigued. I had yearned to have some alone time with him and talk about our future, but that conversation never took place. In fact, the stay there was even more distracting than our lives back in Missouri.

I was jolted into the present by the pilot announcing that we were to prepare for landing. The flight had gone by without a hitch. Once off the airplane, I welcomed Missouri's warmer temperatures. The cold was one thing I would not miss about Door County during this visit home.

Chapter 44

The drive to Perryville in my tiny rental car was an experience in itself. As I drove through the deep rock cuts and foliage, I realized how much further south it was than Door County, as evidenced by the trees and plantings. Entering the city limits took me past the hospital, where Austen spent a lot of his time. I had to convince myself that I didn't need to look at every car that I met along the way, wondering if I would run into him.

Mom was reheating vegetable soup when I surprised her by coming in through the back door. "Oh Claire, I was beginning to wonder when you might arrive," she said, giving me a big hug.

"I'm here. I'm really here!" I declared, knowing we both wanted to cry. "I know how hard Hilda's passing is for you. I can't imagine losing my best friend after so many years."

Mom took my hand and led me to the couch to sit down. Her hands were shaking. "Don't worry about me. You really need to be there for Cher. She's been under a lot of pressure. Having you here will help so much."

"She'll be fine. I sent her a text and told her that I'm here.

She wants me to come to the funeral home early to join her family before the service."

"That's good. I'm going with Doris and Martha. We've played cards together for years."

I nodded.

"Being with them is comforting," Mom said, her voice trailing off as if she didn't know what to say next.

"It smells heavenly in here. Can I have some of that soup? I'll bet there are some homemade biscuits somewhere, too!"

She smiled as we got up to go into the kitchen. It was good to see Mom's face instead of just hearing her voice on the phone. I could tell that the longer I was there, the more she relaxed. I tried to talk about things other than the funeral, and we turned in early after the stressful day. Nothing had changed in my room since the last time I'd been there. Perhaps Mom thought I'd be returning.

The next day, I walked into the same funeral home that everyone in town had gone to for generations. I didn't think I had been there since my father's funeral. There might have been a few updates to the place, but otherwise it looked the same and brought back so many memories. I pushed them to the back of my mind so I could be there to fully support Cher. The greeter at the door sent me to the room where the family had gathered. There was Cher, in tears, surrounded by family members who were consoling each other.

"Claire, Claire!" she called out when she saw me. "I was hoping that you would be here soon."

"Cher, I am so, so sorry," I said as I hugged her tightly.

"Come see her, Claire," she said, taking my hand. "They haven't closed the casket yet. Doesn't she look peaceful? She's not in pain anymore."

I nodded and tried to contain myself. Cher's mother looked the same as the last time I'd seen her. She was wearing pink, which went nicely with her gray hair. "She was my second mom," I murmured, squeezing Cher's hand.

"Yes, just like your mom has been to me," Cher replied. "I can't tell you how much it meant to have her with me through all of this."

"It has to be so difficult for both of you." I consoled her.

By then, family members were moving toward the front of the room. I took a seat and watched each sibling say goodbye for the last time. It was heartbreaking.

The service was held at the funeral home. I sat with Mom and her friends, feeling like I was in a daze through the whole thing. I had to fight back thoughts that personalized everything, making me think of what I would do if the situation were reversed and it were my mother in that casket. I struggled to stay in the moment, again remembering my dad being in this place. Once again, I tried to pull my thoughts into the present. I kept an eye on Mom and was proud of how she kept her cool. Afterwards, I followed the cars out to the cemetery, which gave Mom and me a chance to visit my father's grave. "Where is Michael today?" I finally asked Mom.

"Busy. We'll see him tomorrow for our Thanksgiving meal."

That was just like him. Why couldn't he be here for Mom and Cher? He knew them all as well as I did.

The exhausting day included a luncheon at the church hall. It had all the wonderful dishes I'd grown up with, but I had lost my appetite. It was good to just get back to the house and relax. Mom said our dinner would be simple that night and that we would have a small turkey the next day. After the day's events, simple suited me just fine.

Chapter 45

Mom and I slept longer than usual the next morning, and it felt so good. We met at the coffee counter like we had on so many mornings and munched on rolls from Hoeckele's Bakery & Deli, which had been the town's signature business since the 1940s.

"So, do you have any regrets about your move?" Mom asked, quite out of the blue.

"Not so far. Door County has so many good qualities. One of the members of my quilt group has asked me to help her with her barn quilt business. It's just on the weekends before Christmas because they're shorthanded. They also sell Christmas trees at the same place, which her husband handles. She's been such a good friend since I arrived that I just couldn't say no. I know I told you a little about it before. You should see this place, Mom! It's right out of a Hallmark movie, and I know how you love those. They make the quilt signs in a big red barn on their farm, and a little white Santa house handles greenery and serves as a place for customers to warm up with a cup of hot chocolate or coffee."

"Oh, how special! I can just picture it. You'll probably enjoy working there."

I nodded in agreement. "They gave me a free Christmas tree for helping, and it sits on my porch. I just love it."

"Be sure to send me a picture! Do you have it decorated?"

"No, but I will once I return, if Puff hasn't destroyed it."

Mom giggled. "Yes, that could be a problem. Are the two of you friends yet?"

"After I got your permission, I let her sleep on a corner of the quilt. She just loves it."

"Now that's my girl! Oh, I'd better get that turkey in the oven." She then put on the same calico apron she had worn forever. It was comforting to go back in time, if even for a moment.

I was glad to be able to help prepare all the side dishes, such as creamed onions, mashed potatoes, sweet potatoes, and cranberry salad. I loved my yearly assigned job of setting the dinner table. My grandmother's Haviland china pattern was moss rose, and it was such a sweet remembrance of her. Mom hinted often that one day the complete set would be mine, but when on earth would I use it?

Michael finally showed up an hour before dinner was scheduled. He gave me a quick hug before asking about the funeral.

"You should have been there for Mom," I said simply. "Hilda was so good to us."

"Well, for what it's worth, I tried. We're shorthanded at work, and the paper has to get out. I don't have the staff I used to have, which makes everything more stressful."

"So I guess the newspaper is struggling, like so many other businesses," I replied. "Is yours going to survive?"

"I think so. We have some loyal advertisers, thank goodness. Hey, is Door County everything that it claims to be?"

"I don't quite know what you mean, but it's wonderful beyond words. It's like being at Cape Cod, except that I didn't have to leave the Midwest."

"Nice! So, what do you hear from Austen these days?" Michael asked while pouring drinks.

"Nothing. Over is the best way to describe the situation," I said firmly. "He's gone his way and I've gone mine."

"You sure gave up quite a cushy situation there," he said casually.

"Don't start, brother. He had no intention of marrying me, and the relationship wasn't fulfilling."

"Whatever. I just hope you can survive on pretty paintings."

"Did you mean that to sound as insulting as it did?"

"No, no! I just don't want you to be one of those starving artists."

I took a deep breath.

"Now, you two stop it!" Mom interrupted. "It's Thanksgiving and dinner is served, so be civil."

We did just that and conversed only about things that Mom enjoyed talking about. She belonged to the hospital auxiliary, helped out at church, and had so many friends. All of those were safe subjects. Because Mom had mentioned earlier that Michael might bring a date with him to Thanksgiving, I wanted to ask him if he had anyone special in his life, but as we visited, it became obvious that nothing had changed since I'd seen him last.

As the day went along, I realized that I was enjoying the time the three of us were spending together. I was certain that Michael felt the same way. By seven that evening, he said his goodbyes. After he left, I helped Mom clean up, and then we both said goodnight.

"Claire, I just hate the thought of Hilda being underground and alone during the cold tonight," Mom said as more tears appeared on her cheeks.

"Mom, you can't think that way. Hilda's spirit went to be with God. She was a good Christian and has a place in His home in heaven."

"I so want to believe that," she murmured quietly as she headed to her bedroom.

Once I was settled in bed, I fought to block out thoughts of the burial myself. My heart broke for Cher. I wanted to call her but held back because I hoped she was resting from all the activity. I did the next best thing and began to pray for her. Tears poured down my cheeks as I asked God to comfort and help my mom and my best friend.

Chapter 46

On the way to the airport, it was hard not to replay the sad moments of the visit in my head. As I waited for my departure, I decided to call Cher. "Are you going to be okay?" I asked, concerned.

"I'll be fine. I have a lot to keep me busy right now. I knew this time would come, but I still feel like I wasn't prepared. Thank you so much for coming. It meant so much."

"I'm sorry that Michael didn't make it. He couldn't get away from work in time. He said that they're shorthanded."

"It's okay. He sent flowers with a lovely note attached. I also got flowers from the quilt club, which was a big surprise. I'm glad they haven't forgotten me."

"I'll make sure of that. Ericka wanted to come so badly, but she couldn't get off work."

"Give her a hug from me. I'll get back there one day."

"Oh, Cher Bear, that would be wonderful. You still own my house, remember?" I laughed.

"It's yours for keeps unless you back out. I think it suits you nicely. I do feel guilty about leaving Puff with you."

"She's adjusting. Now, if she destroys my Christmas tree while I am gone, I may return her to Missouri."

Cher chuckled. "I can't promise anything regarding that."

I had to board the airplane, so I said goodbye. As soon as I got settled, the pilot announced that there was snow in Green Bay. It appeared that I was in for another adventure!

The plane landed an hour late. Having left my car parked outside required me to spend another half hour clearing off the snow and ice. That done, I had to drive slowly, as did everyone else. There were accidents along the way. I gripped the steering wheel so tightly that my muscles began to ache. The roads had been cleared, which was enormously helpful, and the scenery with the fallen snow was breathtaking. Cedar and pine tree branches held onto the snow as if it were ornaments. The apple and cherry trees in the orchards had branches half-covered with snow. Early Christmas lights appeared here and there on rooflines. I could envision the cabin with lights strung across the front, making it glisten in the night.

I had missed two phone calls, which I ignored until I pulled into my driveway. It was a relief to stop the car. I took a quick moment to thank God for getting me back safely. I opened the front door, and it didn't take long for me to notice that the tree had fallen forward onto the two chairs. I was sure it would have been flat on the floor had the chairs not been there. "Puff! Puff! Where are you?" No answer.

I took off my coat, dropped my luggage, and started looking for the little mischief-maker. My first thought was to check the bed. When she wasn't there, I looked in the other rooms upstairs. When I went back downstairs, I thought she might be hiding under the couch, but that wasn't the case.

Next was the kitchen. There wasn't any sign of her there either. I went back to the porch to move the chairs and set the tree upright. I looked to see if any branches were broken, but they seemed unharmed. It was then that I saw Puff, who was snuggled in a ball right under the tree. She barely gave me a look when I called her name.

"Oh, Puff. Look what you've done to the tree," I scolded her softly. "Let's get you back to your chair while I work on getting the tree fixed up again." I picked her up and carried her to her cushioned seat just in case she didn't understand English. She gave a meow of discontent, which I ignored. Turning my attention to the tree, I remembered Grayson's advice and was grateful that I had selected the type of tree with the strongest branches.

I went back to the living room to check on my calls. One was from Mom, asking if I had gotten home. I knew she had to be worried, so I called her back and left a message on her voicemail.

The other call was from Cher, asking me to call her. I put it off long enough to make a fire to take the chill out of the cabin, then got a glass of wine and got comfortable in front of the fire. Now I could settle into a conversation with Cher.

Chapter 47

"Cher Bear, how are you doing?" I asked immediately.

"It's so different around here. I find myself going into Mom's room to check on her."

"Oh, I can imagine. How sad for you. Did some of your family go home?"

"Yes, they all left this morning. It's kind of nice to have some peace and quiet. They all have their lives to go back to, and now I have to figure mine out."

"Sure, I understand."

"I'm glad you made it home safely. Was Puff okay?"

"She's playing with my patience," I laughed. "She messed with the tree while I was gone, but luckily, there was no damage. She managed to tip the entire thing over onto the chairs that I had set up as a barrier! When I got home, I couldn't find her at first, but I later found her nestled under the tree."

"Yes, that sounds like her. I should have warned you about that. She never tried to climb my Christmas tree, so I don't think you have to worry. Pets get a bit mischievous when their owners are gone. It's like a parent leaving the kids home alone," she explained. "The main reason I'm calling is because I wanted to tell you that I got a really nice sympathy card from Austen."

"Austen?"

"Yes. He said he heard the news and remembered meeting my mom. He hoped that I was doing well and wrote that if he could be of help in any way, I should just give him a call."

"Well, that's interesting!"

"I guess it was pretty nice of him to reach out, since he knows that you and I are good friends."

"The fact that he took the time to send a card tells me that he's up to something that will benefit him."

"That's not very nice," Cher scolded me.

"He either wants to find out information about me or hit on you in revenge."

"I see," Cher said slowly. Then she added, "Wow, he must have really hurt you. Frankly, Claire, I'm sure this is the last I'll hear from him."

"I wouldn't count on that. I know how he operates. His ego was hurt when I left him. He always wants to have the last word, and he didn't get a chance to do that because of the way I left. I've been waiting for him to strike back in some way."

"Maybe I shouldn't have told you. I'm sorry to have upset you."

"No, I'm glad that you did. Just be careful, and please don't let him know any information about me."

"Sure, Claire Bear."

As we hung up, there was a part of me that wished Cher hadn't told me about Austen's note. What a clever way for him to make contact, thinking he could make me jealous. He knew better than to contact my mother concerning my whereabouts.

I was so tired from the trip that all I wanted to do was relax in front of the fire. I stood and wandered out to the porch again. I started to hang my coat in the front closet when I noticed something out of place. The safe was not exactly where Rob had placed it. Was it just my imagination? I tried to nudge it back into place but couldn't. Feeling uneasy, I became worried that there might be more things out of place. I went upstairs to my bedroom to look around. Everything there seemed normal, but when I went into the office, I noticed that my checkbook was in a different location than I remembered. Had I written a check before I'd left and failed to put it back where I usually kept it? I looked inside the checkbook itself and found nothing unusual. My most recent check had been payment for the work that Rob had completed. Maybe I'd just had a lot on my mind before I'd left. I couldn't tell if my stack of bills and papers nearby had been moved. I didn't want to become paranoid, so I went back downstairs, feeling completely perplexed.

I sat by the fire and tried to settle the uneasiness that had crept over me. It was good to be home, even with a toppled Christmas tree. I was so relaxed that I put my head back and fell asleep until four in the morning! The fire had turned into ashes. I went upstairs to find Puff resting comfortably on the quilt. We settled in together and didn't wake up until eight, when the phone rang. It was Rachael.

"I'm just calling to make sure that you got back in time for our quilt meeting today."

"Today?" I asked in surprise.

"Yes. Did you forget? It's at the library again, and a speaker is talking about Quilts of Valor, remember?"

"Okay, okay, I'd better hang up and try to get there on time. Thank goodness it's close by."

"Great! I'll see you there."

Puff had already taken the clue and scampered down the stairs to wait for her food. I put on some presentable jeans and a sweater, then looked outside. There was even more snow on the ground. It was beautiful. After driving from the airport in the severe weather the day before, a drive to the library would be a piece of cake. After I got Puff taken care of, I decided to leave early and get some coffee at the Blue Horse.

Chapter 48

I entered the café, looking forward to my first cup of coffee for the day. I eyed the pastry options and decided on a hot cinnamon bun that had just come out of the oven.

"Good morning," Grayson said from behind me. "You're out early today."

"Yes, I'm on my way to quilt club," I muttered as I turned to face him, all the while wondering about my hair and makeup.

"I hope you got your Christmas tree home okay," he said, making small talk.

"Yes. Charlie delivered it the same day," I reported. "I had to go out of town the next day, but it survived being left with my cat – I mean, my friend's cat."

"Hmmm. I'll bet that's an interesting story," he said with a smile.

"Thanks for the tip about the type of tree that has stronger branches."

The server handed the coffee and the cinnamon roll to me, and in a moment of embarrassing awkwardness, I turned around and bumped into Grayson!

"Oh, sorry," he said, even though it had been my fault.

"No, I'm sorry," I assured him. "Nice to see you. Have a good day!" I scurried toward the door, feeling the color rise from my neck to my face.

"You too!" I heard him mumble as I retreated.

I got in the car, feeling completely unnerved. I should have known I might run into Grayson there. I probably looked like I'd just gotten out of bed, which I had. I sat there for a bit to gather my thoughts and enjoy a few sips of coffee. Now I had to face the Quilters of the Door, which made me chuckle.

"Good morning," I greeted Frances as we walked in together.

"Good morning, Claire," she said.

It sounded like she was in a somber mood. "Where's Olivia? Doesn't she usually come with you?"

"Yes, but she's down with the flu today," she explained. "She usually drives, so I'm not happy about it. Duty calls."

What did she mean by duty calling? Was this group like a sorority or a military group? I had to chuckle to myself as I went inside. I saw Rachael arrive, so we went to find a seat next to each other. I noticed everyone trying to get a seat in their usual place, but I had upset the apple cart.

"How's it going on the Christmas tree farm?" I asked Rachael, curious.

"It's going well," she answered. "I hope you're still coming out on Saturday."

"I will, I will," I assured her. "Does this snow hurt your sales?"

"No, as a matter of fact, it helps," she replied. "The snow adds a sense of urgency. Customers want to ensure that they get their tree, and it puts everyone in the Christmas spirit."

"Oh, I'm sure it does!"

Greta entered the room, and instantly everyone became silent. She took off her coat and immediately called the meeting to order. It was then that a new woman joined us. I assumed that she was the Quilts of Valor speaker. She sat down to listen to Greta's opening remarks.

"Good morning, ladies," Greta began in a businesslike tone. "I hope you had a nice Thanksgiving."

"Greta, before you start the meeting, Cher said to tell everyone that the flowers were beautiful, and that she thanks you very much," I interjected.

Greta looked perturbed, but nodded with approval. "Thank you, Claire," she said while some members whispered to one another. She continued, "As I informed you last month, I've invited Sylvia Brown from the Quilts of Valor organization in Sturgeon Bay to talk about their mission. Please welcome Sylvia."

A couple of the members clapped, but it felt rather uncomfortable with such a small group. Sylvia introduced herself as a military veteran who had served in the Navy. She described how the Quilts of Valor program started and how it had grown by leaps and bounds. Their goal was to give a patriotic quilt to every veteran. Sylvia explained that many of the elderly veterans had been overlooked for their service and how pleased they were when they were presented with a quilt. She focused on veterans living in Door County. We listened intently, and then she got to her request.

She said help was needed in Door County, so when she'd heard about our group, she'd approached Greta and asked to meet with us. When she explained what kinds of quilts she needed, she then asked if we had any questions. When she saw we had none, she distributed a sheet of information to each of us that included instructions as to where to turn in our donated quilts. I could tell that our little group was not jumping up and down to participate. Each member of the group really focused on their own type of quilts. Would Lee donate one of her intricate appliqué pieces? Marta had a big farm to run, Rachael had to make quilts for her customers, and Ginger had a business to keep afloat. I wasn't sure who would respond to the request despite the wonderful cause.

After Sylvia left, only a few members participated in the show-and-tell portion of the gathering. Rachael was anxious to get back to the shop, so she wasn't interested in going to lunch. Frances was sitting on the other side of me, so I asked if she would be interested in having lunch together. Her look of surprise took me by surprise!

Chapter 49

"Claire, I'd be delighted," Frances said with a big smile.

"Great, because I'm starved. How about The Cookery?"

The Cookery was only a block or so down the street, so we walked. Frances had a slight swagger to her gait. I could tell that some quilt club members thought that Frances was strange, but I wanted to find out for myself. We both ordered chowder and a salad. I told Frances that it was my treat since she had taken me up on my lunch offer. She was surprised, but looked pleased.

"Frances, did you have a nice Thanksgiving?"

She hesitated before answering. "It was just another day. I don't have family nearby."

"I'm sorry. Neither do I. I decided to fly home to be with my family and to attend Cher's mother's funeral. She was like a second mother to me."

"How sad for Cher. She's such a sweet gal. The only place I can go to be with my loved ones is the cemetery."

I wasn't sure I'd understood her correctly. "The cemetery?"

She nodded. "I know you may think it's crazy, but I find

it to be peaceful, and I go as often as possible."

"When did you start doing that?"

"When my husband died twenty years ago. It feels like yesterday. I know he looks forward to my visits. I told him when he was on his death bed that I would not forsake him."

"Do you have other family members there as well?"

"I do. I've also made a lot of friends here who have since passed, and I visit them frequently. Sometimes I take my quilting with me and just work on it while I'm there. Now that the days are getting colder, I don't stay as long."

"Well, I commend you for honoring the people that you love."

She looked astonished at my remark and remained quiet as our food was served. I wanted to change the subject, but once the server left our table, she returned to the topic.

"Did you like the black quilt that I brought to the club a while back?"

I felt that she was testing me. "Yes. I particularly liked that it was creative and personal, which is what I love about quiltmaking."

She smiled. "I made a similar one for a gentleman who lost his wife last year. He misses his wife so much that he goes to the cemetery every day to talk to her. He always admires my work, so one day I surprised him with a quilt."

"You have a special heart, Frances."

"I don't know about that," she said, suddenly looking shy. "Claire, let me hear more about you. How is it working out living in Cher's cabin?"

"It's working out well. Cher and I shared so much growing up. We always referred to each other as Cher Bear and Claire Bear, and we still do."

She looked at me, and I could see that she was surprised at what I had chosen to share. "What will Cher do now that her mother is gone? Will she stay in Missouri?"

"I really don't think so. Cher had said that if something happened to her mother, she would likely move back. I guess I'd have to give up my spot in the quilt club if that happened."

Frances had no response, as if that could easily be the case. "Have you found a gallery for your work?" she asked, changing the subject.

"No. I just haven't had time to pursue that yet."

Frances took a deep breath and smiled at me. "I think you'll have some luck with someone who looks like Clark Gable. You remember that movie star, don't you?"

I chuckled. "Of course," I confessed. "So I should keep my eye out for Clark Gable?"

She nodded, completely serious. I couldn't believe the conversation I was having. I had so many questions I wanted to ask, but as soon as Frances finished eating, she was ready to leave. She thanked me for lunch, rose, and excused herself. She certainly was a different kind of woman.

I decided to have a piece of cherry pie and a cup of coffee before I left. I was tempted to take another pie home but decided against it. It was nice to just sit and think about my conversation with Frances for a bit. The restaurant had suddenly become busy. I was such a people-watching person. I wondered if the staff could tell a tourist from someone who was not. Rachael had said that most of the locals knew each other.

After I took my last bite, I decided that I'd better get home. It was no wonder that I wasn't getting my quilting business going. I was too busy unpacking, reacting to life, traveling to funerals, and going to quilt club!

Chapter 50

A couple of inches of snow had accumulated during the night, so for the first time, I saw a truck pull into my driveway and plow the snow to the side! I was grateful that my neighbors had decided to continue the same favor they had extended to Cher. Today, I wanted to decorate my tree and do a little painting of some kind. I missed painting terribly. Tomorrow, I would be back at Rachael's place.

After I fed Puff, I started popping popcorn to string on the tree. It would complement the cherry garland I had purchased at the Mistletoe Holiday House. I made a fire and got comfortable on the couch to begin the repetitive yet rewarding process of stringing popcorn. Puff was taking a great deal of interest in the process, which was not a good sign for the future.

After putting white lights on the tree, I was tempted to leave it alone because it was so beautiful. It lit up the whole house. I quickly put on my coat and rushed out to see it from the window. It glowed in spectacular fashion. No one could drive by without noticing its beauty. Lights across the top of the cabin would be great if I could find someone to string them for me. Lights towards the end of the driveway might be pretty as well. There weren't any bushes to decorate, but perhaps some lights could be wrapped around a nearby tree trunk. There was something about white lights at Christmas that gave sparkle to my soul. With great satisfaction, I went inside and observed Puff pacing the floor. She was likely planning her strategy for the tree. "Isn't it beautiful, Puff?" I said aloud. "I want you to be a good cat and just look at it." She left the room, ignoring my comment.

My popcorn string would take forever, I decided, so I went ahead and put on the cherry garland. I had just finished when I saw Ericka pull in the driveway. What was she doing here during the day? Maybe she was on her lunch hour.

"Hey, Ericka, what do you think of my tree?" I asked as she came inside.

"I love it! You can see it from way down the street. I think Cher only had a small tree placed on a table."

"Well, I'm a Christmas person, and I'm hoping that Puff will leave it alone. What brings you here this time of day?"

"I was out picking up lunch for the crew at work, but I thought I'd stop by to see if Rob had been around to help you."

"No, why?"

"George said he hasn't been able to get ahold of him, and he thought Rob may be out here helping you. Has he called or anything?"

"No, the last time I talked to him, he said he was busy helping George and didn't have time for me."

"Well, that's not the case," Ericka sighed.

"I really could use him, but he hasn't been dependable, so I need to find someone else."

"If I were you, I'd just go out to Nelson Shopping Center

and pick up some shelving. They may have some handyman names to give you as well."

"That's a very good idea."

"How do you like your part-time job on Rachael's farm?"

"I like it a lot. I'm going there again tomorrow."

"Have you heard from Cher? There's a condo for sale in my building that I want to tell her about if she thinks she'll be moving back here."

"Good thinking."

"Well, I need to move on. By the way, I love what you're doing to this place. I can tell that you're feeling right at home. If you hear from Rob, would you let me or George know?"

"Of course. You and I need to have lunch sometime soon."

"I'd like that."

As I watched Ericka drive away, I wondered what Rob was up to. I knew he drank; I could smell it on his breath when he was around. Perhaps he'd gone on a drinking binge somewhere.

I took a lunch break, ate a turkey sandwich, and decided to start painting. Since it was Christmas, perhaps I should paint something seasonal. Puff walked by, looking very confused. She wasn't used to me camping out on that side of the porch. I then watched her size up the tree, getting closer and closer. I was about to distract her when she found a little place under the tree to curl up! I had to admit that it was quite cute. There was my subject matter. I was sure she'd stay there and nap, so she would be the perfect model. Cher would love a watercolor of Puff. It would make the perfect Christmas present. As I began, I found that I was indeed rusty. It had been too long between brush strokes, but finally it all came back.

Chapter 51

It wasn't until a big truck backfired outdoors that Puff moved. She stretched a bit and then returned to her position. I worked quickly and got better as time went on. The painting was not large, but I knew that Cher would just love it. I worked until evening set in. As I painted, I naturally had Cher on my mind, so I decided to give her a call.

"I was thinking of you, too, Claire Bear," she responded after we exchanged greetings.

"How are you doing?"

"Well, it's up and down, as you might imagine. Your mom was over today, and she helped me make a few decisions regarding Mom's personal things."

"That's good. It had to be awfully hard for both of you."

"Your mom knew a lot of nonprofits that could benefit from some of Mom's things. I'm going to keep all of her quilts, of course."

"That's good."

"I'm pleased that my siblings and I agree about putting the house up for sale. It needs work, and none of us want it."

"So now you'll have to decide where to live."

"I know. Ericka is pressuring me to consider the condo complex that she's in. I certainly love Door County, but I'm not sure that I want to live in that complex."

"You know my feelings won't be hurt if you decide to keep the cabin."

"I think I want a change. Another village might even be good for me. I'm in no hurry, and I have so much to take care of here."

"Sure, but I understand that places are hard to find."

"I have a realtor friend in Ephraim, so I may give her a heads up."

"Good. I hate to ask, but have you heard anything else from Austen?"

"Well, I saw him at the bakery having coffee with friends yesterday. When he saw me, he invited me to join them, but I declined. I really don't want to be around him. I know he only wants information about you. You did the right thing by leaving him."

"Thanks for saying that, Cher."

"I mean it! I never got good vibes around him."

"It's so good to talk to you."

"By the way, I saved something for you when we were going through Mom's things yesterday."

"You did? What?"

"Remember that red-and-white poinsettia cross-stitched tablecloth that you always admired at Christmastime?"

"Yes, of course!"

"Well, I want you to have it. Mom would be pleased. It took her years to complete that thing. You were the only one who complimented her on it."

"Are you sure? I would love it."

"I'll make sure that you have it for this Christmas."

"Thank you so much. I'll cherish it." I felt so happy after talking to Cher. When we hung up, I turned to Puff and said, "Puff, it sounds like your mama will be back in Door County before you know it." She gave me a look that reminded me how crazy I was.

In bed that night, I was grateful that Cher had not taken Austen's bait. I knew how he operated. I appreciated my friend's loyalty and thanked God for my best friend before I fell into a deep sleep.

The next morning brought long-awaited sunshine. I looked out the window at the snow, which glistened brightly in the sun. I could anticipate a nice drive to Rachael's farm. I hoped that Puff would leave the tree alone during my time away.

Upon my arrival at the farm, I found Charlie already loading a tree onto someone's pickup truck. I waved hello and then went into the barn to find Rachael busy with a broom in hand. "Let me do that, Rachael," I offered as I took my coat off. "Help has arrived!"

"There are always pine needles everywhere. It's hard to keep this place tidy. How are you today?"

"I'm good. After my talk with Cher last night, I'm almost certain that she will be moving back here."

"That's awesome."

"Good morning, Claire," Charlie greeted me as he came into the barn.

"Good morning," I responded. "I see you already had a tree sale this morning."

"Actually, that was my second sale," he bragged. "Hey, did

Rachael tell you about our great offer?"

"Offer?" I questioned. "No, she hasn't."

"We want to take you to the Green Bay Packers game this weekend." Charlie announced with excitement.

"Oh, how cool!"

"Charlie, tell her the rest of the story," Rachael warned.

"Okay," he said, scratching his head. "I have this friend, Harry, who's an old college friend of mine. He has season tickets, so Rachael and I get to go quite frequently. Harry's done really well for himself. His family owns quite a few hardware stores here in Wisconsin. He has four tickets."

"In other words, you're fixing me up with this Harry, and you want the four of us to go to the Packers game?"

"Yes, Claire, you've got the picture," Rachael laughed, looking at me to see if I would accept the challenge.

A setup? A blind date? I didn't really feel up to it, but when I looked at their excited faces, I weakened. I drew in a deep breath. "Well, sure, what the heck," I agreed. "It's just a football game."

"Now let me make this clear, Claire. It's not just any game," Charlie clarified. "The Packers are playing their biggest rival, the Chicago Bears!"

I chuckled. "Okay, I get it. It will be fun!"

"Terrific. I'll give Harry a call."

Chapter 52

After Charlie left, Rachael handed me a cup of coffee.

"Rachael, what's Harry like?" I asked.

"He's not your type, so let's start there," she admitted. "He's funny, decent-looking, and richer than all get out. He has several places that he calls home. He even has a cabin on Washington Island. He loves Charlie because he's real, and not just someone who likes him for his money."

"I see. How old is he? Has he ever married?"

"He's about sixty, but looks a lot younger. Sometimes he can come across as a bit callous. He's been divorced twice and is determined to stay single."

"I can handle that. I'm not looking for a husband, and any friend of yours can't be all bad."

Rachael chuckled. "Good. Now would you mind giving these folks a call to tell them that their orders are ready? I need to get a package ready to ship."

"Sure. It looks like business continues to be good."

"It's feast or famine around here," Rachael said, throwing up her hands.

I made the calls, and everyone was happy to hear from me. Christmas tree sales were picking up, and it was fun meeting folks who were excited about their purchases. They couldn't help but notice all the barn quilts on display, so I tried my best to make sales. As I took a sale from a woman who was buying two wreaths, she paused and stared at Rachael. "Isn't that the woman who's giving a lecture at The Clearing in January?" she whispered.

"I don't know, but I'll ask," I replied, my curiosity piqued. I asked Rachael to join us when she finished her sale to a little boy buying his own tiny Christmas tree. It was a small and grubby tree that Charlie had priced for a dollar.

"How can I help you?" Rachael asked the woman.

"Are you the one teaching a quilt design class at The Clearing in January?" she asked with excitement. "It said the teacher had a barn quilt business. I'm signed up for it."

"I am!" Rachael answered. "I've taken classes there, but this is my first time teaching anything. I hope you'll like it."

"Great! Well, it was nice to meet you," the woman gushed. "You both have a merry Christmas!"

"You too! See you there!" Rachael called out.

"Rachael, you're amazing! I've heard about The Clearing from Cher, but I haven't been there yet. Tell me about it."

"It's heaven! Absolutely peace on earth."

"How so?"

"Well, the location is in the woods, for starters. It's in Ellison Bay, just off of Route 42. Jen Jensen, a famous architect, had owned the property since 1919, but created The Clearing in 1935. He believed that the natural environment had a direct effect on people, giving them a place to experience renewal. It's now an independent nonprofit corporation, and it's really grown. People come from all over the country to take classes or spend time with nature. It's perfect in the dead of winter when you get bored and don't have many places to go outside."

"It sounds wonderful!"

"It's a community of its own right here in Door County. There are always fundraising efforts taking place to keep it running. If I can get away in January, I'll take you there. I do love seeing it around the holidays, because their natural decorations are amazing. I buy things from their gift shop all year round. You'll find many books there from local authors. Check The Clearing out online. You'll be impressed."

"How did you get a teaching position there?"

"Their receptionist bought a barn quilt here, and we started talking about quilt block names and their histories. She thought it was a fascinating topic and was impressed with my amazing knowledge, I guess." Rachael burst into laughter at her own joke. "I'm honored to be asked, and I do have a lot of ideas about how I want to teach the class. I told Lee that she needs to teach a hand appliqué class there, but she hasn't done anything about it."

"I'll check it out tonight. Your class sounds like it will be interesting. What about severe weather?"

"They do cancel classes when it's bad. They usually follow whatever the Gibraltar school system does, and they also announce it on local radio and TV."

"Wow, I have so much to learn."

"Anyone can apply to teach a class. They have a board of directors that decides their curriculum. Why don't you apply?"

"Me? What would I teach?"

"How to paint on textiles, for starters. You would just need to think of a simple beginner's class."

"I don't know if that's me. I do want to paint things related to Door County. The landscapes here really intrigue me. I can tell the winter snow and ice will be gorgeous, even though I don't like cold weather."

"Honey, you haven't experienced any cold weather yet!"

"Rachael, can you give me a hand?" Charlie called as he opened the door. "Didn't you hear me ring?"

"Oh, I didn't," she replied. "I guess we were too busy talking." Rachael shrugged her shoulders and put on her coat while I got busy wiping up water from melting snow on the doormats, refilling the hot chocolate carafe, and making more coffee.

Before I knew it, closing time had arrived, and as I prepared to leave, Rachael entered and said, "Take home some of this beer cheese soup. I don't think you took time to eat lunch."

"Don't mind if I do," I responded, happy to not have to fret about what to fix for dinner. I was about to get in my car when Charlie approached.

"Hey, I called Harry, and he's pretty excited about the game and meeting you," he said with a chuckle in his voice.

"Yes, and in that order, too!" I joked back. "I'm looking forward to it. Thanks for asking me." I pulled away, thankful for good friends with big hearts. How had I gotten so lucky?

Chapter 53

When I got home, a sweet reward for the day was seeing Puff still under the Christmas tree instead of a disturbed tree I'd have to rescue. Puff barely looked up to acknowledge me. Had she given up on having her true owner walk in the door? "I'm fine with you camping out there, Puff, but we need to put a tree skirt of some kind under it." Puff rested her head on the bare floor while I got a fire going and then went to the kitchen to put the soup in the refrigerator. It was then that I heard a knock at the door. It was Cotsy, my neighbor. "Cotsy, come in!" I said.

"I love your tree!" she exclaimed.

"It's not finished yet, but it's a beauty, isn't it?"

"We're putting ours up this weekend, and we always put lights on a few of the bushes out front."

"I wanted to string lights across the cabin, too, but I still need to find a handyman to do it."

"Well, if you know what you want, our handyman Tom will be glad to help you."

"Oh?" I asked, hopeful that I could get some assistance with that task.

"Trust me, he'll appreciate the extra money," she assured me. "I don't have your phone number, and I wanted to invite you for cocktails next Tuesday. When I saw you drive in, I thought I'd just come over in person."

"Thank you, I'll come. And thank you for sharing your snow removal guy."

"No problem. He always did it for Cher," she said, dismissing the subject. "Now, back to the party. You're welcome to bring a date if you like."

"Not a concern there, but thanks. I would love to come and meet some new people."

"By the way, I wanted to thank you for putting that outdoor light in the backyard. With all of these break-ins, we can't be too careful. Last night, Husby's in Sister Bay got broken into."

"I hate to hear that. These break-ins seem to happen late at night when we're all asleep."

"They say that the thief has to have some inside information on these places."

"Well, hopefully the Christmas lights will help keep them away from the cabin," I said.

"It will. And I'm so glad that you can come to the party."

"Can I bring anything?"

"And take all the glory away from Dan, who cooks up a storm for this event?" Cotsy chuckled. "It's from five to nine, so come anytime."

"Thank you!" I responded. After she left, I went back to the fire and poked the logs. I said a little prayer of thanks for such nice friends and neighbors. As I warmed the soup, I got a text reminding me of the chamber breakfast meeting the next day at Chives restaurant in Baileys Harbor. The only time I'd seen that little village had been on my way to Marta's farm. Did I want to go? I decided to text Rachael to see if she was going. She immediately texted back and said Charlie would kill her if she left him alone at this time of year. She did encourage me to go. As I thought about it, I decided that I could attend and then explore more of that part of the county. Perhaps I could take the time to stop and talk to some gallery owners.

Before I prepared for bed, I opened the blanket chest and saw my red-and-white Ocean Waves quilt. I thought Mom had told me that Grandmother Stewart had made it. It looked rather festive, so I pulled it out, thinking it might be striking under the Christmas tree if Puff behaved herself. Puff stood and watched as she waited for me to settle in for the night.

Eager to see how the quilt would look with the tree, I headed downstairs and arranged it at the base. It looked amazing. I liked it better than any commercial tree skirt. I smiled, thinking how surprised Puff would be in the morning. She might think that Santa Claus had come! I guessed I didn't mind sharing just one more quilt with Puff.

I headed to bed and fixed Puff's corner of the quilt. "Sweet dreams, Puff," I said before I fell asleep.

Chapter 54

I didn't wake to sunshine the next morning, but I happened to glance at the clock and realized that I had just enough time to dress and get to the chamber meeting. I felt fairly confident about finding the place. Puff patiently waited for her food as I tried to make myself presentable for the meeting. Just before I left, Puff had gone to her new place under the Christmas tree. "Did you see that Santa Claus left you something last night? Do you like the quilt?" There was no response, but as soon as Puff settled on the quilt, I snapped a picture to send to Cher.

Hungry for a good breakfast, I scraped the windshield of my vehicle and left for the meeting. I certainly missed the attached garage that I'd had in Missouri. Once the car was warmed up and I was on my way, it was a pretty drive on Route 57 to Baileys Harbor. Most of the leaves had dropped off of the trees. As I got to the little community, I started looking for Chives. I saw cars lined up and parked on the side of the road. I then saw the restaurant, which was perched on a low cliff close to the road. It wasn't a big place, and it had an excellent reputation. I pulled behind the car in front of me and began my long walk to the door. Lake Michigan was across the road, affording customers a spectacular view. As I walked, the wind was brisk, and it played havoc with my hair.

Once I got in line inside, I saw how crowded the place was. I recognized a few faces, but in the back of my mind, I was looking for Grayson. The buffet looked amazing, and my stomach was growling for attention. Who served eggs benedict on a buffet? They were beautifully presented, and everyone was helping themselves. The hash browns were smothered with onions and smelled divine. Lovely fruit and iced Danishes were there for the taking as well. As I waited my turn and observed my surroundings, I saw that some people were having to stand while eating. I began to wonder what I was going to have to do. When I finally got through the line, I saw Grayson looking at me. He motioned for me to come and take his place. When I got to him, he stood up to leave. "Please take my seat," he said graciously. "I can't stay for the meeting, but I didn't want to miss this breakfast."

I smiled, grateful for his thoughtfulness. "Are you sure?" I asked in disbelief. For a moment, it felt like our eyes were having a conversation.

"I need to be on my way," he said, moving close enough to brush against my coat. "The food was delicious, as always."

"Have a good day!" I responded as he left. I greeted a few other people who were sitting at the table, but I sensed that I was interrupting their conversation, so I began eating. In no time, the president got our attention by using his gavel and began speaking. It began with the usual reports from officers and committees. There was a new member from Sturgeon

Bay who was introduced. Someone was then introduced from the Winter Committee who announced that they were collecting coats and cans of food. The Door County Coffee and Tea Company in Carlsville was the designated drop-off point. That was another place I wanted to revisit. A woman then got up and announced the dates of the spring Art Crawl in Egg Harbor. At first, it really interested me, but as she spoke, I realized it didn't appear that it was for artists like me but for those who had galleries in Egg Harbor. However, I needed to attend that event so I could see what was selling.

After the meeting ended, I decided to stick around to see if there were any networking possibilities. I missed having Rachael with me. It seemed like she knew everyone. I left the meeting feeling unsatisfied. Was the chamber the best use of my time? The group seemed cliquish to me. I had gotten to see Grayson, however. He could have offered his seat to anyone, but he'd had his eye on me. Hmmm.

I stopped at the post office to get my mail and then traveled on to get gas before going home. When I arrived, I was pleased to see a man on a ladder putting up lights across the cabin.

"Ms. Stewart?' he asked as he turned to look at me.

"Yes. You must be Tom," I said, smiling. "I really appreciate your doing this. I don't own a ladder, or I might have tried doing it myself."

"I wouldn't advise it." He grinned. "I'm glad to do it. I've been helping the Bittners for many years." He finally came down to talk face to face.

"I don't suppose you do any other kind of work, do you? Any carpentry?"

He took off his cap and scratched his head. "My daddy

was a carpenter, and I learned just enough from him to be dangerous."

I laughed. "I need some shelves put in a couple of rooms."

"I'll have time when the Bittners leave for Florida after Christmas."

"Great! Here's my business card. Would you write your phone number on this other one so I can call you?"

"Sure," Tom said cheerfully.

Back up the ladder he went, and I couldn't wait for darkness to fall so I could see the lights!

Chapter 55

When I entered the cabin, Puff was still under the tree. I wanted to give Rachael an account of the chamber meeting, so I gave her a ring. She put me on hold while she finished with a customer. Part of me missed being there with her.

"How was it?" she asked.

"The food was amazing, just like you said it would be. The meeting was a bit boring, and frankly, I think that group is rather cliquish."

"Well, I'm glad you had a good breakfast," she said.

When I told her about Grayson offering me his seat, she got excited. "You're definitely on his radar, Claire Bear," she stated.

"You called me Claire Bear. No one calls me that but Cher."

"Well, the more I get to know you, the more your nickname seems quite fitting," she joked. "I just think that it suits you."

"Well, as far as Grayson is concerned, it was very sweet of him, but don't you think he would be that way to just about everyone?"

"No, I don't think so. It sounds like he had many others there that he could have offered the seat to."

"Okay. I'll take that as a bit of good news. I also met the Bittners' handyman. He put my Christmas lights up and said that after Christmas, he'd be available to help me with other things. Do you remember Rob from the Bayside? He helped me with a few things and then said he was too busy helping Ericka's brother George."

Rachael replied, "I think there's something odd about all of that. Rob had been somewhat of a regular at the Bayside, and when he didn't come in with George anymore, I asked about him. George said that he hasn't heard seen or anything from Rob for quite a while. In fact, Rob had promised some people that he would do some work for them and hasn't shown up. The customers have been calling George and complaining. George seems worried that Rob has gone on a drinking binge."

"I'm sorry to hear that. He must have problems to just disappear like that."

"He surely must! Listen, we'll pick you up tomorrow for the game at about one. We have to get there early, or your seat will get covered up with people's coats."

"Seriously?" I said, laughing.

"Yes, seriously. Dress warm and wear green, of course."

"Oh! I don't have anything Packers-related."

"Go to On Deck Clothing down the street. They'll have things."

"Thanks, I will." I hung up the phone with a mission. The weather was clear enough to walk, and I needed the exercise! I bundled up and flew out the door. Puff didn't even look up.

I loved the On Deck stores in each village. I went to the men's side of the store and found Green Bay Packer sweatshirts, scarves, and hats. A young sales associate offered to help me. I was sure that he'd easily sized me up as a woman trying to look cool at an upcoming Packers game. He threw himself into the challenge, and fifteen minutes later, I left with a sweatshirt, a sock cap, a scarf, and gloves that fit like a charm.

When I arrived home, I displayed everything on my bed. I felt like I was about to go on an adventure. I had never been a football fan, or any kind of sports fan for that matter. Austen was a big St. Louis Blues hockey fan, and every now and then, he'd tried in vain to get me to go to a game with him.

As soon as it got dark, I rushed outside to check out the lights on the cabin. My home looked like a Christmas card! I took some photos to send to Cher and Mom and went to bed that night with twinkling lights in my dreams.

I woke up the next morning with Puff's hairs tickling my face. I sat up quickly and saw that it was half past nine. It was later than I usually slept, but I had nowhere to go today. Puff obviously had other plans for me, because she continued to walk around the bed until I vacated it and served her breakfast. After I had breakfast, I felt energized and began to decorate the house with greenery. There was nothing like the fresh aroma of cedar. When I completed the look with a few red bows, I would be all set.

Before I knew it, I needed to get ready for the big game. Rachael had assured me that there would be plenty of food. She had also told not to bring a purse unless it was see-through. The air was spitting snowflakes, which would set the tone for an average Green Bay Packers game. I had to admit that I was getting excited.

I looked up the team's record for the season thus far, and it was very promising. Their historic stadium was named Lambeau Field in 1965 after the death of Curly Lambeau. He founded the team in 1919, played for the Packers in the early years, and was the team's coach for thirty-one seasons. That sounded amazing to me. There was a famous statue of him outside the stadium, and now I would get to see it in person.

Chapter 56

At one, Charlie, Rachael, and Harry arrived at my door. The introductions were awkward, but I was prepared for that and got through them.

"Nice little cabin," Harry said, smiling.

"Thanks," I replied.

"Your place looks so festive," Rachael said. "Even in the daylight you can see your Christmas lights down the street."

"Okay, ladies and gentleman, we need to get going," Charlie said, looking at his watch. "Did Rachael tell you that we have a place to tailgate?"

"No, but that sounds like fun," I said.

We got into Harry's black Hummer. I had never been in one before and didn't know what to check out first. I felt like I was going to war in an Army tank. I sat up front with Harry, noticing that he had a large build. Perhaps it was all the heavy, warm Packers garb he was wearing. He had a hearty laugh and seemed to be a man's man.

"Harry's got some steak kabobs and sausage links to grill," Charlie said with excitement. "We won't go hungry, and others will share their food as well."

"I'm getting hungry just hearing about it," I responded.

For the rest of the drive, I mostly listened to the others talk. As we got closer to the stadium, the traffic became thick and the crowds were more intense. It was an exciting atmosphere. As soon as we parked, I could tell there were plenty of intoxicated people. Some faces were painted green, and of course the famous Cheeseheads appeared.

A chilly wind picked up and snow flurries painted the ground white. The fire from our grill helped take away some of the chill, but my toes were freezing. I knew it wouldn't get any better. Food and drink appeared and took my mind off of the cold. I wondered if my taste buds were frozen. I could tell that Rachael was watching my reactions, and I did not want to disappoint her. Eating outdoors did increase my appetite, so I did my best to sample everything.

"How are you doing, hon?" Harry asked as he put his arm around me.

"Fine, fine," I said, determined to be a good sport.

Just before the game started, Harry knew exactly where we needed to go since he had season tickets. When we arrived at our row in the stadium, I couldn't even determine which seats were ours. I guessed that with season tickets, I'd expected to see something more comfortable. Harry told us the numbers of our seats, and we made our way through the unruly crowd. Earlier in the day, Charlie had bragged about the view we would have from our seats, but once there, I didn't see what made them special. I just wanted to sit and be warm, but that didn't happen either. It seemed that people mostly stood during the game.

The fans were bundled up like we were, so our four seats

on the concrete bench were hard to find. In unison, we all sat down, shoulder to shoulder. Well, that part was cozy, which I didn't object to.

When the national anthem was played, we all rose together with the thousands of others. Fans continued cheering and remained standing. Harry forgot all about me. I began to realize that winning this game was serious business. I didn't understand the intensity I felt around me until Rachael reminded me that the Packers were playing their big rivals, the Chicago Bears. She said they would be out for blood. As the game went on, the Bears were winning, and the crowd around me was getting restless and foul. I thought Harry was going to have a heart attack just watching some of the plays. Then we lost! Needless to say, there was no conversation as we made our way back to the vehicle.

Traffic was slow and heavy on the drive back to Door County. Finally, Harry spoke to me. "Well, Claire, we didn't get a win, but how did you enjoy the experience?" he asked.

"It was fun, and I'm glad I went," I responded. "I'm sorry they didn't win."

When we arrived back at my place, I insisted that I just hop out of the Hummer, which wasn't that easy, but I managed.

"I'll give you a call, Claire," Harry said. "We didn't really get a chance to get to know one another."

"I had a fun time, and I feel like a real Cheesehead now," I kidded. The others chuckled as I waved goodbye. They waited until I got inside the cabin to drive away. I was glad to be home. It was even good to see Puff lounging under the tree. I couldn't wait to take off my costume and change into my pajamas. It had been quite a party, and I'd thoroughly enjoyed seeing the passion that this state had for their home team.

As I settled into bed around eleven, my head still rang with the loud sounds I had experienced hours earlier. I hoped that Harry wouldn't call. Although he was a nice man, he wasn't my type. I really appreciated Charlie and Rachael looking out for me. I was just getting comfortable and ready to fall asleep when my cell phone rang.

Chapter 57

"Claire, it's Harry. I hope you're a night owl like I am."

"Well, I just turned in for the night."

"I kept thinking about you and wanted to apologize for not being as attentive as I should have been today. I'm a pretty passionate Packers fan. You're a beautiful woman, and I assure you, I was a lot smoother when I was a younger man."

The unexpectedness of the conversation made me laugh. "You have nothing to apologize for. Your food was amazing, and the experience is something that I will never forget."

"Well, that's something, anyway. I'd like to make it up to you and take you out for a nice, fancy dinner."

"Oh, Harry, that is absolutely unnecessary."

"I want to. Really. What do you say?"

"I'll think about it, but right now I'm busy getting settled in the area and getting ready for Christmas. Helping Rachael out on the farm is also a priority." I paused, and Harry didn't speak, so I added, "This isn't a no, but not right now."

"I'll remember that. Rachael has said so many wonderful things about you."

"She's just being a good friend. If I don't see you before, have a merry Christmas!" I could feel that he was reluctant to hang up. What had I gotten myself into? I needed to put that call out of my mind and get some sleep. I had to get up early and get to work at the farm. I looked at the foot of the bed and saw that Puff was curled up and sleeping well. That call sure hadn't disturbed her, and I was determined to keep it from disturbing me!

The next day was sunny, and I was greeted enthusiastically when I walked into work. "Perfect timing," Rachael called when I arrived. "Charlie just rang the bell. I think he thought you were already here."

"Did Charlie recover from yesterday's loss?"

"Not quite. You were a good sport yesterday, Claire Bear."

I smiled and told her about Harry calling me the night before.

"Setting you up with him at a football game was unwise, especially since we lost."

"I really have no interest in him, Rachael, but I appreciate your effort, and I certainly don't want to hurt Harry's feelings."

"I know. Hey, I've got to get outside!"

"Go! I'll get started cleaning up."

"There are some customers to call, and I'll send some people in here to pay since Charlie and I have other things to do this morning."

"Great!"

Rachael flew out the door, and I looked around to see what I should do first. It was kind of fun playing store, and I started thinking about what I would do differently if the business belonged to me. The time passed quickly. I had just finished lunch when Harry walked in with three little girls.

"Hi, Claire," Harry said cheerfully.

"Hi there! So, what do we have here?" I said, glancing at the girls.

"I'd like you to meet my three granddaughters, Mary, Mindy, and Misty. They're five, four, and three." The little girls giggled at their grandfather's enthusiasm as he introduced them.

"I'm pleased to meet you! My name is Claire."

"We just picked out Papa Harry's Christmas tree," Mary informed me, her eyes wide with excitement.

"You did? Wow!" I responded.

"It's really tall," Mindy offered.

"Oh, I can't wait to see it!" I exclaimed. The blonde-haired, blue-eyed children must have had a real adventure picking out the tree. Their cheeks were still rosy from the cold.

"Girls, Claire is an artist like you like to be sometimes, and she helps Rachael sell her barn quilts."

The girls eyed me curiously, and I could tell that something else was on their minds.

Chapter 58

"Rachael said you would give us some hot chocolate," Mary mentioned shyly.

"Absolutely!" I responded as I led the way. The girls gathered around as Harry and I poured each of them half a cup of hot chocolate. Harry was especially attentive to Misty, who had every intention of aimlessly running around the shop.

"I think I know where there are some cookies," I informed them. I went to the back room, opened a bag, put cookies on a plate, and presented them with anticipation.

"What do you say to Claire?" Harry asked the girls. His question was followed by a series of three polite expressions of thanks.

"You're welcome," I responded, watching the little girls enjoy their snack. "Harry, how many grandchildren do you have?"

"Just these three little beauties," he answered proudly. "My son divorced last year, so when he has the girls, I try to help him out. They're a handful most of the time."

"I can see that," I said, laughing. Within minutes, the girls had abandoned their hot chocolate and cookies in favor of scattering themselves throughout the shop.

"Papa Harry said we can decorate the tree today," Mary reported, bouncing back to where we were standing.

"Oh, that will be such fun," I said. "I got my tree from here, too. It was so much fun to decorate it."

"Who helped you decorate?" Mary asked.

"It was just me and a cat named Puff."

"You have a cat?" Mindy asked when she came running by.

"I do!" I said, shaking my head at her boundless energy.

"I love cats!" Mary exclaimed. "We just have a dog."

"Oh? What's his name?" I said, stooping down to her level.

"Skipper."

"Mary, will you find Misty? We need to be on our way," Harry said. "Miss Claire has work to do. Thanks so much for the treats. Charlie insists that I take the tree for free, but take this fifty-dollar bill. He'll never make any money being as generous as he is."

I nodded. "I know. I felt bad as well," I agreed.

"Do you know that on Christmas Eve, he gives the rest of his inventory away to anyone who doesn't have a tree? Some people who know that take advantage of him, but that's how generous he and Rachael are."

"I know," I said as Harry zipped up the girls' coats.

"All aboard!" he called out.

Just then, Rachael came in. "Did they get their hot chocolate?" she asked.

"Yes, and cookies," Mary exclaimed.

Rachael laughed.

"Thanks for everything, Rachael," Harry said kindly. "We'd better get started on that tree; don't you think?" At that question, all three girls ran to the door ahead of Harry.

"Nice to meet you," I said to the three retreating bundles of energy. "I hope Santa Claus brings you lots of goodies." The statement caught their attention, and they turned and began to enthusiastically inform me of their Christmas lists. Harry scooped Misty up in his arms and herded the other two closer to the door. Just as Mary reached the threshold, she turned around and ran towards me.

"I want to give Miss Claire a hug," she insisted.

"Me too!" Mindy agreed, following her sister.

It was a sweet and unexpected moment. When was the last time a child had hugged me?

"Goodbye," Rachael said with a wave as they made their way out the door for a second time. "So, what did you think of that?" She smiled, looking to me for an answer.

"That was a side of Harry I didn't expect to see."

"He's a teddy bear despite his large stature. His son really depends on him."

"He's really good with those girls."

"You know that you and I are old enough to be grandparents, don't you?" Rachael teased.

"I guess you're right. I have a few classmates who are."

"Claire, I know we haven't known each other long, but why haven't you married? If you don't want to talk about it, I understand."

"Well, Rachael, I'm the 'almost' girl. I almost married my first love in high school before I realized that he didn't have to be the one. Then I almost married Bill, who really broke my heart. Brian almost convinced me to marry him until I realized that he wouldn't stop drinking. Last but not least, I was hoping to marry the successful Dr. Page, but after five years, I realized it wasn't ever going to happen. I felt used, which is not a good feeling."

Rachael eyes were huge as she tried to take in all that I had shared. "Oh, I'm so sorry. Actually, you might consider yourself rather lucky."

"Yes, I do. I could have married one of those bad choices and really would have been stuck. I see so many divorces for those very reasons."

Chapter 59

On the way home from Rachael's, I stopped to pick up a pizza from The Wild Tomato in Fish Creek. I was sad to see that they were going to close for the season after Christmas. Wasn't pizza a year-round thing? When I arrived home, I was beaming, just like all the lights coming from my cabin. I poured myself a glass of wine and turned on the TV while I enjoyed the pizza. Unfortunately, the six o'clock news reported another break-in near Green Bay. They suspected that it was related to the ones in Door County.

The next night would be Dan and Cotsy's open house. I had to think about what to wear. Surely this was not your usual jeans-and-sweatshirt affair. I knew I'd be meeting other neighbors from Cottage Row before they left for the winter. I had to make a good impression.

After the news ended, I went upstairs and began going through my closet. Puff anxiously followed in case I was thinking of going to bed early. I knew I had to wear my black dress boots, because I would be walking over in the snow. That meant that my outfit had to go with black. I had a black knit dress, but it was really too plain. After all, it was Christmas. A light bulb went off in my head, and I rushed downstairs to remove a fur collar from one of my coats. I thought it would fit perfectly, and it did. It changed the look completely.

I had decided to get ready for bed when I got a call from Cher.

"Hey, Cher Bear!" I answered. "How are you doing?"

"Doing better. How are things there?"

"I worked at Rachael's today, which is always fun, and now I'm deciding on an outfit for tomorrow's cocktail party next door."

"Oh, I wish I could be there. It's always really nice. Dan loves to cook, so the food is always outstanding."

"Well, hop on a plane and join me! I don't mind sleeping on the couch."

"You're crazy, but I am thinking more and more about how I can arrange to move back to Door County. My siblings and I have all agreed to put the house on the market, but it's not that easy. There's so much to do."

"That's a start. Have you thought about where you'd like to live?"

"I haven't said I'm moving back for sure. I'm thinking hard about it. This house is too big for me to live in."

"You have to. The quilting club would love to have you back."

"I've always been attracted to Egg Harbor, so just for fun, I asked someone I know there to just keep an eye out for me. I'm shocked at the prices that they can ask for places, though."

"I love Egg Harbor! I hear that they have an art crawl that is immensely popular."

"Yes, and its well-attended. Hey, you haven't told me how you liked the Packers game. I hated to see them lose to the Bears."

"It was a blast, and quite an experience. I'll tell you more about it as time marches on. How is Mom doing?"

"She's great! I saw her having dinner last week with Mr. Vogel at Park-et."

"Again? Well, I'll be! They seem to have something special going on."

"I think it's wonderful. You don't know how lucky you are. Your mom's as sharp as always. She looks really good."

"I haven't been to the Park-et for a long time. Do they still have decent food?"

"For this town, yes!" she said sarcastically. "You know it's all about the pie around here."

I chuckled. Just like that, an hour went by, much like when we were teenagers. I hung up hoping that in just a brief time, Cher would be joining me in Door County!

Chapter 60

The next day, I was energized by the thought of going to a party in the evening. I busied myself with domestic chores and then got back to my painting of Puff. I was incredibly pleased with how I'd captured her eyes. If I were planning to sell this painting, it would sell immediately since so many people had cats, but this one was going to my special friend. Around noon, I saw Ericka pull in the driveway.

"Have you had lunch?" she asked as soon as she entered. "I'm off today, and I really need my fix of some whitefish chowder from the White Gull Inn. Will you go with me?"

"Oh, I wish you had called. I'm such a mess from painting."

"You're fine. Just put on a coat. The place is casual enough. Is this Puff that you've painted?"

I smiled and nodded. "Yes, it's Cher's Christmas present."

"It's wonderful. She'll love it."

"I heard from her last night, and she seems to be looking at places in Egg Harbor. I don't care where she's looking. I just want her to move back here."

"Darn. I guess my condo complex is out."

"I think she decided against that idea since she wants to try another community in the county. Well, I think I will go with you. I'm rather hungry." I changed into a sweater while Ericka played with Puff. I could only imagine how thrilled Puff was to see someone besides me.

The New England-style restaurant had a wonderful fire going in their fireplace, so Ericka requested that we get the table for two right in front of it. It was available, and we settled in by the warmth of the fire.

"Good, my friend Brenda is working today," Ericka observed. "You need to meet her. She's a quilter, by the way."

I smiled, and seconds later an attractive woman came to our table and greeted us.

"Brenda, this is Claire Stewart, the person who moved into Cher's cabin," Ericka said. "Claire, this is my friend Brenda."

"Well, nice to meet you," I said as I extended my hand.

"Welcome to the White Gull Inn," Brenda responded. Her short blunt-cut hairstyle suited her.

"I'm happy to be here," I replied.

"I've always admired that little house of Cher's. What can I get you to drink?"

Ericka and I both ordered iced tea. Brenda told us that the special of the day was whitefish chowder and the pilgrim sandwich. Ericka encouraged me to try both, so I did. Ericka began our conversation by asking about Cher's mother's funeral. We covered a lot of ground, and I even got some advice as to where to find a good hairstylist. Then she brought up Rob's name.

"George thinks someone should call the police and report Rob missing," she divulged.

"Perhaps so." I nodded. "This sounds like more than a

drinking binge."

"George finally told me that Rob had a falling out with a girl he had been dating, and as he typically would, drank his troubles away."

"That's really sad. He was so nice to me and was willing to help me with things."

As we were eating lunch, Brenda came by to check on us. "How's the lunch?" she asked. "Don't forget, we have fantastic desserts."

"The lunch was fabulous," I praised. "I couldn't possibly handle any dessert."

"I'm glad you liked it." She nodded. "So, Claire, are you getting settled in?"

"Pretty much," I replied. "It's nice to meet new people. Ericka and her friends have gone way beyond the call of duty."

"Ericka told me that you belong to that quilt group at the library," Brenda said. "I don't know how you managed that, but many of us would love to join."

"I lucked out, thanks to Cher," I confessed. "I was able to take her spot."

"I go to the hygge on Fridays at the Egg Harbor Library," Brenda revealed. "It's not just for quilters, but for anyone who wants to hang out and work on something around a fire. It's wonderful!"

"What's a hygge?" I asked, curious.

"It's from Norwegian and Danish culture and encourages you to slow down and enjoy life with a cup of tea or hot chocolate."

"Now that sounds enticing!" I responded, intrigued by the idea.

"You should come," Brenda said. "Sometimes my daughter

comes with me. It's from ten to two, but you can come and go anytime. If you're not working on anything in particular, you can always look through books."

"I wish I could go," Ericka said, sounding disappointed. "I haven't had a Friday off in a long time."

"I'll be sure to come, if I can remember," I responded. "It sounds wonderful, and I'll look for you there."

"Great," Brenda said warmly. "Thanks for bringing her here, Ericka."

I snagged the check and told Ericka how much I appreciated the lunch and the introduction to Brenda. When I arrived back home, I realized that I was starting to feel like I was fitting into the community. Now it was time for a neighborhood Christmas party for my evening activity.

Chapter 61

After I got dressed, I looked in the mirror and realized that it had been some time since I had put on a dress. I wanted to make a good impression and look somewhat festive for the holidays. I added some silver accessories to the black, which I liked. I looked out the front window and saw quite a few cars. Despite the snow on the ground, I was going to walk next door, all the while hoping I wouldn't fall.

A man answered the door when I arrived. "Welcome, Claire. I'm Dan," he said kindly. "It's nice to finally meet you. Welcome to the neighborhood."

"Thank you for inviting me tonight," I responded.

"Amy, our niece, will be happy to take your coat," he offered. "Help yourself to some food and drink, and enjoy yourself."

"Thank you, I will," I said, glancing around the crowded rooms. I walked towards what I recognized as the bar and saw Ginger and her husband.

"Merry Christmas, Claire," Ginger greeted me. "I think you've met my husband."

"It's good to see you again," Allen said as he gave my hand a friendly shake.

"I'm glad to see some familiar faces," I confessed. "How do you know the Bittners?"

"We've known them a long time," Ginger said. "Dan and Allen play golf together occasionally."

"How do you like your place?" Allen asked politely.

"I like it a lot, and I'm intrigued with its history," I replied. "It was reconstructed here in the 1940s, but it originally came from Peninsula State Park."

"Very interesting," he responded. "You like history, and I have a love of antiques in general. I buy the antiques for the shop while Ginger does the arts and crafts."

"How nice." I nodded. "I can't wait to see your shop."

It was my turn to order something to drink. As I took my first sip, I couldn't believe who was standing on the other side of the room. It was Grayson, looking extremely handsome in his finery. He was talking to a very pretty woman who seemed to be gushing at his every word. Of course he would be here with a date. What had I been thinking? I turned away from Ginger and Allen when Cotsy approached me.

"Claire, I want to introduce you to some people," she offered. "I know what it's like to be new to an area. By the way, you look very pretty tonight."

The introductions began, and I was right in thinking that the guests would mostly be from Cottage Row. The Alexanders, who lived just four houses down, said the Bittners' party was traditionally the last gathering before the snowbirds left for Florida. Cotsy then steered me in a new direction. What happened next was a bit awkward.

"Claire, this Grayson Wills," she said. "The boaters around

here can't do without Grayson's expertise. Also, he's quite the chef, if you're lucky enough to experience any of his culinary creations."

"Really?" I said, pretending we hadn't met. "Well, nice to meet you, Mr. Wills." Grayson gave me a big smile and just nodded.

"This is Meredith O'Connor, one of our artists in Door County," Cotsy said, sounding especially delighted. "Her studio is in Ellison Bay."

"A pleasure," the woman next to Grayson said. Her voice had a funny intonation, like she really had no interest in meeting a new person.

"Nice to meet you, too," I said as I briefly shook her hand.

"Claire is our next-door neighbor in that cute little log cabin you saw all lit up so pretty," Cotsy explained.

"That cabin is yours?" Grayson asked in surprise.

I nodded. "It belonged to my best friend, who had to move back home to take care of her mother," I explained. "You may remember Cher Clapton, who belonged to the chamber of commerce." I could see that he was trying to recall if he knew Cher. "I was looking for a change, so I took it off her hands."

Before Grayson could respond, Cotsy moved me on to a charming older woman who said she was one of the board members in Fish Creek. Cotsy quickly noted that she was the first woman to be elected to that position. As we chatted, the woman revealed that she owned some rental cottages on Main Street in Fish Creek not far from me. I wanted to learn more from this delightful woman, but then Dan interrupted us and said that Cotsy was needed in the kitchen.

"Claire, have you had something to eat?" Dan asked.

"No, but I'm looking forward to it," I said, smiling.

"Well, let's get started," he said, leading the way. "Cotsy makes the best crab dip."

I inched my way along the buffet table as I drooled over all the wonderful choices being offered, making sure I tried the dip.

"Isn't this spread of food amazing?" Ginger said as she joined me. "Dan and Cotsy both love to cook and entertain."

"I hate that they're leaving for the winter," I said.

Chapter 62

Ginger and I found a couple of empty seats together in the living room where we could enjoy our food. "Ginger, do you know the artist Meredith O'Connor?" I asked.

"No, I don't think I do. Why?"

"She was talking to Grayson Wills, and I was introduced to her," I answered.

"Have you found a gallery for your work?" Ginger asked, changing the subject.

"No, I've been too busy helping Rachael at her barn," I explained. "I hope to get out and about soon to do just that."

"You should try Art of Door County," she suggested. "I think they have more than one location. The manager's name is Carl. He's so nice and is very enthusiastic about promoting local artists."

"Yes, I know the place, but when I looked in the window, it looked so crowded," I complained. "Where would they even hang a quilt?"

"Well, he might get you connected with someone else if he couldn't help you," Ginger suggested.

"That would be great. I'll try to get there tomorrow. Thanks for the suggestion." I noticed that some guests were leaving, and I certainly didn't want to be one of the last to leave, so I got up from my seat.

"I could sit here and eat and drink all night, but knowing Allen, he's ready to go," Ginger said, also rising.

"Well, it was good to see you here. I guess I'll see you at quilt club," I said as she left. "Have a merry Christmas if I don't see you."

"You too, Claire," she said.

I went to retrieve my coat when I saw Grayson coming my way.

"Are you cutting out, too?" he asked.

"Yes, I think it's time, before I make a glutton out of myself with all this delicious food," I joked.

"Here, let me help you with your coat," he offered.

"Thanks," I said as he came closer. He was wearing an aromatic cologne.

"Can I walk you to your door? It's pretty icy out there."

"Thanks, but that's not necessary. I wore these boots, so I'm good," I said, realizing Grayson was going home alone.

Dan approached us. Smiling, he said, "Hey, you two! You're not leaving without saying goodbye, are you?"

"Not at all," I answered quickly. "This was a wonderful party. Thanks so much for inviting me."

"Thank you, Dan," Grayson added. "Please tell Cotsy thanks, and I hope the two of you have a merry Christmas and enjoy your time in Florida."

Grayson and I walked down the beautiful front steps together, which felt odd. I felt Grayson holding my elbow to steady me in case I slipped. "Are you sure I can't walk you to your door?" he asked once more.

"I'm good," I assured him. "Where are you parked?"

"Just down the road a piece, as they say," he chuckled. "Be careful, and merry Christmas."

"You too, Grayson," I responded.

As I walked to the cabin, I could feel his eyes watching me, making certain that I didn't fall. Why hadn't I let him walk me to the door? Was he just being courteous, or was something more developing between us? When I got inside, Puff was standing by the stairway like she had been expecting me sooner. I sat down and called for her to join me by lightly patting the couch. She had other plans and scampered up the stairs.

I took a few moments to reflect on the evening. It had been nice to socialize with professional people in a beautiful home. Then there was Grayson, who had come alone after all. Why did I care? It reminded me of when I was available – before I connected with Austen. Austen and I had attended grand parties together, but this was different. I felt drawn to Grayson, and I liked that we were taking baby steps as we were getting to know one other. On the other hand, maybe he had just offered to walk me to my place out of simple politeness. I needed to get upstairs, but before I did, I looked out the window to see how many cars were left at the party. It has been a good evening. When I finally went up to bed, Puff was already settled in her spot, hoping the quilt would keep her cozy. She was not disappointed, and neither was I.

Chapter 63

The next morning, the sun greeted me while snowflakes swirled gently every now and then. It was a beautiful day in Door County. I knew most of the shops opened around ten, so if I left earlier than that, I could stop at the Blue Horse for coffee. I wouldn't be early enough to catch Grayson, but that was fine.

When I arrived at the busy café, I felt adventurous and tried the pumpkin-cinnamon coffee. I added a few pastries to take home and made my way to find a seat. I then saw Ava from quilt club sitting with a friend, so I walked her way.

"Claire, join us," Ava graciously offered. "Meet my friend from Florida. Dee, this is Claire."

"Nice to meet you," I responded. "What are you girls up to?"

"Whatever Ava has planned," Dee said, shrugging her shoulders.

As we made small talk, I couldn't help but notice when Ava put a few drops of something into her coffee. Ava remained a bit of a mystery to me. She was so different from the rest of the quilters, with her glitzy accessories and deep

V-neck tops that revealed a fair amount of cleavage. Rachael had once told me that Ava lived in a Victorian house that was decorated much like Ava accessorized herself.

"Well, Dee, we'd better get started," Ava said after the two of them had finished their coffee. She rose and collected her purse from the back of the chair.

"Yes, we should," Dee agreed as she dropped a ten-dollar bill on the table as a tip. "Nice to meet you, Claire."

"I'll see you at the next club meeting," Ava said to me as Dee started to walk away.

The next thing I knew, Ava picked up Dee's ten-dollar tip and slipped it into her pocket! I pretended I didn't notice, which was difficult because the action was rather obvious. Then a thought struck me. Had Ava added enough alcohol to her coffee that she was tipsy at this hour? Ava picked up her pace to join her friend. I waved them on and took a big swallow of my hot coffee. I'd thought I'd wanted to get to know each of the club members in a personal way, but perhaps I should rethink that notion. How many more secrets would I learn about this club?

I got back in my car and headed for a parking spot in front of On Deck Clothing. For the first time, I checked out their basement discount department. There was nothing I needed, so I reminded myself that it was galleries I was looking for. I left there and came across a cute, colorful shop called Sailor Sam's. The shop carried jillions of glass yard ornaments. I thought I would have called it Trinkets.

In the next block heading down Main Street, I saw a sign for Art of Door County. I walked inside and was struck by the number of items to view. The walls were covered, and the aisles were full. I checked, and the prices were very reasonable. I didn't see any textiles, but everything I looked at was wonderful. What a place for tourists to find Door County souvenirs!

The young woman behind the counter asked if she could help me. I told her I was an artist who had just moved from Missouri and that I was looking for a place to sell my work. Since I was now local, I asked if the gallery would consider purchasing my work.

"The way it works here is that if Carl likes your work, he's willing to try to sell it on consignment," she explained. "If it does well, he'll usually then purchase it outright."

"Oh, yes, my friend said I should ask to speak to Carl," I remembered. "Is he here?"

"He sure is." She nodded. "He's downstairs in the storeroom, but I'll tell him that you'd like to see him."

"That would be great. Thanks so much," I responded. As I waited, I saw such a mix of art. There was beautiful pottery, painted scarves, paintings, and even handmade jewelry.

"Hello, I'm Carl," a man said as he walked towards me.

"Carl, it's nice to meet you," I said, shaking his hand. I then nervously began telling him about myself, explaining that Ginger Greensburg had suggested that I approach him about some of my work. He listened intently. In the back of my mind, he reminded me of someone.

"Great, so did you bring some of your work with you?"

"No," I answered shyly. "I wanted to meet you first and see what kind of merchandise you might be looking for. I live close by, so I can come in soon and show you some examples."

"Anytime," he agreed. "We have a nice local following of people who shop here, but the tourists especially love to see work from local artists."

I found him to be very charming. I figured he must be around sixty to seventy years old. It then hit me that he must be the Clark Gable that Frances had mentioned. He must be!

"So, if I understood you, you purchased Cher's little house?" he was asking.

"Presumably so. However, she may move back here at some point, if that makes any sense."

He smiled.

"I'll try to bring in some things next week," I assured him.

"That's fine. Weather permitting, I should be here," he said.

I left feeling like I had taken a step forward in my life! I'd met the Clark Gable I was supposed to meet. How about that? I stopped by the post office on the way home. There, I was beginning to see many of the same people, and they were beginning to say hello to me. That building had many meeting rooms in addition to being home to my little quilt group. I also made a point to pick up the newspaper while I was there. It did a wonderful job covering local news and human-interest stories, and it also included a huge calendar of events.

When I got home, I felt inspired to get back to my quilt work. I needed to make some things to show Carl. I had left him information about my website so he could see the wide range of quilted art that I had done in the past.

I noticed that when I worked on the porch, Puff was not comfortable in her chair. I thought she felt like I was invading her space. She moved to her spot under the Christmas tree. I glanced again at my watercolor of Puff. I thought I should probably consider painting pets, even though I only had one to claim. I had to remind myself that this painting was made for Cher and was not meant to sell at Art of Door County.

Chapter 64

As I got ready the next morning to help at Rachael's, my mother called. "What a pleasant surprise, Mom."

"Well, I wanted to catch you before you ran off somewhere. You help out at the barn today, right?"

"Yes, I'll be leaving soon. Is everything okay? How is Cher doing?"

"Well, the two of us are dealing with everything okay. I give those siblings credit for getting organized quickly and putting the house up for sale."

"Yes, that's one step closer to her moving back here."

"Well, that's not such good news for me. You know how much I think of her."

"I know, Mom, but she loves Door County, and I know how hard it was for her to leave here."

"I know my daughter would have done the same for me."

"You bet! Now, why are you calling?"

"You've got mail!" she announced.

"What's new about that? Just send it on to me if you want."

"It looks like a Christmas card."

"Well, is there a return address?"

"Yes. It's from Austen."

"Austen?"

"I'm afraid so. What should I do with it? Do you want me to send it on?"

"Throw it away."

"Claire! That's not nice. Do you want me to open it and read it to you?"

"No! Absolutely not! I don't want to hear from him."

"It's the holidays, for heaven's sake. It may be perfectly harmless."

"It's a trap. Just do as I say, Mom."

"If you insist. You know your situation better than I do."

"Yes, I do. Thanks. I've got to get going. We'll talk later, okay?"

"I love you!"

"I love you too."

As I did my makeup, I didn't want to think about Austen. I said goodbye to Puff and got on my way.

The traffic was unusually slow on my way to Rachael's. Unfortunately, it gave me time to think about Austen's card. It had been almost a year since I'd left him, and I'd done him a favor by leaving. What could he want? It could be a threat – or maybe an insincere note of affection to try and get me back. I would never know because I wasn't going to look at it. Honestly, it just didn't matter, or at least it shouldn't have.

The parking lot in front of the barn was full, so I pulled around back and found a space there. "Rachael, I'm sorry I couldn't get here sooner," I apologized. "Traffic was awful."

"We're good," she said. "Everyone has been patient. Get yourself some coffee."

I skipped the coffee and relieved Rachael behind the cash register so she could go out and help Charlie. A stern-looking woman approached me and said her last name was Wilson. She went on to say that she was there to pick up the wall quilt that she had been due when she purchased her barn quilt. "Sure." I nodded. "Wait right here, and I'll look for it." When I couldn't find it, I rang the bell for Rachael to come in and help me. I turned to the woman and said, "I can't find it, but Rachael will be in shortly to get it."

"Oh, for heaven's sake. I bought my barn quilt a couple of months ago. I should have had it by now."

"Hey, Claire, what's up?" Rachael said, entering the room.

The woman recognized Rachael and immediately started complaining. She provided quite a litany of things that she was displeased about.

Rachael listened intently and then said, "It's a remarkably busy time of year for us. I'll get to you as soon as possible."

"That quilt is the main reason I bought the sign," the woman exclaimed. "I'll be back on Wednesday, or I'm returning the sign." With that, she flew out the door.

Rachael looked at me in despair.

"I'm sorry I didn't handle that for you, Rachael," I said weakly. "I just couldn't find it for her."

"No, I'm sorry that you had to deal with her," she responded. "She's not the only unhappy one. I'll have to stay up late and get hers done."

"Is there anything I can sew for you in the shop? Would it help if I could sew the bindings on?" I offered.

"Well, perhaps," she said, thinking about the possibility. "I've done a lot of them and do a pretty good job."

"For now, I need to get back to Charlie," Rachael said,

making her way to the door. "We have paying customers out there."

Not long after she left, Allen came in. "Good to see you again," I said cheerfully, determined to not let the previous customer ruin the day.

Chapter 65

"Well, Ginger said this is where I had to get a Christmas tree for the shop," Allen informed me. "There's a line out there, so Rachael sent me in here to pay."

"Absolutely! Would you like some hot coffee while you're here?"

"Man, that sounds good."

"I sure hope to get to your shop sometime soon before you close for the season."

"I hope you can, too. We clean the place out and nearly start over so we're ready for the tourist season with additional items each year."

"Yes, so does the antique mall on Route 42. They make all of the vendors clear out and start over in the spring."

"It keeps everything fresh and new," Allen said as I handed his charge card back.

"Nice of you to buy your tree here," I said.

"We business folks need to support one another. I know it hasn't been easy for them." He chatted for a few minutes and then was off to set up the tree at his shop.

The rest of the day went quickly. Rachael came in around five, feeling pleased about their sales.

"I'll be happy to take some quilts home to work on if you want," I offered.

"It's not necessary. I plan to stay up late tonight and finish some of them. I'm usually so beat from working that I don't have much energy for the night. I don't know why folks are so critical sometimes. After all, it's a free gift from me."

"I hear what you're saying."

"I worry about Charlie, though. He's such a hard worker, although he does have a little break after the tree season is done."

"So when do you have your Christmas?"

"Well, we're busy on Christmas Eve, so when we finally close around five, we have a little party for anyone who has helped us and any good customers who want to stop by. I hope you can help us that day and have a bite to eat with us."

"It sounds great. I don't have anyone coming for Christmas, so I'll be glad to help you out."

"What about Cher?"

"She and my mother will likely be together. It will be a hard year for them this Christmas."

"I lost my mother on Christmas day, so I almost always just want the day to be over."

"Oh, how sad. I plan to visit the Moravian church tomorrow. The little Episcopal church by my house is already closed for the season."

"Yes, they have rotating pastors. I, too, am intrigued by the lovely Moravian church."

"Well, they have a ten o'clock service that I hope to attend."

"Let me know how you like it."

"I will. I'm pretty excited about spending my first Christmas here in Door County."

"Have you seen all the lights in Sister Bay? They really went all out this year."

"Not at night, but I will. I'd better get going."

"Thanks so much, Claire!"

I left with mixed feelings about that wonderful place. It was perplexing to see them so busy and yet still struggling to survive. I stopped at the Egg Harbor Main Street Market. It was like a small-town store with sophisticated merchandise. I always found something new to try.

From a distance, I saw Grayson and a young teenager. They were near the meat counter, and I could hear them laughing with the butcher. I began to gather a few items that I needed while watching Grayson out of the corner of my eye. Could the teenager be his daughter? Should I pretend not to see him, or approach the counter and order some sliced ham? I made my decision quickly before I lost my nerve. "Save some for me," I joked as I approached him.

"Hi, Claire!" he said with a big smile. "I'll be sure to do that."

"Dad, get some of those hot dogs," the girl reminded him.

"Yes, six will do," Grayson instructed the butcher. "Claire, this is my daughter. Her name is Kelly," he said, looking at the girl. "Kelly, this is Claire, who just moved here from Missouri. She's a quilter. Claire, Kelly is taking some craft classes at The Clearing, and one of them is quilting."

"Oh, how fun!" I responded. "There are no rules in

quilting, which is one of the things I like about it. One day, I hope to take some of The Clearing's classes as well."

"Cool!" Kelly said. She had a pretty smile and her daddy's dark blue eyes.

"Here you go, Grayson," the butcher said as he handed Grayson two packages.

"Well, we'll be on our way then," Grayson said. "You take care."

"Nice to meet you, Kelly," I said as the two of them turned to go down an aisle. Then, I had to turn my attention back to my own grocery list and order some Christmas ham.

Chapter 66

Sunday morning arrived, and I was determined to go to church. Mom would be pleased. She never missed a Sunday. I had driven by the beautiful building many times. The historic church was on top of a cliff that overlooked the bay. A side road took me up to a place to park. I couldn't wait to enter.

I was immediately greeted by a friendly group of church members. One of them handed me a visitor's packet. The charm of the small church was enhanced by lovely Christmas decorations. I sat in one of the tiny pews, which would only hold two people. It was near the back of the church. I was early, so I had a chance to read some of the materials.

In February 1853, Reverend Andreas Iverson and several others traversed over the ice from Green Bay to a tree-laden wilderness that would later become known as Ephraim. Rev. Iverson used a five-hundred-dollar loan to purchase four hundred and twenty-five acres of government land for his parishioners. A house was built for the Iverson family and was used for church services and school classes until the church building, also built by parishioners, opened its doors in 1859. It was the first church on the Door County peninsula. I took a break from my reading to look at the structure. Rev. Iverson had designed the building and had also participated in the building process. Interestingly, the church had been built close to the water but was later moved to its current location in 1883. What a vast amount of history this one building held!

The service began, and before long, I was captivated by the sermon. The pastor, a woman, delivered a wonderful talk, which was surprisingly short compared to the sermons I'd grown up with. This appeared to be a very musical church. A young man played a solo on his French horn. It was so special. When he was finished, the congregation applauded, something else that took me by surprise. Then, there was a sweet baptism. Afterwards, the pastor walked down the aisle, holding the baby for everyone to see. It was a lovely celebration. I was touched by God's presence. At the end, communion was offered to those of all faiths, which I thought was nice for those visiting. As I left, people stopped me and encouraged me to return. I was uplifted by their friendliness. I left, truly feeling I had found a church that had welcomed me.

On the way home, I stopped at the Blue Horse to pick up a sandwich to take home for lunch, but when I saw a few empty tables, I decided to eat there. I ordered a turkey sandwich with mango chutney and lettuce on focaccia bread. I was tempted to add a bowl of soup to my order, but passed. I was pleased that those working at the restaurant considered me a regular and called me by name. I took my time as I ate and enjoyed looking out the window, watching people come and go. Once back in the car, I drove by the library. Quilt club would meet the next day.

My cell phone rang as I got closer to the house. "It's me," Cher greeted me.

"Hey, what's up?"

"I think I have a good lead on a condo in Egg Harbor!"

"Great! Tell me more."

"It's called Meadow Ridge. The woman who lives there now is going into an assisted living place. By January or February, it should be available."

"Oh," I said, feeling a bit disappointed. "Not sooner?"

"Hey, it's not easy to get a place like hers. It's rather pricey, but thanks to my inheritance, I think I can do it."

"Oh, that's just wonderful! Where in Egg Harbor is it?"

"It's on Route 42. Drive by and take a look. It's a two-bedroom on the first floor, and I like that idea."

"If I can do anything to help, let me know. Any nibbles on the house?"

"No, but we're making a lot of progress getting it cleaned out. How is Puff?"

"Well, she's under the Christmas tree most of the time, just like in the photo I sent you. She will be so happy to see you. They do allow pets at the condo, don't they?"

"Yes, of course!"

"Quilt club is tomorrow, so I'll drop a little hint that you may be coming back."

"Oh, it may be too soon to say anything. How is it going with them?"

"Well, I'm trying to get to know each of them, but it isn't easy. The meetings are so formal. Tell me more about Frances."

"Why?"

"I asked her to have lunch with me. She told me about

going to her husband's gravesite every day and that she sometimes sits there and quilts. I think she also has a gift for telling the future. Did you know that?"

I could hear Cher chuckle. "What in the world would make you think that?"

"Well, we were talking about finding a place for my work, and she said that a man who looks like Clark Gable would be glad to help me."

"Oh, she must be referring to Carl at Art of Door County," she said, giggling. "She probably just couldn't think of his name."

"Well, she was correct. I'm going to show him some of my work next week."

"I'm so excited that you may be able to work with him and sell some of your work. Hey, let me know how club goes tomorrow."

"I will. Keep me posted on the condo."

"Sure thing, Claire Bear," she said, hanging up.

Chapter 67

The next morning, the temperature was only thirteen degrees. There was snow in the forecast for the afternoon, so I was glad the quilt club was meeting was in the morning. I dressed in warm clothes and then sat down at the kitchen table to enjoy coffee and an English muffin with cherry jam.

I had to start getting serious about what gifts to send home for Christmas. Mom was my biggest challenge. She didn't need another thing to sit around the house, but she would love the music box I had purchased for her from the Tannenbaum shop. I'd made her a flannel quilt years ago, which she kept by her recliner. I had a nice picture book of Door County that I could give her, or I could always give her gift certificates to some of her favorite places around town, like Rozier's, which had been there forever. I wondered what Michael was planning to get her; I hadn't talked to him since Thanksgiving.

I did want Mom to know more about Door County and hoped to get her here for a visit soon. I thought that once I got her here, she wouldn't be that anxious to go back home. After all, her best friend was no longer there, and Cher and I would both be here. I glanced at the clock and knew that I had to get moving if I planned to be on time for quilt club.

When I arrived, I went to get my mail from the post office inside the building. As I glanced through the envelopes, I saw what appeared to be a formal invitation to Lee's Christmas party. When I walked into the meeting room, I went up to her and showed her that I had received it.

"I hope you can make it, Claire," she said, smiling.

"I plan to," I assured her. "Thanks for thinking of me." As I found a seat, I wondered if anyone else in the club was invited. It was a hard group to read.

"Good morning," Greta said loudly enough to get our attention. "I see that everyone is here except Rachael." As if on cue, Rachael hurried into the room. "Oh, here she is," Greta said.

I motioned for Rachael to sit next to me. "Sorry I'm late," she whispered. "There was an accident, and it's slowing everyone down."

"Before we do our show and tell, there is a little item to take care of," Greta said, businesslike as always. "We have been asked to contribute to a fundraiser that the library is having right now. As you know, we have no dues in this group. The library is very generous to allow us to meet here free of charge. Considering that, I would like to ask everyone to leave a donation today, and I will present it to them. Does anyone object to that idea?"

"Will they take a check?" Marta inquired.

"That's no problem." Greta nodded.

"If they'll take a charge card, I can leave a bigger donation," Ava offered.

"I would suggest that you talk to Ms. Taylor in the office. She's taking the money," Greta responded. "The second thing is that we have received two formal requests to join the club," she then revealed. "You all know the answer we typically give concerning new members, but I always tell you when we have these requests."

"I get asked about joining in the shop all the time," Ginger mentioned.

"Well, while we're on that topic, I have a bit of news to share," I said. "I heard from Cher, and she has her eye on a condo that may work out for her. It may be a month or so, but I'm sure she'll want to come back to the group."

Greta eyed me evenly and said in a matter-of-fact tone, "Of course we'll be happy to have her back, Claire. However, the agreement was that you would only take her place while she was gone."

There was silence, which I broke by stammering, "Of course. I've certainly appreciated the opportunity to be a part of this group." I swallowed hard and kept my eyes focused on Greta, not allowing myself to glance at other group members. I could feel color spreading up my neck and onto my cheeks. An awkward silence followed.

"So Claire has to leave this group when Cher returns?" Rachael asked in disbelief.

"Every club has rules," Greta said simply. "We never made an exception until Cher asked us to. Claire understands."

I swallowed again, feeling vastly uncomfortable. "I do, I do." I nodded. "I'm just so tickled that Cher's moving back."

"I'll bet you are," Greta replied. Her tone indicated to everyone that the discussion of my membership was resolved satisfactorily. Then she said, "Ava, you can start the show and tell."

Ava's quilt was stunning to say the least. She had completed a small wall quilt covered in beads and seashells with the ocean as the backdrop. It looked heavy with adornments, but everything she had so laboriously applied to the background fabric seemed to have found a home.

"That is gorgeous, Ava," I said. "Is it for you or for someone else?"

"It's for my Florida friend. I love going to the beach when I visit her."

"Marta, you're next," Greta announced, moving the meeting along at a good clip.

"I just got this off the frame this morning," Marta said. "I did this Trip Around the World in all solid colors because I think the quilt stitches show so nicely."

"It looks Amish," Olivia said. "Is that a king-sized quilt?"

"Yes," Marta replied. "One day, I had my neighbor and her two daughters come to quilt, and we really made headway. You can't tell one person's stiches from the others'."

"I just love it," Ginger said as she looked closer to admire the hand quilting.

"Okay, does anyone else have something before I show mine?" Greta asked. She waited a moment to see if anyone else spoke. When there was silence, she shared, "We have three babies due in my family this year. There will be two girls and one boy. I decided to make each of them a Log Cabin quilt, but with all three quilts having their own variation. This pink-and-green one uses the Barn Raising pattern. The other girl gets this yellow-and-blue quilt in the Courthouse Steps variation. The boy gets Sunshine and Shadow in blues and reds."

"How do you work so fast?" Olivia asked.

Greta seemed a bit embarrassed. "It was quite easy to do," she said with a hint of a smile. "I hope the parents like them."

For just a moment or two, I saw Greta beam with pride as everyone made a fuss over her quilts. They were well done, and I shared her hope that the parents of the babies would admire them as enthusiastically as the members of the quilt club did.

Chapter 68

After the club adjourned, I could tell there were some who wanted to say something to me about Greta's comments, but I had a goal to exit quickly. I had almost reached my car when Rachael took my arm, pulled me to face her, and looked me straight in the eyes.

"You are not leaving this group – Cher or no Cher," she stated emphatically. "Everyone likes you so much, and that was no way to treat someone we've invited into our group."

"Rachael, it's okay. I know how difficult it must have been for this group to accept me in the first place. Cher isn't here yet, so let's not worry about it."

"Well, you only may have one more meeting," Rachael reminded me.

"Maybe so. Do you have time for lunch?"

"No, Charlie has already texted me asking when I'll be back. He knows that once I'm out and about, I find all kinds of places to go. As you know, I also have some quiltmaking to do."

"I'll be there on Saturday. It should be one of your busiest days!"

"Yes, come early if you can."

I walked to my car and saw Frances waiting for me.

"Don't you worry none about what Greta told you today," she said, shaking her head. "You aren't going anywhere!"

"Oh, Frances, that is so sweet of you, but I truly understand," I said, touching her hand.

"She isn't the only one who has a say here," she said in disgust. "You just keep coming!"

"By the way, Frances, I found Clark Gable at Art of Door County. He's willing to look at my art quilts."

Her face lit up. "Oh, that's wonderful! You should do well there." When Frances was leaving to go to her car, I saw Olivia in the car waiting for her. I wondered how Olivia felt about my leaving the group.

Feeling rejected, I decided to treat myself to lunch at the White Gull Inn. I would be close to home if the weather turned bad. The place was always crowded, but I lucked out with a table for two by the fireplace. I looked for Brenda, hoping she would be working. I eventually saw her at work in another part of the restaurant. I looked at the menu for a few minutes. When I had decided what to order, I looked around and couldn't help but notice a lot of businessmen having lunch.

"Good to see you again, Claire," Brenda greeted me. I was pleased that she remembered my name. "Are you alone?"

I nodded.

"Well, I'll chat with you when I can, but we're pretty busy," she explained.

"That's fine. It's good to see you," I said as another waitress arrived to take my order. I had decided on tomato bisque and a grilled ham sandwich.

"Is this Claire Stewart that I'm running into again?" Grayson's voice said as he came by with two other men. "It's nice to see you."

"You too! I love this place," I gushed, knowing my face was turning red.

"This is Claire Stewart," Grayson said to the two men with him. "She's a new member of the chamber of commerce."

"Nice to meet you," they both responded.

"Welcome," the taller of the two added. "We need some new blood in that group."

"Well, we'll let you enjoy your lunch," Grayson said with a smile. "We do business together, so we'd better get started."

"Nice to meet you," I said as they went to their table.

Of course, I thought of how I must have looked coming from quilt club. The men were in business suits and I looked like I had been mountain climbing. Once again, I felt that silly flutter all over my body when Grayson was around. What was he really like?

My food was served, and it was delicious. Eating by the fire was comforting. Would I ever, ever be able to share a meal with Grayson? Without hesitation, I ordered the cherry bread pudding and a cup of coffee. I guessed I felt like I deserved it. When the waitress saw that I was finished, she came towards me with what I thought would be my check.

"Your lunch is taken care of by that gentleman at the corner table," she said with a smile. "I hope you enjoyed it."

I turned around to look at Grayson. He gave me a smile and a wink in response as the other men kept talking. I smiled and mouthed a silent "Thank you."

Chapter 69

I was about to leave when Brenda approached me, saying, "I'm sorry I was too busy to talk. These are busy days, and we have a fish boil tonight, so I have to stay for that. Have you been to one of those?"

"No, I haven't," I replied. "I've read about them, but I'm not too crazy about the menu, if you know what I mean."

She laughed and nodded. "Maybe I'll see you at one of the hygge events," she said.

"I hope so, but Christmas is coming, and I need to catch up on some work, so I'm not sure when I can make it. It does sound like my cup of tea, though."

"Well, just holler if you ever want to get together," she offered. "I have a fair amount of free time since I only work part time."

"Sometimes I feel like I'm burdening the few people I know here with so many questions. I have your number in my phone, so we'll see."

I left the Inn feeling much better than when I entered. Everyone was so friendly, like Brenda. Even if the club kicked me out, I would still have my own circle of friends. Perhaps even Grayson would be within that circle. It had been awfully kind of him to buy my lunch.

With the harsh weather still holding off, I decided to drive to Ginger's shop near Sister Bay. It might be a place where I could find some Christmas gifts, and she might even bring up the quilt club meeting.

"So glad to find you open!" I said, entering the vintage shop.

"Hi, Claire! Long time no see," Ginger joked. "I'm glad you finally made it here."

"I had lunch and decided to drive out here before the forecast gets worse. Is Allen here?"

"No. When I got back from the club, he went to run errands."

"Well, I want to look around. I already see some clever things. This place is great, Ginger."

"Well, we have some new products, crafts, antiques, and repurposed items. We try to make sure everything is in good condition."

"That's great!"

Another woman came into the shop and needed help from Ginger, so I started looking around. Christmas decorations were everywhere, and some were indeed vintage, which was neat to see. There was a handmade craft section, and I immediately recognized some of Ginger's work. She used a signature cherry-print fabric to make many of her items. I had kitchen curtains made out of the same fabric, so I picked up some potholders and placemats for myself.

One of the craftspeople made unique items out of narrow tree branches. One tree-shaped design was quite clever and intricate. It needed to go home with me and perhaps be given away. I saw a very clever wine rack that made me think of Rachael and Charlie. I had never been in their home, but I knew they would appreciate the handiwork. As for my gift to Mom, I wanted to give her something that would make her think of me. Perhaps a quick watercolor of my log cabin would be personal enough.

"Claire, you're doing pretty well there, I see," Ginger said, noticing my collection. "Be sure you see some of the homemade jewelry that my sister makes. It's over here in this display case."

"I will." I nodded. "I wish I had more room in the cabin. I see some antique pieces I would love to have. Your prices are very reasonable."

"Thanks. We try to keep it that way," she claimed. "Claire, I just want you to know that I will do everything I can to keep you in the club if Cher returns. Greta was just plain rude today."

"Well, those are the rules, and because you've restricted the number of members, everyone wants to join."

She nodded, looking sad.

"It's a group like no other, I have to admit, but anyone could start their own group, for heaven's sake. I'm trying to get to know each one of you, but I don't think that is encouraged."

"There are reasons, but I won't go into them right now. Let's just leave it at that."

Someone came into the shop, and Ginger went over to greet her. I wanted to ask Ginger if she had been invited to Lee's open house, but now that I had visited with her, I thought I'd better not. When Ginger was free again, she added up my purchases, and I could tell that she was pleased.

"I'm so glad that you like the hot pads and placemats I made," she said. "They sell very well to tourists because of the cherry fabric."

"Well, I must still be a tourist in my new hometown," I joked.

I left with a big bag of goodies. The snow flurries had started. I needed to get a few groceries at the Pig, so I hurried on.

Chapter 70

I wasn't the only one thinking of stocking up for the big snowstorm. The store was packed, making it more difficult for me to concentrate on what I really needed. I rarely used milk and bread, but there was something about this urgency that made me feel as though I should buy it! I stood in a lengthy line while waiting to check out and finally got on my way home.

By the time I left the store, snow was already accumulating on the roads. I had to encounter some hills and curves, so I took them at a snail's pace. I wished my Subaru well, and she was doing just fine. I finally arrived home safe and sound, then took the groceries inside and started a fire before removing my coat. Puff was following me around as if she knew something was going on. Papers and a small box fell to the floor as I unpacked, and Puff found that amusing and started to play with them. At last she had something to entertain herself with.

I heated the beef stroganoff I'd purchased from the deli, and the aroma was so comforting. Life was good at this moment. Let it snow, let it snow, let it snow. I sat on the couch and turned on the weather channel. Being snuggled up against some pillows gave me a sense of peace in my cozy home. I looked at my unfinished quilt nearby and decided that I would make a serious effort to get something done the next day, when the weather would keep me inside. Then I got a telephone call from Cher.

"Hey, Claire Bear! How was quilt club?" I rolled my eyes and briefly caught her up on the membership situation. Cher listened intently but did not readily comment. She seemed to be thinking about what I'd shared. Finally, she changed the subject by saying, "I heard that you're getting a pretty big snowstorm."

"Yes, indeed! It has begun."

"Remember what I told you about keeping the drip going in the faucets."

"Oh, that's right! Thanks for the reminder."

"What about the driveway?"

"I'll find out in the morning if anyone shows up to clear it. It's dark out now."

"I had so much snow on the roof one year that I had to get George and his friends to push it off. Keep an eye on that. That roof is over ten years old. Hopefully, you won't have any leaks."

"Well, you're just full of good news, aren't you?" I teased. She laughed.

"I just got back from the Pig, so I have plenty of supplies."

"That's good. I hope that includes wine," she joked. "I still feel bad that Greta was rude to you at the meeting."

"Oh, Cher, forget about it. I'm getting to know each member personally on my own, because I sure don't get that experience when we meet as a group. The group seems to have no purpose, or am I just missing something? What makes them bond together in the first place? Is it just being able to say they belong to this very old, traditional quilt group?"

"Its purpose is to accept diversity within the industry, and I have to say, they've maintained that."

"Okay, fine, but I sense no love between them. They don't even have a title for the group, which could unite them. You wouldn't believe the different titles other people give them!"

"Those things might all be true, Claire, but I've learned a lot from each of them."

"That's good, but how did Greta come to have so much power?"

"It started long before my time. Now, no one seems to care that she's in charge. Someone has to take the reins when a group doesn't elect officers."

"Well, at least several of the others have approached me and said how bad they feel about Greta's rudeness," I said. "Were the show-and-tell parts of the meeting cold and structured when you were in the group?"

Cher burst into a giggle. "Well, you're seeing things with fresh eyes, that's for sure. It's been a while since anyone new has joined," she commented, then asked, "How would you feel if Greta asked you to leave?"

"Well, I wouldn't be surprised, that's for sure!"

Chapter 71

"Now, Claire Bear, you don't want it to get out that you were kicked out of such a prestigious club," Cher laughed.

"Tell me, did you ever try to change anything when you were a member, and why aren't there more quilters in this winter wonderland? Surely out of over twenty-seven thousand people, there would be more evidence of some."

"They're out there. I got to know a nice woman named Judy who owns that pizza place in Sister Bay. She belonged to a quilt group that met at some fire station. Have you ever been to Joe Jo's Pizza there along Route 42? Judy and her husband are both quilters, and they display some of their quilts on the walls."

"I haven't been there, but I'll check it out. I just wish I could see quilts and other textiles in some of the galleries. Hopefully, Carl will like what I'm working on."

"Well, good luck. I'm meeting with painters and a fix-it guy who can make this house presentable for selling."

"Tell my mama hello for me if you see her."

"I will. Don't forget the faucets."

"Thanks, Cher Bear. Love you!"

"I love you too!"

Before I went back to my project, I got the drips going so I could put that out of my mind. I then sat down at my machine and started doing some piecing. The whole time, I kept thinking about the quilt club. Cher had never been a person to enact changes, but I had a streak in me that caused me to always be on the lookout for something different or better. I hadn't thought to ask Cher if anyone else had ever tried to change anything in the group and how that had turned out. Were they run by Greta's Rules of Order or Robert's Rules of Order? If I did want to propose a change, I'd better do it soon before they asked me to leave! It was obvious that most of them were happy with the status quo – or were they?

I set up my portable flannel design wall, and Puff hurried to check it out. I did a simple layout of what I wanted to accomplish and got back to putting it together. The sooner I could get away from the machine and do the work by hand, the better.

I made the mistake of looking out at the snow. From the glow of the Christmas lights, I could see that it was accumulating very quickly. My car must have been buried in snow by now! When would I ever get out again? I took a deep breath and reminded myself that I was having a new experience in Door County, and I should just relax and enjoy it. I had everything I needed to be warm and secure.

My phone rang. I had to search to find it because it was hidden under so much fabric.

"Claire?" a man's voice asked. "This is Grayson Wills."

"Grayson, thank you so much for the delicious lunch! What's up?"

"I hope you're enjoying the snow," he began. "The reason I'm calling is that the chamber of commerce is putting together some focus groups before they do their long-range planning. I'm one of the chairmen, so I need to get a few folks together to discuss some topics. Since you're new to the area and would have a fresh perspective, I thought you would be an excellent person to have in my group."

"So are you asking me to participate?"

"Yes, if you're not too busy."

"Sure, I'd be happy to. Where and when are you meeting?"

"I'll have to let you know. I just left a meeting at Husby's in Sister Bay, but the weather got so bad that we had to end early. Have you been there, by the way?"

"No, I haven't. There's so much I want to see and experience here."

"Well, you need to get one of their 16-inch pizzas. Actually, it's the only size they make, so you need to go there when you're really hungry. I'll give you a call and let you know the details of the focus group meeting. I just wanted to get my list of names secured."

"Sure," I said. "By the way, how long do these big snowstorms last?"

He chuckled. "As long as they want to."

"I feel bad not getting out to Rachael's to help her. I'd thought I might drop by and surprise them by offering an extra hand, but my car is snowed in."

"You should stay where you are. I feel bad that they're having a rough time. I know how important this season is to them, and I hope they don't lose it. Well, I'll talk to you later."

At that, he hung up. Lose it? Were Charlie and Rachael in grave financial trouble?

So, Grayson had thought of me for his committee. Was I an easy target, or did he want to get to know me better? Why hadn't he offered to share one of those 16-inch pizzas with me? I had too many questions to think about as I got back to my sewing. Puff had found enough fabric on the floor to make a nest. What was with her?

Chapter 72

At around six, I stopped sewing. The wind was howling, and I prayed that the power wouldn't go out. From the snowy windows, I could see nothing but white. There were snowdrifts everywhere. I warmed some soup and then made a fire. I turned on the TV, but it didn't make me feel any better. Could this little cabin just disappear? It made me nervous, and I had more questions for Cher. I knew it would make me feel better just to talk with her again.

"I wondered how you were doing," Cher said. "If you still have power and no frozen pipes, you're good. I have to say, I'm glad I'm in Missouri right now."

"Of course you are. That's not helpful." I managed a laugh.

"Well, there was one year when the electricity did go out for quite a while. You do have candles if you need them, right?"

"I have candles, but I can't remember where I put them after I unpacked them. I'll look for them as soon as we hang up. Any other warnings, Cher Bear?"

"Well, I hope you have plenty of firewood."

"I think I do, but God help me if I don't. The rest of it is outside all covered with snow."

"You'll be fine. Don't hesitate to call. I understand that going through this for the first time is stressful."

I hung up feeling more frightened than ever. I needed to find candles and matches somewhere, and maybe I needed to start rationing the firewood. Would Tom ever be able to shovel me out of here?

After I found candles and placed them around the house, I decided to crawl under the covers early. Puff followed me, and I guessed that she likely felt the same way I did. The branches were beating against the windows, which wasn't comforting.

It didn't take long until I fell into one of those deep sleeps that caused me to dream. I dreamed that Rachael and Charlie's farm was completely snowed in. I tried to rescue them by pushing mountains of snow aside. Then, of all people, Harry happened by, grabbed me by the arm, and pulled me through the snow and away from Rachael and Charlie. I woke myself up by crying, "No, no!"

I was shaking and unable to settle back into sleep, so I gathered the quilt around me and went downstairs. Puff reluctantly followed. I went to the coffeepot even though it was only four in the morning. Thinking better of that, I made a cup of hot chocolate, thinking it would relax me, then walked to the front porch with the warm cup in my hand. I might have been in the North Pole from the looks of things. Bushes and trees were bent over from the heavy snow.

I curled up on the couch. Only a few embers were still burning in the fireplace. This could have been romantic if I didn't live alone. My mind naturally went to Austen. He had been the last man to hold me close and tell me sweet things to comfort me. Why did I feel I needed more of a commitment?

Why didn't he need more? Had he preferred to not talk about the future because he didn't see me in his future? I knew I had made the right decision. He hadn't even felt the urge to talk me out of it. He'd let me go so easily, and that hurt. I wanted to be with someone who wanted to just be with me. Was that asking too much?

Eventually, the hot chocolate did its thing, and I curled up on the couch for a couple more hours of sleep before I woke up from my cell phone ringing on the floor where I'd left it. It was Rachael.

"Claire, are you doing okay?" she asked.

"Yes, but I'm pretty snowed in."

She chuckled. "It's a bit early for this time of year, but here we are. Charlie has been plowing the parking lot for any brave customers. Please don't try to come out here. I'll put your check in the mail."

"Oh, Rachael, you don't have to pay me. I don't mind helping at all."

"What? Absolutely not! We agreed, and you've really been helpful! If I don't see you before, please come to help on Christmas Eve and then stay for the party."

"I wouldn't miss it!"

Chapter 73

I wasn't sure how I could really help Rachael and Charlie, but I would do everything I could. If Grayson knew about their financial problems, many others probably did as well. Suddenly, I heard a lot of racket outdoors. I went to the porch and saw Tom shoveling the front steps! I tried to open the door, but it was snowed shut. I called, "Thank you, thank you!" Tom's face was covered with a sock cap mask, but he nodded to let me know he'd heard me. It was a great relief to know that I could get out of the house if I needed to.

I dressed for the day, ate a quick breakfast, and got back to my sewing. I really wanted to take Carl some pieces this week. I knew I couldn't expect any quick sales since I'd missed the tourist season.

As I started quilting, my mind returned to Rachael and Charlie. I wondered if there had ever been a quilt raffle in Door County. In Missouri, we made quilts and raffled them, giving the proceeds to all kinds of causes. It wouldn't be much, but even a little bit could help. I'd never heard anyone mention a quilt raffle in the quilt club. Perhaps they considered it gambling.

Rachael and Charlie could plan an event at their place to increase revenue. Perhaps Grayson could help me figure something out when I met with him.

By six that evening, the snow had stopped falling. The wind had calmed, and moonlight brought beauty that glistened in the night. I made a fire and put a frozen pizza in the oven. The ringing of my phone broke the silence.

"Claire, this is Lee. I hope this isn't an inconvenient time to call."

"I'm certainly not going anywhere!" I joked.

"Well, that's why I'm calling. We've cancelled our party due to the weather. The caterer is snowed in, and I don't think we would have many guests who could get out."

"No worries here. I just appreciate your inviting me."

"While I have you on the phone, I just want to apologize for Greta's response to you at quilt club."

I sighed. "Thank you. I honestly didn't feel like it was necessary. I do understand rules, and I'm just happy to have Cher return to Door County."

"Well, let's just see what happens. If I don't see you soon, have a very merry Christmas!"

"You have a merry Christmas as well." After we hung up, I checked on my food and began thinking again about how each member of the club was reacting to Greta. The pizza was done, and I ate it, still perplexed about the quilt club situation. After watching some TV, I started to yawn and was considering moving upstairs when a call from Rachael came in.

"Are you still up?"

"Sure. What's up?"

"I just wanted to tell you that I'm bartending at the Bayside tomorrow night and wondered if you wanted to come by. It'll be slow with this weather, but I didn't want to pass up the work."

"Well, the idea of getting out of the house sounds wonderful. I could even walk there. Maybe I'll give Ericka a call and ask her to come with me so I don't sit there like a barfly."

She chuckled. "That's a great idea. If I get busy, you'll have someone besides the regulars to talk to."

"How was business today?"

"In spite of the snow, we still had some customers. Christmas must go on! The roads are finally getting cleared."

"That's good. Okay, my friend, I'll see you tomorrow night. Thanks for thinking of me." Even though the hour was getting late, I then gave Ericka a call. "Are you in bed?" I asked quickly.

"Heavens, no. I'm on the computer. What's on your mind?"

"Rachael wants me to stop by the Bayside tomorrow night when she's bartending. Would you go with me? We could just meet there. I went alone the last time and felt a little uncomfortable. I love their hamburgers."

"Actually, that sounds great. I was going to give you a call to meet up anyway. We can talk then. I get off at five, so what if I meet you there at six?"

"Perfect. I'll see you then!"

Chapter 74

The next day, I was pleased that I'd been able to complete a few small quilts to show Carl. One was a wholecloth that I called Quilted Snow. I had taken assorted sizes of snowflake quilting designs and connected them. I loved it so much that I considered keeping it for myself. The delicate hand-quilted stitches added to the overall soft look of the piece.

After a full day's work, I looked at the clock and realized I needed to get in the shower and get ready to meet Ericka at the Bayside. I dressed in my warmest sweater and my best blue jeans, and chose warm snow boots since I was going to walk there.

The walk to the Bayside was rather difficult, but when I arrived at the warm, cheerful tavern, I forgot all about it. I waved to Rachael, who was mixing drinks like they were going out of style. I then saw Ericka waving to me from the back corner of the bar, and I joined her.

"Hey! I'll bet you're freezing!" she greeted me. "I got us a table back here where it's a little quieter."

"Great!"

It wasn't long before our orders were taken.

"I'm so glad you asked me to come tonight," Ericka said. Her tone had turned serious. "I need a little cheering up. You won't believe what I have to tell you."

"What?"

"I'm not sure where to start, but the bottom line is that George has been questioned by the police more than once about the disappearance of Rob," she divulged.

"Why?"

"They think he's a possible suspect for all the robberies here in Door County."

"Rob?" I asked in surprise. "That's awful! Have they found him?"

"No, but they're seriously looking for him," she whispered. "There seems to be a trail of evidence that links the robberies to him."

"Do you think he's really capable of that?" I asked in disbelief, keeping my voice low as well.

"I don't know what to think," she said, her eyes wide. "George said he thinks Rob got into drugs. That, along with his drinking habits, means that he had to have money coming in from somewhere. He probably needed more and more money to support his habits. When George realized that Rob was hiding from him and not answering calls, he knew something more serious was up."

"How awful! Where could he be?"

Ericka shrugged her shoulders. "George also mentioned that Rob might have had a girlfriend who called the relationship off," she added. "He thinks she lived out of state, so maybe Rob went to see her."

"This gives me the creeps!" I said. "To think that he was

supposedly helping me because I was afraid of the break-ins! It's really scary."

"You never noticed anything missing, did you?" Ericka asked, curious.

"No, but..." I stammered.

"What?"

"Well, it's odd. Rob moved my safe into the downstairs closet because he said that my bedroom would be the first place that burglars would look for a safe," I explained.

"He was probably right," Ericka agreed.

"Well, the creepy part of the story is that he shoved it back into the dark corner of the closet when he placed it there, but recently, I noticed that it had been moved into a different spot," I said. "It's so heavy; there's no way that I could move that thing."

"It was! I remember George carrying it up your stairs," she recalled. "He really struggled with that thing. Would or could Rob even do that while you were gone?"

"Or while I was asleep!" I cringed. "I couldn't budge it even if I tried."

"Why didn't you say anything?" Ericka asked. "Was there anything else?"

"Yes. There were papers moved on my desk upstairs," I admitted. "It could be my imagination, but when you live alone, you know where you leave things because no one else is around."

"Yes, I know. I live alone. You're absolutely right," Ericka agreed.

"I've not had anything happen since, but if it was him, now I know how those things got moved," I said slowly, thinking back to that night when I had walked downstairs after I'd heard the noises. "I wonder what he was thinking when he put the light up behind my house. Maybe the safe was too heavy for him to get out of the house and he changed his mind. I wonder if he heard me coming down the stairs and ran. I've thought of all kinds of scenarios since then." Then I told her about the footprints.

Ericka shook her head in disbelief. "I'll have to tell all of this to George," she said. "He'll be furious if he thinks he put you in harm's way by referring Rob to you. If Rob truly is guilty of these break-ins, consider yourself lucky."

"I suppose you're right." I nodded. "The scary part is that he's still out there somewhere."

Chapter 75

Rachael finally came over and joined us for a few minutes while on her break. "It feels good to sit down for a few minutes," she said as she pulled up a chair. "You girls look so serious over here. I hope I'm not interrupting anything."

"Not at all," Ericka assured her. "You know, Rachael, I've wanted to get out your way to pick up a small tree for my apartment. My little artificial one is looking pretty pathetic."

"We can give you one for free at this point in the season," Ericka offered. "We have a lot of smaller ones left. Charlie can even deliver it if it need be."

"Well, I may not get off until Christmas Eve," Ericka noted.

"I'm working out there that day, so if it doesn't fit in your car, perhaps it will in mine," I offered.

"You're working on Christmas Eve?" Ericka asked, surprised.

"Well, it's not just any Christmas Eve," I said with a smile. "I hear there's a great party that starts when everyone gets off work."

Rachael grinned.

"Well, that's pretty cool!" Ericka responded.

"If you come out, you're invited," Rachael said. "Charlie fries and bakes turkeys and everyone else brings a dish. It's quite fun."

"I usually go over to George's that evening, but we'll see," Ericka said. "Thank you so much."

"If he wants to come over, the more the merrier," Rachael offered.

She was always so generous. I wondered if Rachael and Charlie's generosity contributed to their financial problems.

"Well, I'd better get back to the bar," Rachael said as she surveyed the crowd. "Let me know when you leave, okay? There might be some folks you'll want to say hi to before you leave, like Fred and Nettie." She said as she returned to work.

"You know some of the regulars?" Ericka asked me.

"Not really. I just met them here one night. They're a sweet older couple who come in every week."

"Well, it appears that Cher is on track to be back with us soon," Ericka said, changing the subject.

"The condo sounds wonderful!"

"The complex that she's looking at is nicer than mine, that's for sure!" Ericka commented. "You know, Cher once mentioned in passing that you had a long-term relationship before you moved here. You've never mentioned it."

"No need to. We've both moved on."

"I understand that he was a doctor?" she asked. "That's quite an adjustment for you, I'll bet. To be up here as a newcomer, living in a tiny cabin…" Her voice trailed off.

I laughed, knowing that she was fishing around a bit for information. "It's a change for the better, trust me," I assured her. "So back to Rob. Do you think I need to worry about him showing up at my place?"

"Would he return to the scene of the crime? I doubt it. I wouldn't worry about it."

We decided to leave, so I motioned to Rachael that we were going and blew her a kiss. Ericka decided that I didn't need to walk back to the cabin at that time of night, so she offered me a ride. Because the temperatures had dropped even more, I was happy to take her up on her offer. When she dropped me off, she waited until I was safely inside the house before driving away. Of course, when I went inside, I wondered about Rob returning, mostly because we had just talked about it. Before I went upstairs, I turned on the local news to see if I could learn anything about Rob. There was no mention of the break-ins. I had to remind myself that he might be perfectly innocent.

I happened to check my cell phone and noticed that I'd missed a call from Grayson. The noise from the tavern must have drowned out the ringtone. He had left a simple message saying that his focus group was meeting at the library at ten on Monday morning. He closed by saying that he hoped I would be there. I liked the sound of his voice and realized that I wanted to be there for more than one reason. When I got upstairs, Puff was waiting for me. The first thing she did was jump on the bed and make herself comfortable on the quilt. I guessed it was the little things in life. The quilt was comforting indeed as we snuggled into its warmth. In the moments before I fell asleep, it was much more pleasant to think of seeing Grayson at a meeting than it was to worry whether Rob would show up.

Chapter 76

The next morning, I gathered my newly made quilts together to take to Carl. My next challenge was pricing them. I had never done consignment before, but I knew the bottom line was what I needed for each piece. Most galleries charged twenty to forty percent, so the final retail price could get out of hand. I then made a list of what I was taking before I called to make sure Carl was there. Since it was Sunday, I knew the gallery wouldn't open until noon, but at least I was finally ready to approach Carl.

The rest of the morning, I marked another Quilted Snow quilt so I could have another on hand to quilt. I was interrupted by a phone call from Greta.

"Claire, this is Greta," she announced. "I'm calling to tell you that we will not be having a meeting this month like we'd hoped."

"Oh, I'm sorry to hear that," I responded.

"I hope you have a merry Christmas, and we'll see you in the New Year."

"You too, Greta," I said as she quickly hung up. Just like

that, the quilt club would not have any celebration for the Christmas season. That didn't seem normal. It would have offered an opportunity to socialize. Greta had given no reason, so maybe it was cancelled just because she'd decided to do so. I breathed in a deep sigh and shook my head. I needed to get it off my mind, so I began to put on my coat to go see Carl when my phone rang again.

"Claire, this is Brenda from the White Gull Inn."

"Hello," I said, surprised to hear from her.

"I thought of you because there will be Christmas caroling at the Noble House tonight. I was going to walk down there after work and wondered if you wanted to join me."

"Oh, I hadn't heard anything about it," I replied.

"You know where it is, I'm sure. They have a big lit tree in front."

"Yes, I do know where it is."

"Well, they have a big outdoor fire in the pit with Christmas carolers and hot cider for everyone. It generally draws a nice crowd. The house is also open, if you haven't seen inside."

"I would love to go. Should I just meet you at the tree?"

"I know where you live, and I'll be passing by, so I'll just knock on your door when I get there. Dress warm!"

"Great!" I responded, excited at the prospect of an evening out. As I hung up, I realized I had another new friend. It had been so sweet of her to think of me.

I then got on my way to Art of Door County. Luckily, my Subaru was up to the task and knew what to do with all the snow still on the ground. Carl had a big smile on his face when I walked in. "I'm so glad that you're open today," I greeted him.

"Well, just until Christmas Eve. I may open for Winterfest, but otherwise, we stay closed until early spring."

"I know I could have waited, but I do know that you sell some things online, so since I had a few quilts finished, they're yours!"

"Well, let's see what you have."

Carl helped me open each quilt. He remained silent as he looked at them. When he saw the Quilted Snow quilt, he held it up and examined it closely.

"This is quite beautiful, Claire," he complimented. "I don't know much about quilting, but this speaks to me about Door County in the wintertime. It looks like fireworks, but it's snowflakes."

I beamed with pride. "That's a wonderful compliment, Carl," I said, relieved to get his approval. "I loved doing it, especially when I was snowed in for a couple of days. I have to admit, I almost kept it."

"I suggest you continue on this path. I would like to purchase this piece for myself."

"Seriously? I haven't shown you my list of prices yet."

He looked over the list carefully and nodded. "It's sold, so you'd better get that needle going."

I had to keep myself from jumping up and down. We chatted a bit about each of the other pieces. When I asked what was selling these days, he shrugged. "What sells is something that makes a connection with our visitors' experience here in Door County. It can capture a beautiful memory, like a sailboat ride or something they discovered on a hike in a park."

"Maybe that's why I did Quilted Snow. The beauty of my first snowfall in Door County was going through my mind."

He smiled and nodded. I thanked Carl for his partnership. The highlight of the visit was when he handed me a check. Quilted Snow had become the first sale I'd made since I'd arrived in the county.

Chapter 77

Inspired by Carl's comments, I spent the rest of the afternoon quilting on my second Quilted Snow. I also had the evening to look forward to with going to the Noble House with Brenda. I really wanted to get to know her better. The thought of meeting up with Grayson and his committee also gave me a tinge of joy. I couldn't help but wonder if I popped into his mind every now and then. I still wondered what it had been about him when I'd picked him out in the crowd with his red wool scarf that day. Each time I'd run into him, he'd been polite and very careful in his communication. If I had to guess, I supposed he was one of those attractive men who didn't know they were attractive. Seeing him with his daughter that day just confirmed to me that he was a kind person. For me, kindness meant a lot.

After quite a session of hand quilting, I took a short nap and then woke to see that Puff had taken advantage of the situation by snuggling up next to me and taking a nap as well. Why did she want to be right next to me? She certainly had other special places she'd adopted around the house. I gently stroked her fine hair. She started to purr, which I thought meant that she liked it. Perhaps we were both looking for love.

I looked at my watch and saw it was time that I got dressed for the evening. I munched on a bag of popcorn as I thought about what warm clothes I should wear. I made my decision and got ready for an evening outside. Brenda arrived a little earlier than I'd expected, so I invited her in.

"Your tree and lights are amazing, Claire," she commented. "You look like you live in a Christmas house."

"Thank you! That's probably one of the best compliments you could give me. I could enjoy Christmas all year long. Would you like to have something to drink before we go?"

"Oh, that would be great! Frankly, I'd just like to get off my feet for a bit. I was busy nonstop today. I'm glad I asked you to go before my shift ended today, or I may have chickened out!"

"Well, you relax." I went into the kitchen to fix us two glasses of wine. From there, I explained, "I didn't make a fire since we're leaving." I returned and handed her a glass while I sat on the other end of the couch.

"This is so nice. Your place is so cozy."

"Listen, we don't have to stay there long if you're tired. I must have been frostbitten as a kid, because I go crazy when my fingers and toes get cold."

She nodded as if she understood. "Thanks, Claire. This hits the spot," she said, lifting her glass and taking another drink. "Are you happy here?"

"I am. It's terribly small and so different from what I've been used to, but I love many things about it, like all the light on the front porch where I paint."

"Claire, what is this? Are you quilting on this?" Brenda asked, looking at my wholecloth quilt.

"Yes. I'm pleased to say that Carl purchased a bigger version of it for himself, so it inspired me to make another. It's called Quilted Snow. Do you really like it? It's pretty simple."

"It's very lovely. Your stitches are so small and consistent. Mine are never that good."

"I know that hand quilters are nearly extinct, but I do it for relaxation. It's almost like drawing with a pen when I see the design come alive in stitches. A quilt isn't a quilt until it's quilted, they say."

"I have to say, it sure speaks of Door County, with all the snow we get."

"Brenda, why don't I see much quilting going on in this county? Are there closet quilters here?"

She burst into laughter. "Oh, they're here, trust me. It doesn't seem to draw the same attention as other crafts for some reason. There are a lot of small groups of quilters out there. I see folks quilting at the hygge, and there's a group that meets at a firehouse that has a fairly strong membership, I hear. I think the quilt shop in Sturgeon Bay also does very well."

"Why aren't there more events where quilters can show their work? Most quilters want to share. It's a reward for their fine work, like any artist wants."

"Well, Claire, fresh eyes see things more clearly sometimes. Perhaps you should think about how to change that."

I shook my head. "Funny you should say that. Grayson Wills said the same thing and hooked me into coming to his focus group for the chamber of commerce's long-range planning."

"See? I told you! Hey, perhaps we should be going. I don't know the schedule."

While I put on my coat, Brenda noticed Puff curled up under the tree. She took a moment to stoop and pet her. At that, we stepped into a very cold evening. It was a short walk, but with each chilly step, I wondered whether it would be worth it.

Chapter 78

"Don't you just love this charming house?" Brenda exclaimed. "Let's hurry and get some cider to get warm."

We got in line for cider and chimed in as everyone sang "We Wish You a Merry Christmas."

"I'll bet we could go inside the house to warm up, don't you think?" I suggested after we finished the carol.

"We can't take our drinks inside, so let's stay here for now and enjoy the caroling," Brenda said as we got closer to the carolers.

"Silent Night," one of my favorites, was the next song. It made me homesick to think of Mom being alone for Christmas. For a second, I wondered if I shouldn't try to get home and surprise her.

The cider was warming me up a bit, and more people joined us around the firepit. All of a sudden, Santa Claus came out of the Noble House, and the children ran towards him. I felt their excitement, remembering my own younger days of believing in him. We then joined in with "O Come, All Ye Faithful," after which Brenda and I decided to enter the house.

The entrance felt small and crowded as a throng of people traversed in and out. A costumed woman greeted us, saying, "We have a wonderful Victorian bridal exhibit displayed in each of the rooms. You will also see what domestic life in the Greek revival farmhouse was like. Three generations of the Noble family lived in this house, and it's now on the National Register of Historic Places. On each floor, there's a docent to answer any questions you might have."

"I'm embarrassed to say that I've never been inside this place," Brenda confessed as we walked through the house. "I wonder how many children lived here. Everything looks so small."

"I don't know," I responded. "I'm fascinated by these bridal gowns. They're amazing."

"I wore one, but none as fancy as these," Brenda said quietly, almost to herself.

Well, that told me something about Brenda. We didn't talk much after that, but were able to get warm and toasty as we explored the ten rooms of the structure. When we finished, I asked Brenda if she wanted to go somewhere else. She declined, saying she'd had a long day at the restaurant and needed to head home. I was happy to hear that answer, because I knew I would be ready for the solitude and warmth of the little cabin after walking back home in the cold.

Sure enough, there was urgency in our steps as we struggled against the freezing wind. I thanked Brenda for inviting me to the caroling, and we parted ways. It felt like it was really Christmas after hearing all the music. When I got back inside, I grabbed some cheese and crackers to take upstairs and got prepared for bed. While Puff watched me snacking, I wondered if I should be buying treats or toys for her.

My cell phone rang, but it was silent when I answered, although I could hear someone breathing. After a while, I just hung up. Would Rob or Austen do such a thing?

I crawled under the covers and said my prayers, hoping for a good night's sleep. The next thing I knew, morning light was pouring in through the window. I heard Puff scampering down the stairs to wait for breakfast. I looked at the clock, wanting to get up early enough to take my time dressing for the meeting with Grayson.

After I fed Puff, I went upstairs and chose a red knit sweater and black wool pants to wear. The outfit didn't come together until I put on red lipstick. After all, it was the Christmas season! I wanted to go early enough to mail a few packages at the post office while I was there. I hadn't finished the log cabin painting for Mom, but she did have a birthday in February, so I could save it for then.

I arrived at the post office and took care of business there, then said hello to some familiar faces before I entered the meeting room. There stood handsome Grayson, wearing a red sweater vest under his sport coat. That touch of red was perfect for him. Did he always dress that way? He looked quite stylish for a boat repair businessman.

Chapter 79

"Good to see you," Grayson said as I entered.

"I'm glad to be here." I smiled and took a seat, and Grayson made sure to introduce me to everyone else. One by one, they rose to shake my hand. I noticed that I was the only woman in the group, but that did not make me uncomfortable. I was just interested in making a positive contribution.

Grayson found a chair and began the meeting by saying, "I printed off an agenda to keep us focused this morning. Please help yourself to coffee if you like."

Sam Norris, who represented a marketing company, was the first to comment about how the chamber wasn't doing enough to promote local businesses and was more interested in tourism. Grayson agreed with him, but the owner of a bed and breakfast did not. I was too new to discern who was right and who was wrong.

"So, Ms. Stewart," Sam began.

"Please call me Claire," I interrupted.

"Okay. Claire," he began again. "You arrived here just a few months ago. Were you attracted to the area as a tourist, or did you see this as a favorable place to cultivate a business?"

I paused. "My reason for moving here was personal, but I have to say that the warm and fuzzy aspects outnumbered any business aspirations I might have."

"Good answer," Grayson responded.

"I like the business-after-hours events that the chamber offers, because I think that referrals from other business owners are extremely important. I'm all about relationships. I come from a small town, and the relationships that I had with business owners there made those businesses my go-to for any services that I needed."

"She's right," a representative from the Egg Harbor Market agreed. "I have to depend on the local market to sustain my business. Anything I get from tourists is 'gravy' as far as additional income is concerned."

We went to other topics as Grayson continued to take notes. There were transportation concerns, low-income housing problems, and the ever-present requests from nonprofits in the area that needed help.

"It's important to realize that the chamber of commerce can't be everything to everyone," I offered. "Their focus needs to be on commerce and doing business, not charity. There are many needs out there, and we should support them as individuals, but not as an organization."

"Well, that sounds a bit harsh," Sam protested. "I hear what you're saying, but many nonprofits expect our support."

"Therein lies the problem," Grayson said. "I agree with Claire." From there, he continued to lead the meeting quite well, giving time and opportunity for people to express differing views. As things progressed, I began to worry that I had overstated my opinions. At noon, the meeting adjourned, with Grayson thanking everyone for coming and being willing to help him with his project. He mentioned that there would be another follow-up meeting. As the others were getting up to leave, Grayson caught my eye and said, "Can I buy you lunch, Claire?" The volume of his voice was low. Maybe he didn't want the others to hear.

"Sure! That would be great."

"Let's meet up at the White Gull Inn. It happens to be my favorite, but if you have another suggestion, we can go there."

"Oh, I love it too! I think that's where I saw you last. By the way, I think I owe you a lunch, so this one's on me."

"That's not necessary," he replied.

Was he blushing? I couldn't tell for sure. As I left the building, I didn't think my feet touched the ground. Grayson Wills had just asked me out to lunch! Before I entered the restaurant, I freshened up my lipstick. When was the last time I had done that for a man?

Brenda noticed me right away when I entered the room. "Hey! Good to see you!" she said happily.

"You too." I smiled. "I'm meeting Grayson Wills here for lunch. We just finished up a chamber meeting."

"Way to go, Claire!" she teased. "I know Grayson. He's here a lot and is one of the handsomest men around." She winked.

"Oh, it's not what you think." I blushed. "He asked me because I'm helping him out."

"Don't give me that," Brenda said, shaking her head. "Grayson has been coming in here for years, and the only other woman I ever see him with is his daughter."

As soon as I was seated, Grayson walked in the door.

Chapter 80

"That was a good meeting," Grayson said. "I was impressed with your observations and opinions, Claire."

"I felt a little intimidated, being new and all, but I figured that's why you asked me to participate."

"Hi, Grayson," Brenda greeted him when she came to our table. "We have your favorite lobster bisque today for our special."

"Great!" he responded. "Brenda, I don't know if you've met Claire Stewart."

We exchanged knowing smiles. "We were just together last night at the Noble House, as a matter of fact," Brenda reported.

"It was cold but fun, and I got to see the inside of the house for the first time," I added.

"It's an interesting part of the history here in Fish Creek," Grayson noted.

We gave Brenda our order of lobster bisque and house salads before we continued our somewhat awkward conversation.

"So, tomorrow is Christmas Eve. I'll bet Kelly is excited."

"That she is. What are your plans?"

"Well, tomorrow is a busy day at Rachael and Charlie's farm, so I'm helping them until closing time. After that, everything turns into a big party for their help, friends, and good customers. That should be fun."

"They're an amazing couple."

"Yes, they are, and it troubles me to hear that they're struggling financially. They work so hard. I want to help them and work for no pay, but they won't hear of it. What else can I do?"

"There's an example of a business that the chamber might be able help."

I nodded.

"Unfortunately, they're headed for the winter months that cause many businesses here to struggle."

Brenda served our food. She had a smile on her face, which I surmised was because of Grayson and I having lunch together.

"Do you like to cook, Grayson?" I asked.

He nodded. "I have no choice. I'm raising a growing teenager! Kelly's taken an interest in making simple things like pancakes and spaghetti."

I smiled. "She's quite pretty."

"Just like her mother, which is hard for me when I look at her sometimes," he said. "Now let me hear more about your adjustment to Door County."

"Well, I finally have a gallery that's accepting my work," I said, and I couldn't keep from smiling at the thought. "Carl from the gallery on Main Street liked my work so much that he bought a piece from me."

"Well, that's a nice compliment," Grayson responded. "I would like to see your work sometime."

"That would be great. I'm hoping to introduce the county to quilt art," I said more seriously. "I just feel there should be more of that medium, and I haven't seen much of it in this area."

"I'm sure you'll figure out a way to do that. My grandmother was a quilter, as is my mother. Mom is also quite the seamstress."

"That takes real talent."

We turned down the complimentary dessert from Brenda, and Grayson said he needed to get back to work.

"I have to ask if you dress this dapper every day in your line of work."

He looked surprised as he said, "I'll take that as a compliment. I didn't use to years ago, but now my position is such that I'm always meeting with suppliers and clients, not to mention taking care of civic duties like today. I grew up in this business. My grandfather started with just a small little place along the bay. My father had a much bigger vision and took on bigger boats. Now we have to turn away work."

"How nice," I responded. "Do you ever have time to get out on the water yourself?"

"No. I did plenty of that in my younger years," he answered.

I was surprised at that answer. We decided that it was time to leave, and I picked up the bill.

"Thanks for the lunch, Claire. That was an unexpected treat."

"My pleasure," I said. Then, just as we had several times before, we shared a moment of awkwardness trying to figure out how to end the lunch.

"How would you feel if I gave you a call sometime?" Grayson mumbled.

"Like a date?" I teased, lifting my eyebrows in surprise and giving him a smile.

"I guess you might call it that. I don't know what that means anymore."

"You're not the only one!" I said almost sarcastically. "Call me anytime. I appreciate any local who can show me around."

"That I can do!" he said, putting on his coat.

"Have a wonderful Christmas with that daughter of yours."

"Thanks, and have an enjoyable time at the farm," he said as he left.

Chapter 81

I knew Brenda had been keeping an eye on us. She smiled as I waved goodbye to her. I then decided to stop at the market on Main Street to get some things I needed for the potluck the next night. Green bean casserole would be a big hit. It was then that I noticed a small rack of pet supplies, so I grabbed a couple of things that I could give Puff for Christmas. It seemed like a silly gesture, but it made me feel a little excited to see what she would do with them.

When I got home, I decided to call Mom to make sure she had plans with Michael for Christmas. There was no answer, so I left a message. I figured that Cher might know her plans, so I decided to give her a call. Again, I had to leave a message. My next approach was to call Michael.

"Michael, it's Claire," I began. "Is this a good time to talk?"

"Well, I'm a little out of breath. I'm outdoors at a ski resort in Colorado for the holiday."

"You are? You aren't going home to see Mom?"

"No, I'm with a few guys, and we've had this trip planned for some time. It's gorgeous here. How's the weather in

Door County?"

"It's fine, but tomorrow is Christmas Eve. I guess I'm feeling guilty now that I didn't fly home to be with Mom."

Michael paused. "I don't know what to tell you," he said.

"Well, it's too late now," I shot back. "I didn't know you weren't going to Mom's, or I would have made plans to be there." I felt exasperated by our lack of communication. Poor Mom! I ended the call with a frustrated "Have fun out there – and Merry Christmas!"

"You too, Sis!" he said, hanging up.

I rolled my eyes. That behavior was so typical of Michael. He liked to keep his distance from family. Hopefully, Cher would call me back with some better news.

As I got busy making the food, I gathered my thoughts and revisited my lunch with Grayson. He'd asked if he could call. Had he thought I would tell him no? I was right in assuming that he was very shy and totally dedicated to his daughter. I had to admit, it felt odd to be having lunch with a man again. It made me feel a bit shy myself! I was pleased that he'd liked what I'd had to say at his meeting.

As I made a fire for the evening, I thought it odd that I hadn't heard from Cher or my mother. Maybe they were out together. Cher had a cell phone, but Mom did not. I made some angel hair pasta for dinner and opened my favorite brand of marinara sauce. Puff looked up at me like she was expecting something.

"Santa will come on Christmas morning, Puff. If you've been good, he may bring you something." She gave me a meow and walked away. I had a big day coming up, so after I cleaned up in the kitchen, I headed upstairs. My phone rang.

"Claire?" a man's voice questioned.

"Oh, hi, Harry," I answered.

"I got to thinking about you and hoped you would be coming out to Charlie and Rachael's tomorrow for their big party."

"Yes, I'm helping them all day, so I did plan to stay for the party."

"Hot diggity!" he said with a nervous laugh. "I'm going to be there most of the day myself, playing somewhat of a Santa Claus."

"That's great! What is 'somewhat' of a Santa Claus?"

He chuckled. "Good question. I'm wearing part of a Santa outfit, including the hat, of course, but I also have to keep in mind that I have to help Charlie outside when he needs me. It will be extra fun with you there."

"I just hope they have a big turnout."

"They should. I think the weather forecast is good."

"Harry, can I ask you a confidential question?"

"Shoot, sweetheart."

"I've heard from folks that Charlie and Rachael are having serious financial difficulties. I worry about them and want to help. Can you advise me on that, or am I just hearing rumors?"

"Well, I can't break any confidentiality with Charlie. He's my best friend. I feel your concern as well."

"So it's true?"

"Charlie is a proud man. I don't think Rachael knows everything. I try to help them when he lets me."

"I admire that, Harry. I want to think of something to generate some winter business for them."

"You're a real sweetheart, and if you think of any way I can help, just let me know."

"Thanks, Harry. I'll see you tomorrow."

Whether I liked it or not, Harry was going to be around the next day. He was a good old boy with a heart of gold, and unfortunately, he'd confirmed what I had heard.

Chapter 82

I put on one of my two red holiday sweaters and wished Puff a merry Christmas Eve as I went downstairs to leave. "Santa will bring you something if you're good. I won't be back until later tonight."

I gave Mom another call before I left for work, hoping to catch her at home, but she didn't answer. I grabbed the wine rack that I'd bought for Rachael and Charlie's Christmas present and put it in the car before putting in my two green bean casseroles. As I got in the car to leave, I was reminded that the forecast had pretty much assured us of a couple of inches of white Christmas.

Despite my early arrival, cars were already in the parking lot. Harry was already there and approached my car when I pulled into a space.

"Can I help you with anything?" he asked thoughtfully.

"Yes!" I responded, thankful for the help. "Please take these casseroles into the kitchen for the party tonight. Thanks so much!"

"Glad to do it."

"Merry Christmas!" I called as I walked into the barn.

"The same to you, friend," Rachael replied. "I'm still arranging everything."

"Here's a gift for you all to put under that tree over there. I brought a couple of green bean casseroles, too!"

"And I helped," Harry added, emerging from the kitchen.

A woman came into the shop, so I quickly stashed my purse under the counter. "May I help you with anything?" I asked.

"Oh, I'm just fascinated by these signs," she gushed. "I need a last-minute gift, and I think this one will do just fine."

"It's very nice," I agreed. "This pattern is called Jacob's Ladder."

The woman seemed to be in a hurry, so I took care of her quickly, securing the first purchase of my workday. From then on, the pace of customers was steady. Most were on a mission since it was Christmas Eve.

"Well, I made it!" Ericka announced as she entered the shop.

"Wonderful!" I responded.

"Charlie picked out a perfect tree for me and insisted that it was free of charge, but I don't feel right about it," Ericka shared.

"He's way too generous," I said, shaking my head. "If you want, just make a donation. It would be appreciated."

"Sure!" she agreed. "Pick out one of those cute little quilt signs for my neighbor, would you? I forgot to get her something, and she loves quilts. She's always bringing me leftovers of some kind."

"Now that's a nice neighbor to have," I said as I chose an Eight-Pointed Star design.

"Yes, the blue one," Ericka said, agreeing with my suggestion.

I went right to work to finish her sale and told her how much Rachael and Charlie appreciated her business.

"Hi, Miss Claire!" one of Harry's granddaughters called, running towards me.

"Merry Christmas!" I replied, giving her a hug.

"Do you still have cookies?" she questioned.

"We sure do!" I told her. "Let me finish here, and I'll get you some. Where's George today?" I asked Ericka.

"He wasn't up to coming this morning. I think he has a hangover, to be honest."

"Any news about Rob?"

"Nothing that I know of," she said, shaking her head. "I would love to stay for the party, but I need to be with George. I'll say goodbye to Rachael on my way out."

"Thanks for showing up, and have a merry Christmas!" I said, giving her a hug. I went to get the girls their cookies. They were eager to tell me about Santa coming to their house that night.

In the afternoon, sales slowed down, but folks still kept coming in to wish everyone a merry Christmas or to drop off food for the party. It was quite touching to know that Charlie and Rachael knew so many people. Since I was free, I went to the back room to make the punch.

Fortunately, Charlie had enough work to keep Harry busy outdoors for most of the day. As closing time came around, I could tell that Rachael was totally exhausted. I didn't know anyone who worked as hard as this couple.

"Time to relax and enjoy the party!" Harry declared enthusiastically as he entered the room.

"Claire, Charlie and I will open your gift tomorrow morning, if that's okay," Rachael interrupted. "I don't want anyone to think they were supposed to bring a gift."

"Oh, I understand," I said as she took it to the back room.

Chapter 83

"You got big plans tomorrow?" Harry asked. His voice was jubilant, his energy for Christmas matched only by the excitement of his granddaughters.

"Not really," I said. "I'm having some regrets about not flying to Missouri to be with my mom."

"I'll be with my son and those granddaughters," he said proudly. "It should be nonstop fun!"

"It certainly will be," I agreed. "Enjoy every moment. Being around children at Christmas is especially wonderful."

"If you don't want to be alone tomorrow, we'd be glad to have you join us," Harry offered.

I was touched by his sincerity. "No, I'm truly fine."

"May I have your attention please?" Charlie was standing on a chair to be more easily heard. "Rachael and I are so pleased with this great turnout tonight. We want to thank you for everything you've done for us throughout the year. You know who you are. Thanks for bringing all of this wonderful food. Celebrating Christmas with you and with my sweetie by my side makes all this worthwhile. We both wish you a merry Christmas!"

The crowd clapped and then continued to enjoy the gathering. I slipped away from Harry and joined Rachael in the back room, where she was cleaning some dishes. I began to help her.

"Claire, this party is for you, so get out there and enjoy," she insisted. "You've been such an immense help."

"I am enjoying it," I said, giving her a hug. "You're blessed with so many friends! Folks are slowly leaving, so the two of you will be left alone soon, unless Harry decides to stay."

Rachael chuckled. "I hope he doesn't bother you too much," she lamented. "He means well, and I think he doesn't really want to give up on you."

"Forget Harry! You just enjoy your day tomorrow with Charlie. We'll get together some ideas for the winter."

Rachael looked at me questioningly.

"You have a Merry Christmas!"

"You too, and thanks for the gift. That wasn't necessary."

I walked away and found Charlie so I could give him a Christmas hug. That done, I got home around ten and was totally exhausted from the long day. I wasn't used to being on my feet all day long on a concrete floor. When I saw that Puff wasn't under the tree, I went upstairs and found her waiting for me on the bed.

"I told you that I would be late," I reminded her as she looked at me.

It didn't take me long to get under the covers and provide a spot on the quilt for Puff. My intent was to get to the Moravian church in the morning for their Christmas service. To do that, I needed to get a good night's sleep.

The next morning, I was awakened by a phone call from Cher. She'd remembered me on this special day, which boosted my spirits.

"Merry Christmas!" she greeted me. Her voice sounded upbeat.

"Merry Christmas, Cher Bear. I'm still in bed."

"Well, you'd better get up, because I'm leaving the Green Bay airport in a rental car to come to see you."

"What?" I blinked, trying to comprehend what she had just said.

"Tell Puff her mama's coming home for Christmas! I should be there within the hour, so put the coffee on!"

"Oh, I will. I can't believe it!"

"See you soon, Claire Bear!"

I jumped out of bed as if Santa Claus had come during the night and I was in a hurry to claim my presents! "Puff, Puff!" I called out. "You won't believe who's coming! Let's get your breakfast going."

After I fed Puff, I prepared a pot of Door County coffee using the cherry creme, which was Cher's favorite, then went upstairs to change. Back downstairs, I got out the toys I had purchased for Puff. She observed very carefully as I rolled the ball to her and demonstrated how the little mouse toy squeaked. I couldn't tell if she thought I was nuts or if she approved. She finally responded, but with a fair share of hesitancy. I looked at the clock and rushed around to straighten up the cabin. How weird it would be for Cher to return to her previous home. I planned to give her my bed for the night, and I would sleep on the couch. I turned up the Christmas music and got out a frozen cherry pie to serve with the coffee. Cher would likely be hungry.

My cell phone rang. I thought for sure that it would be Mom, but it was Ericka.

"Ericka!" I said before she could say hello, "Cher will arrive here any minute! Did she tell you that she was coming?"

"She actually did, but she wanted to surprise you. Isn't it great?"

"Oh, I have to go. I think that may be her at the door right now. Merry Christmas, by the way!"

Ericka laughed. "You too, Claire! Have a wonderful Christmas."

As I got closer to the door, I couldn't believe my eyes. Not only did I see Cher approaching, but she was accompanied by Mom!

"Mom!" I cried out. "I can't believe it!"

I opened the door and flew into my mother's arms. It was an emotional moment that left both of us in tears and hugging one another again and again.

"Well, I'd better get a hug, at least!" Cher said, coming near me.

"I don't know what to say!" I responded, giving her a warm embrace. "Merry Christmas, and please come in."

"Well, look who's under the Christmas tree waiting for me," Cher said, scooping Puff into her arms. Puff had no reaction.

I ignored the reunion and indicated for Mom to come and sit down. "Welcome to my home," I said, squeezing her hand.

"I'm so happy to be with you, honey," she said softly. "Cher insisted that I come with her, and your place is just as cute as in your photos. I didn't know if it could all happen, so I didn't want to get your hopes up."

"This is the best Christmas surprise ever!" I said, putting my arm around her.

"Claire, the place looks great, and it's so festive with all the lights," Cher declared. "Why didn't I think of that? I can't wait to see each room."

"Are you happy to see Puff?" I asked with a smile.

"I'm not sure that she's happy to see me," Cher said. "She couldn't wait to jump out of my arms. She may not remember me."

Chapter 84

We finally made it into my tiny kitchen to enjoy coffee and pie at the table. I was proud of the cherry-print placemats I had purchased at Ginger's shop. When I mentioned Ginger's name, it triggered all kinds of questions about the quilt club.

"I'm so grateful to have had Ericka, of course, but Rachael has been the one who's really gone out of her way to welcome me here," I told them.

"Hey, how was the Christmas party?" Cher inquired.

I tried to describe in detail what it was like as Mom watched with a big smile on her face. We shared lots of stories between the three of us as we enjoyed our coffee. I then said to Mom, "I can't believe that Michael went off on a ski trip and left you alone at Christmas."

"Honey, it wasn't like that at all," Mom explained. "I told him that my intent was to go with Cher to surprise you for Christmas. He seemed pleased, so he decided to make plans of his own. He gave me beautiful new luggage for Christmas, which you'll see when we unpack the car."

"Okay, I forgive him – for the moment," I said, feeling a little chagrined.

"I'm going to poke around for old times' sake, if you don't mind, Claire," Cher stated.

"Go ahead, but just remember that you didn't give me much time to clean up the place," I warned. "My office is a mess." As Cher began looking around the cabin, I asked, "More coffee, Mom?" as I poured myself another cup.

"You called this cherry creme?" she asked as she took another sip.

"Yes, it's Door County coffee made right here. Maybe we can stop by the coffee place. How long will you be here?"

"We'll leave on New Year's Eve, if that works for you."

"Not long enough, but that's okay."

"Well, Cher has to accomplish a lot regarding her new condo while she's here. She's pretty much packed, so I hope the timing works out for her."

"You would love it here as well, Mom," I said with a smile. She knew that I was hinting for her to make a big decision. "I'm sure I would, but I'm too old for that kind of change. You're still young enough to adapt to a new area. I love my town, my church, and all my friends."

"I know you do, and you should. I'll try to come home more frequently, it's just that I had to leave the town where Austen is so well-known."

"I completely understand, and I see how happy you are."

"Are you talking about Austen?" Cher interrupted, joining the two of us. "Linda saw him with another woman at a restaurant in Cape, so maybe he's moved on."

"Hopefully," I said. "I didn't think it would take him very long."

"Now tell us about any prospects here in Door County," Cher requested rather matter-of-factly, but with a telltale smirk on her face. "You're not the only one who's single around here."

It was fun to laugh together again. I decided to open up a bit about Grayson. "Well, I've been admiring a very nice man who owns a boat repair business in Ephraim."

"Is this the guy with the red scarf?" Cher asked with a giggle.

"As a matter of fact, it is." I nodded.

"A red scarf?" Mom inquired.

"So, what's the deal?" Cher asked. "Is he divorced, widowed, has children, or what?"

"He's widowed with a young teenager," I stated. "I haven't asked anyone how his wife died."

"Well, I want to hear more," Cher encouraged. "Maybe he has a friend."

"Hey, it's Christmas day!" I announced. "That means that there are presents!"

"Now, wait a minute, you already sent presents," Cher reminded me. "I loved the painting of Puff! Where is she, anyway? I think she's ignoring me. I brought her some treats that I know she likes."

We went into the living room with our coffee.

"Here are a couple of things for you," Cher said as she handed me some packages. "This one is from my mom."

I knew it was the poinsettia tablecloth she had made that I had always admired. When I opened it up, it was just as I had remembered it. "Thank you so much," I said, clutching it close. "I'm going to use it on the table this very day."

"She did pretty work," Mom said. "I miss her so much."

We looked at one another and took a quiet moment to remember Hilda. She had been a wonderful mother and friend. All three of us were trying to keep from crying, but we had telltale tears tracking down our cheeks.

Cher bravely picked up the conversation and, as was her way, used humor to change the tone. "Now here's something you can cry about," she teased as I opened the second gift.

It was a framed collage of Cher and I growing up together. I couldn't even describe my delight, but I knew I needed to try. "This is a real treasure," I said. "Mom, did you see this?"

She nodded, smiling proudly. "Actually, I had the frame, and I knew it would work perfectly for this," she revealed.

"Here's one that I almost kept for myself, but I wanted you to have it," Cher said more seriously as she indicated for me to open the third gift.

When I tore the paper off, I saw a painting Cher had done of the log cabin when she'd first moved in.

"I love it! Thank you!" I said, holding it up. "Speaking of a log cabin, there's something I want you to see, Mom."

She followed me to the porch, where I had the painting of the log cabin that I was originally going to give her for Christmas. "This was supposed to be done in time, but I just couldn't finish it," I explained.

"I'll be happy to have it when it's finished," she exclaimed. "You already sent me that wonderful coffee table book on Door County. I really enjoy looking through that, and the music box was delightful."

"I knew that you would love the music box," I said, smiling.

"This one is from your brother," Mom said, handing

me a heavy package.

"Michael rarely gets me anything," I said, feeling perplexed.

"Just be gracious about this," she counseled me.

I opened what appeared to be a book, which I thought was odd. It was probably about something Michael liked.

Chapter 85

"*Let the Whole Truth Be Told,*" I read aloud. I looked at Mom for an explanation.

"Read the whole cover, honey," she encouraged.

"*Let the Whole Truth be Told* by Michael W. Stewart," I read aloud, letting the words sink in. "When did this happen?" I asked in astonishment.

"You knew he was working on a book, right?" Mom questioned.

"All his life he's been saying that he's been working on a book!" I joked.

"Well, he decided to self-publish it," Mom explained.

"Good for Michael," Cher cheered. "Why didn't he tell you on the phone earlier?"

"I think he wanted it to be a real Christmas surprise for his sister," Mom remarked.

I opened the cover, and there was an autographed message to me. It read, "To my little sister Claire: let the whole truth be told that I love her very much. Michael." I was speechless and wanted to cry. I just sat there in silence for a moment. "This is such a shock," I admitted. "I can't wait to read it."

"I'm so proud of both of you," Mom said quietly. She then handed me a large gift bag. "Here's a little something from me."

I reached in and felt something soft. "A quilt, Mom?" I questioned.

She smiled and nodded. "Don't get too excited," she cautioned. "I didn't make the whole thing. At church, the quilting group made blocks for this. Our names went into a hat to see who the lucky owner would be, and it happened to be me!"

"You won this beautiful Log Cabin quilt?" I asked in disbelief.

"Everyone said it was meant to be since I was going to give it to you. They know you live in a log cabin."

"I love those reds and browns together," Cher remarked. "That will go well in your bedroom."

"Mom, thank you so much," I gushed as I gave her a hug. "I love it, and it means even more since you helped make it."

"I even know the variation name. It's Barn Raising, right?" Cher asked, receiving a nod from Mom.

"Please tell the ladies how much I love it," I said, feeling overwhelmed. I heard a knock on the door and opened it to find Ericka.

"Guess who else is here?" I asked with excitement. I could tell by the look on her face that she knew about Mom coming on the trip as well. Ericka and Cher embraced each other. "Ericka, this is my mother," I said proudly.

"Nice to meet you, Ericka," Mom said. "I've heard so

much about you. Thanks for all you've done to help Claire."

"Any friend of Cher's is a friend of mine." Ericka blushed. "To be honest, I did know about this little surprise, so I prepared a simple Christmas meal at my house this evening. I don't think there's a restaurant open for miles around. I have a delicious ham and all the trimmings."

"How thoughtful!" Mom exclaimed.

The merriment continued as we showed off our gifts and drank more coffee. At two, Ericka went home to prepare for our arrival later in the evening. This was turning into the most perfect Christmas ever! I left Mom and Cher for a bit and went upstairs to call Michael and thank him for the book. I felt sure he'd never gotten so much praise and affirmation from me, and it really caught him off guard. I talked to him for a while and then took my phone downstairs so he could wish Mom a merry Christmas.

Chapter 86

When we arrived at Ericka's condo that evening, I could tell she had tried to outdo herself to make her place look nice. George was there to share the meal with us, but then he announced he had other plans and had to be on his way. That made me much more comfortable. I had tried to avoid him ever since he'd asked me out.

Ericka's small Christmas tree was perfect in her compact living room. We had many fun toasts and laughs about old memories and new moments shared together. We didn't leave the dining room table until nearly eight that evening. Everyone pitched in to clean up, just like family. As I observed Ericka and Cher together, it was interesting to see their close friendship. Cher and I had been best friends since grade school, so it was hard for me to think that she had another best friend in her life.

"I plan to stay here with Ericka, and your mother can stay with you," Cher announced.

Truthfully, sharing Cher made me feel just a bit jealous. "That's great!" I said, hiding my initial resentment.

After all, it made sense. The cabin only had one bed and a couch, so three people staying there for a week would be close quarters. I tried to swallow my sadness and put on a brave face. Plus, Cher was correct; it would give me more time to spend with Mom.

"I have an appointment tomorrow to take a look at the condo in Egg Harbor," Cher said. "Who wants to go with me?"

"You girls go ahead," Mom said quickly. "Puff and I will be fine by ourselves."

"I want to go," Ericka said quickly.

"I'm curious to see it," I said, weighing in last.

We made arrangements for Ericka and Cher to pick me up the next day. I knew all the excitement was making Mom tired. It had been a long day for her. I suggested that it was time to leave, so we said our goodbyes and thanked Ericka for the special Christmas dinner.

When we arrived home, Puff was already upstairs on the bed. Mom got a kick out of seeing her reaction when I told her to move off the bed so I could put on my new Log Cabin quilt. "Oh, it's perfect!" I beamed. "Thank you again, Mom. You know how much I love your quilts. I'll use the other one on the couch, which will make Puff very happy."

"I'm perfectly capable of sleeping on the couch," Mom offered.

"I won't have it," I insisted. "Puff and I have slept on the couch before."

Before Mom prepared for bed, I showed her around the small upstairs. I cautioned her about the narrow staircase and urged her to hold onto the railing while going down the stairs. After I changed into my pajamas, we said goodnight.

Puff and I got comfortable on the couch. I was thankful for a wonderful Christmas day. The photos, the quilt, Michael's book, and a surprise visit from Cher and my mother had made it a Christmas to remember. God had certainly been good to me this year. My mind wandered, and I began to think about Charlie and Rachael. I hoped that they'd enjoyed the day despite their financial worries. Who had Austen spent the day with? Then my mind flipped to thoughts of Grayson. How had he enjoyed the day? I imagined that his energy was spent in devotion to his daughter and making the day special for her. Did the thought cross his mind that it would be nice for him to have someone else to share the holiday with?

I must have really fallen into a deep sleep, because when I woke up the next morning, Mom was already moving around in the kitchen. It woke Puff up, too, and she went flying into the kitchen for her food.

"Good morning," I said, joining her in the kitchen.

"Oh, I didn't mean to wake you," Mom apologized. "I hope you slept okay on the couch."

"I slept really well. How about you?"

"I did fine, but I think your kitty cat is ready for her breakfast. I brought a surprise from Hoeckele's Bakery."

"Not the peanut coffee cake! Seriously! Mom, you thought of everything."

"It traveled pretty well, the way they have it packaged. I found the coffee, so it should be done any minute."

Mom and I settled in at the kitchen table like we had done so many times before at her house.

"Are you feeling okay these days, Mom?"

She smiled. "I'm fine, just slowing down. Losing Hilda

was a wake-up call for me. It's taken a bit of the wind out of my sails."

"I'll bet it has. Have you seen Mr. Vogel lately?"

She smiled shyly. "We played cards at the senior center last week."

"That's nice. How is his health?"

"I worry about his heart. He's always been overweight. I try to get him to do a little more activity than he normally does."

"I'm sure that it's hard to pick up a new routine at that age, but I'm glad that the two of you are friends."

"We go way back, and your father trusted him with so many things throughout his life."

"After I get back from Cher's condo, we'll go to out to eat at one of my favorite places nearby. Would that be fine with you?"

"That will be nice, and it'll be my treat," Mom insisted.

When we finished breakfast, I showed Mom the Quilted Snow quilt that I was working on. She loved the whole idea and complimented me on my quilting stitches, even though I knew they weren't the size quilted by Mom and her group at church. She offered to mark or bind any of my quilts while she was visiting.

Chapter 87

I was pleased to join Ericka and Cher to take a look at the condo in Egg Harbor. When I asked them about their evening, it seemed that Cher had been exhausted from the trip, and Ericka was ready to get some rest after spending the day preparing Christmas dinner for everyone. They had visited for only a brief time before turning in after Mom and I had left.

Cher's chosen condo was quite impressive. If she liked what she was offered, all she had to do was sign on the bottom line. Ericka and I remained reserved as Cher carefully checked things out. It was a big financial decision.

"Being on the first floor is important to me," Cher explained. "When I enter, it feels more like I'm walking into a house."

The unit had been updated and looked brand-new, and Cher was incredibly pleased. "Okay, Egg Harbor, you're going to get a new resident," Cher announced at the end of her inspection. We cheered. "Now I just have to arrange for a mover."

"I told Mom that I wanted to take her to the White Gull Inn tonight for dinner. Why don't you join us and celebrate your big decision?"

"What do you say, Cher?" Ericka asked, excited for her friend. "I'm game!"

"Sounds terrific!" Cher said, giving me hug.

Ericka dropped Cher and me off at my place so she could go to work. We found Mom busy with little chores around the cabin.

"Mothers will be mothers," she admitted sheepishly. "Puff follows me around as if she wants to help."

"Come here, Puff," Cher cooed, gesturing towards the cat.

Puff looked at her, made a quick decision to fly in my direction, and leaped onto my lap.

"Puff, that's not nice," I scolded. "Your mama is talking to you."

"She's different, Claire," Cher said, disappointed. "She's fallen for you, and even though it's sad for me, I'm glad she's happy with you."

"Oh, I don't think that's the case," I assured her. "I'm the one who feeds her, so she's sticking with me."

"Well, back to dinner plans," she said, changing the subject. "I suppose I can go to dinner in what I'm wearing, so I don't have to go back to Ericka's."

"You look great!" I said. "I'm going to call and make a reservation."

Cher and Mom proceeded to look at the projects I'd started. I called Ericka and told her our reservation time.

"This small white quilt is lovely, Claire," Cher noted. "I don't know how you make such tiny stitches. I'm finding myself doing more and more machine quilting."

"Oh! There's a blood stain," I gasped. "I wonder when I did that! Now what?"

"That's no problem, Claire," Mom said as she looked closer. "Haven't you heard the old wives' remedy for taking out blood spots?"

I stared at her, hoping she had some magic cure.

"Your saliva is supposed to remove your own blood."

"I've heard that," Cher agreed.

"Get a cotton swab or a cotton ball," Mom instructed. "Let's try it."

I went in search of either of those two items and quickly found a cotton swab. We then held the quilt in direct sunlight so we could see it better. As crazy as the suggestion was, it started to work! I couldn't believe it.

"Well, that's amazing!" I gushed. I couldn't believe that the problem had been solved so simply.

"We have to do this all the time at church. It works most of the time, especially if the blood stays on the top layer," Mom claimed.

"Cher, did you look in the bedroom? I put the Log Cabin quilt on my bed."

"No," Cher replied. "I'd love to see it." We went to the bedroom, where Cher exclaimed, "Claire, it's perfect in this room. I also like the way you've arranged some things. I was never very clever that way. You've made this place quite charming. I'm so glad that you like it here."

"I do for now, at least." I smiled. "I still think that once you get moved back here, you need to take Puff with you."

She looked at me oddly. "I can't do that. I'm sorry," she responded. "This is her home. I can always get another cat."

Chapter 88

Off we went to the White Gull Inn, ready for a great dinner. I didn't see Brenda, but I remembered that she rarely worked the evening shifts. Ericka arrived shortly after we got seated. Mom was impressed with the charming decor. Someone was playing the harp, which added a nice touch.

Knowing we were celebrating the return of Cher caused each of us to feel lighthearted. The rest of us gave recommendations to Mom as to what she should choose to eat. Cher and Ericka also told her all about the fish boils that the Inn had in the summertime.

Ericka's cell phone rang, and she said that it was George. She got up from the table and went into the front reception area to talk to him. We decided to wait until she returned to place our orders. Cher began sharing how she planned to decorate the new condo. She had covered every room in her conversation, and Ericka had still failed to return to the table. In the lull, the three of us looked at one another while wondering what could be keeping her.

"Something must be wrong for her to take this long,"

Cher decided. "I'd better check on her." At that, Cher left the table, and Mom and I continued chatting and listening to the lovely music. I could tell that Mom was really enjoying herself. Finally, Cher and Ericka returned, wearing stone-faced expressions.

"Is everything okay?" I asked as they sat down.

"Ms. Stewart, forgive me for interrupting our nice dinner in that way. I just got some sad news from my brother," Ericka explained.

"No, that's fine," Mom assured her. "We've enjoyed the harpist, and it's always interesting to watch people come and go. No problem." Then Mom eyed Ericka and said, "Are you ok, dear?"

"They found Rob," Ericka blurted out as if she couldn't keep the news in any longer.

"My goodness! Where?" I asked.

"Alabama," Ericka said, shaking her head. "He went to see the girl who had broken up with him. George thinks that the police were staking out the place, knowing that he might show up there. It obviously worked."

"Did they arrest him?" I could feel my head beginning to spin. Surely it wasn't actually true that the same kind man who had helped me get settled was the one wanted for so many break-ins!

"Yes, and he confessed to the robberies," Ericka said, trying not to cry.

"Robberies?" Mom asked innocently.

"Rob is my brother's friend," Ericka explained, taking a deep breath. She paused. "He's my friend as well." She paused again to gather her thoughts. "He was an alcoholic and got involved in drugs. That's when he disappeared, so we knew something was up. He likely had to support his habit and was running short on funds. We also think he became very depressed after his girlfriend broke up with him. The result is that he committed some burglaries around Door County. Now he's confessed to the crimes."

"Oh, how sad," Mom said in a consoling tone.

"He was really a nice person, Mom," I chimed in. "He did some work for me around the house. He did an excellent job."

Upon hearing this, Mom glanced at Ericka.

"I'm sorry about that," Ericka said, shaking her head. "I had no idea that things would turn out this way. I was kind of worried that he'd that come back here. Even though he's my friend, I felt uneasy about him being back."

"Would he have been dangerous?" Mom asked, concerned.

"No, I actually don't think so," Ericka expressed.

"If there are drugs involved, I wouldn't be too sure about that," Cher, who had been silent until this point, said. "I barely remember him."

"George is very upset," Ericka continued. "I think it would be best if I spend the evening with him. You all enjoy your dinner. I'm so sorry for this interruption." At that, Ericka stood and said to Cher, "Listen, you stay and enjoy. I'll be home after I leave George's, and I'll be up late. Claire can drop you off."

"Sure, I can do that," I agreed. "Please tell George how sorry we are. Is Rob still in Alabama?"

"Yes, for now, but George may know more when I talk to him a little later," Ericka answered.

I gave her a hug before she left. I hated to see her going

through this. When she was gone, the rest of just looked at each other. Despite losing some of our appetite, we ordered dinner. The news had added a different tone to the evening, but we tried to make the best of it. After dinner, we dropped Cher off at Ericka's. When we arrived home, I knew Mom would have more questions concerning Rob. I didn't want to frighten her, but I did disclose that I had been concerned when he was at large.

"In a new area, you can't be too careful about the folks you meet," Mom cautioned. "I suppose that if he's been arrested, everyone needs to go on and not worry about it." She sighed and shook her head as if she couldn't think about it anymore. "I'm really tired, honey, so if you don't mind, I'm going to turn in."

"Good idea. I want to take you to the Blue Horse for breakfast in the morning. You'll love it. It has a beautiful view of the bay and every kind of coffee you can imagine."

"I'll look forward to it. Good night, sweetie."

I fixed my bed on the couch as Puff eagerly watched. "Well, Puff, I think your stay here might be permanent. Your mama has moved on and wants you to stay here." Puff looked at me and jumped up on the couch. I stroked her soft hair, and she purred as if to indicate that she was okay with the new arrangement.

It took me a while to get to sleep. I kept thinking of Rob inside the jail in Alabama. Who would have thought that things would have turned out like this? Poor George.

Realizing that Christmas was over was always a bit depressing. I wanted to keep my tree up forever and keep the outside lights on the cabin. I also wanted to keep my mom here with me. I didn't want Cher to leave. Yes, it is difficult to say goodbye to Christmas.

I finally fell into a deep sleep, still thinking about Rob. I had a dream about him breaking into the cabin, brandishing a gun, and threatening to shoot Mom and Puff! At the height of the tension, a man wearing a red scarf burst in to rescue us. I tossed and turned and finally woke myself from all the drama. I nearly fell off the couch as I came back to reality.

Chapter 89

The next morning, I told Mom about my restless night.

"I didn't sleep that well myself," she claimed. "I almost came down to have a cup of warm milk."

"Mom, do you still do that?"

She nodded, smiling like she was privy to a secret that I was completely unaware of. "Read the literature," she laughed. "It works!"

I laughed along with her and said, "Well, the sun is shining on this very frigid day, so we need to venture out of this cabin for breakfast. Are you up to it?"

"Of course. My arthritis acts up until I get moving around, but then I'm fine."

"You're a trooper, Mom. I'm so lucky to have you, and I'm so thankful that you're in good health. I know that Cher misses Hilda something terrible."

"I miss her, but towards the end of her life, I don't think she knew who I was."

"How sad," I said, shaking my head.

We finally got ourselves together and headed to the Blue

Horse. It was crowded, but many customers were getting their coffee to go. Later in the morning, it would be more crowded with tourists. I spied a table for two on the porch, so I told Mom to save it for us while I ordered. Mom wanted black coffee and an English muffin with honey. I chose hazelnut coffee and a cinnamon bagel.

"Good morning, Claire," a man's voice called from behind me. I turned to see Grayson.

"Oh, good morning!" I answered.

"Say, hold up a minute after you order," he requested. "I want to ask you something, but I need to get my coffee to go, so I won't be staying."

"Sure. My mom is with me," I announced with a smile. "She and Cher surprised me on Christmas morning. I'd like you to meet her." By then, I had placed my order, and Grayson was moving closer to the counter to do the same.

"How nice for you. Let me put my order in, and then I'll join you."

That done, we stepped away from the line of waiting customers. My heart was beating way too fast. Grayson's eyes caught mine, and we held each other's gaze for a moment. "You had something to ask me?" I said absently, not wanting the gaze to end.

"Yes," he said, clearing his throat. "Do you have any plans for New Year's Eve?"

"New Year's Eve?" I repeated, taken by surprise.

"Yes, I have a small group of friends that gets together every year, and I usually go alone," he explained. "I thought I might ask you, being new to the area and all. I mean, I just thought you'd fit in. If you have plans, it's no big deal."

I smiled. He sounded so unsure of himself. I would have

guessed that he'd practiced what he was going to ask me, but when the moment arrived, he seemed to have forgotten his own script. "It sounds perfect!" I responded. "I wondered what folks did here for New Year's Eve. I did see some restaurants advertising special dinners."

"Are you sure you want to go?" he asked in disbelief.

"I would love it. Thanks for asking. You have my number, so just let me know what time."

"I will. We just enjoy heavy appetizers and drinks until midnight. After that, Liam serves his homemade jambalaya to start the New Year."

I chuckled. "It sounds like a wonderful way to celebrate the occasion. I'll look forward to it. Come and meet my mom," I said. "She's probably wondering what happened to me."

"There you are!" Mom said when I showed up.

"Mom, this is Grayson Wills. We met in this very café."

"Nice to meet you, Ms. Stewart," he said, shaking her hand. "How nice of you to surprise your daughter for Christmas."

"She was really surprised," Mom admitted. "Please join us."

"Thanks, but I'm taking plenty of things back to the office, and I'm sure they're anxiously waiting for me to return," he replied. "Nice to have met you, and I hope you enjoy your visit."

"Nice to meet you, Grayson," Mom responded.

"I'll be in touch," Grayson said before he turned away.

Mom waited for him to walk away before she got an impish look on her face. "This must be the man with the red scarf," she teased. "He's quite handsome, and very much a gentleman."

I blushed. "Isn't it funny how I first saw his red scarf? Then I saw this dark-haired, handsome man. I'm sorry it took so long for you to get your coffee, but he had a question to ask me."

Mom kept the same look on her face as she asked, "What did he have to ask you, pray tell?"

I could tell that she was quite amused by the excitement that I was trying to keep tamped down. The words came tumbling out of my mouth in a rush as I exclaimed, "He very awkwardly asked me out for New Year's Eve! Can you believe it? I can't!"

"Oh, honey, that's just great! This could be the start of something!"

"It's a small party with friends, which makes me feel more at ease. He seems to be rather shy and private, from what I can tell. You never see him with any women."

"All the better, Claire. If he has a teenage daughter like you said, he has other priorities."

Chapter 90

"I can tell that you're overwhelmed, aren't you?" Mom teased. "I'm so happy for you. An unpleasant experience with someone shouldn't discourage you from going forward with someone else."

"It won't," I assured her. "To be honest, Mom, I don't think that there are very many eligible men around here. George asked me out, but he's not my type. If I don't have another relationship again, that would be fine with me, too."

"Don't say that," she said, patting my hand. "Even at my age, I enjoy having a man's attention. I don't want you to be alone for the rest of your life."

"That's sweet, but I don't want you worrying about me."

"A mother never stops worrying about her children," Mom said matter-of-factly.

We took our time finishing breakfast. On our way out, we ran into Ginger. I introduced her to Mom and told her that we might stop by her shop if we had time.

Mom's request for the day was to go to a market where she could buy cheese, jars of cherries, and cherry jam for her friends. I knew she would enjoy Seaquist Orchards in Sister Bay, so I headed in that direction. She loved all the scenery and commented more than once about how it reminded her of Cape Cod. Mom was like me in that she liked to be around water, but not in it.

"Well, I still fear it may set off my vertigo," I told her. "That means I no longer go on any boat rides. When I flew home for Thanksgiving, I had to give myself a heavy dose of meclizine."

"It's good you know what you need to avoid," Mom assured me.

There was a tasting counter at the market. Mom was amazed at all the things to taste, and she was determined not to miss any of them! I went in search of a shopping cart while she got her bearings.

"Where do we start?" Mom asked, feeling overwhelmed. "This place is huge!"

"Just take your time and get anything you want," I encouraged her. "I can always send home what you don't want to take on the airplane. You wanted to get some Door County coffee, and they have quite a few choices here."

"Yes, it's amazing!" she responded as she chose several assorted flavors.

We walked the aisles of baked goods, which was my weakness. There were slices and slices of apple samples to choose from. They were all labeled. I never knew there were so many kinds of apples. Mom examined many sizes of canned cherries and had a tough time choosing which ones to purchase. There was nothing like this in our small hometown. I stopped in the aisle where they had pretty pastel sweatshirts. I needed clothing that could be layered, and these were very soft. I bought a pink one and a yellow one.

Together, we chose a quiche to eat for supper.

"I wish we had this market at home," Mom said with a sigh.

We loaded up the car, and I could tell that Mom had had a marvelous experience. "Shall I continue our adventure?" I asked when she got in the car.

"I'm pretty tired, Claire. Would you mind if we headed home?"

"Not at all. Perhaps we both need a nap after our restless sleep last night."

Cher called while we were unpacking the car. I told her where we had just gotten back from and that we were both exhausted.

"Ericka and I are going for a late lunch. Would you care to join us?" Cher asked.

"We'll pass. You enjoy yourselves. Has there been any more news regarding Rob?"

"George did mention that Rob's bail is so high that he'll have to stay in jail."

"That is so sad."

"Ericka has plans tonight, so do you want me to pick you up for dinner?"

"Mom and I picked up a quiche from the market, and we plan to make a salad to go with it. Why don't you join us?"

"How nice! I will."

While Mom took an afternoon nap, I got back to my quilting and thought about every word Grayson had said to me at the café. My phone startled me, and I saw that it was Rachael.

"I miss you! How's it going with Cher and your mother?"

"Just great," I answered. "Mom said she wanted to see where I worked, so I thought we'd drive out there tomorrow so you can meet her."

"Sure! I'll be manning the shop. I think Charlie is going into Sturgeon Bay to get supplies."

"Did you have a nice Christmas?"

"Christmas Eve is really our Christmas, so we rest the next day. Thank you so much for the wine rack. We have the perfect spot for it."

"Great! Can I bring anything with me tomorrow?"

"Just yourselves. It sure was a shame that our quilt club skipped Christmas."

"Yes, I agree. Well, we'll see you tomorrow!"

Chapter 91

Cher joined us for a light supper. Mom fixed a tossed salad and her homemade salad dressing. I threw in some sliced fresh strawberries, which delighted her. Cher brought leftover chocolate cake from Ericka's house. As we started to converse, Mom couldn't wait to for me to tell Cher about being asked out for New Year's Eve.

"Mom, it's not that big of a deal," I protested shyly.

"Oh, it's a big deal if you have a date with Grayson Wills," Cher argued. "I wish we were still going to be here to see how it goes. Hey! Maybe we should stay a little longer!" she teased, winking at Mom.

"Don't worry, ladies. I'll tell you every detail."

They laughed. Then I brought up a different subject, partly to get them off the topic of my dating life and partly to seek some advice from Cher.

"Cher, you're such a good promoter," I began. "I could use some advice."

"From me?" she questioned.

"Seriously, I think Rachael and Charlie are about to go

bankrupt. I'm trying to think of ways that I could possibly help them."

"My goodness!" she responded. "Things certainly don't appear that way."

"Well, I can't do a lot, but I thought that if they had some kind of winter event at their location, it would bring folks out and would be good for the barn quilt business," I shared.

"Like what?" she asked.

"Something like a chili fest," I suggested. "Everyone has to eat, and there aren't many places open in the winter. There could also be a chili contest. I'll bet restaurants would want to compete once the word got out. There could be other attractions as well. I want to really develop the vision before I present the idea to them."

"You're a friend indeed," Cher bragged. "My first thought is to add beer and brats."

"Great idea!" Mom chimed in. "Local vendors could do that."

"That's all good, but everyone has to realize that this is a fundraiser for Charlie and Rachael."

"Of course, and as well-known as they are, I think a lot of people would pitch in," Cher replied.

"You know how in Missouri they hold a quilt raffle for every cause known to man? Do you think the quilt group could put something together?" I asked Cher.

"I have no idea, but I can tell you that they've never done anything like it before," Cher warned.

"Exactly! They've never done anything before that I'm aware of," I said. "Am I missing something about this group?"

"You're right. No one suggests anything that hasn't been done before," she agreed.

"Well, that's odd," Mom said.

"They want to be so unique, but for the life of me, I can't figure out what makes them so special," I stated.

Cher nodded and chuckled.

"Claire, I think that you need to think it through before you stir things up," Mom warned. "They were nice enough to let you in after Cher moved."

"You have a great idea here, Claire," Cher said. "Just so you know, whatever you come up with, I'll back you all the way. You just have to get past Greta first."

"No doubt about it," I agreed.

"As to the chili fest, I would proceed," Cher encouraged. "You'd better first approach Charlie and Rachael."

"It's a good thing that I'm going home, or I'd be put to work," Mom joked. "I'm too old, but Claire's heart is in the right place on this."

"Yes, it is!" Cher agreed. "I almost forgot! I brought a couple of toys for Puff. She always liked playing with my balls of yarn. I'll let you deal with the mess!" Cher chuckled.

"Great!" I responded, rolling my eyes.

"Oh, and there's a squeaky toy that she likes," Cher added.

"Well, you two go play with Puff while I clean up the kitchen," Mom suggested.

We did just that. Cher was excited to introduce the new toys to Puff. At first, Puff was hesitant to respond, but then she caught on. Was Cher trying to win Puff's attention back?

A half hour later, Cher decided to get back to Ericka's. I appreciated getting her input on things, and now my imagination could go wild.

Chapter 92

The next day, there were serious threats of snow, but I was convinced that we needed to go out to Rachael's. Mom whipped up a tasty omelet before we left. I knew these moments would be lovely memories for me once Mom returned to Missouri. We both dressed warmly, and if the weather held off, I wanted to show her some other sights along Route 42. I texted Rachael when I left the house to let her know that we were on our way. I cautioned Mom that the conversation could get awkward when I brought up the idea of helping them.

"Well, you must be careful not to hurt their pride, Claire. When it comes to financial things, folks sometimes become sensitive."

"I know. I need God to help me choose the right words."

Mom smiled and didn't say any more on the subject. As we neared Rachael's place, she admired the big red barn and the spacious property. Even she could see the possibilities.

"Welcome!" Rachael greeted. "I've heard a lot about

you, Ms. Stewart."

"You and Charlie have been a godsend to Claire, and I thank you for it," Mom gushed.

"Well, we think the world of her," Rachael responded.

Just then, Charlie burst into the room in a flurry of energy, surprising me. "I hear that we have company!" he cheered. "I was supposed to go to Sturgeon Bay, but I didn't like the forecast."

"Yes, I'm hoping it will hold off," I agreed.

"You sure pulled off a surprise for your Claire, Ms. Stewart," Charlie boasted.

"I'm so glad I kept it a secret." Mom smiled, clearly pleased with herself.

"Well, let's have some coffee, shall we?" Rachael suggested. "I have some cinnamon rolls if you'd like."

"Mom made a big breakfast for us, so no thank you," I replied. "I'm dying for Mom to see your shop with all the barn quilts, but we don't want to keep you from your work."

"Nonsense," said Charlie.

As Mom strolled around the shop for a bit, the rest of us sat around the lunchroom table. I knew this was the time to bring up my idea.

"While the two of you are here, I'd like to bring up something for discussion," I began.

"Sure." Rachael nodded.

I took a deep breath. "While I was working here, I had a lot of ideas about how to get customers here after the Christmas season."

"Yes?" Charlie asked.

"Mom even noticed what a nice setup you have on this property, with the barn and all," I continued. "When

I saw the crowd of friends and customers who came to your party, I began to consider other occasions that would draw them back out here."

"That would be fun!" Charlie said.

"The thing I've been most excited about is a chili fest," I announced.

"A chili fest?" Rachael repeated.

"Yes, an outdoor occasion in the dead of winter," I explained. "Everyone loves chili, so there could be a contest – and I happen to know that Harry makes a mean chili that could be packaged and sold. There could also be other foods, like beer and brats."

At that, Charlie sat up in his chair and looked more interested.

I continued, "I'll bet that you know contacts and vendors who would be eager to have the exposure. I personally want to get a quilt made to be auctioned or raffled off. I could see an event like that grow and grow over time."

"Claire, I don't know," Rachael said, looking doubtful.

"You know that women would likely come inside and buy some barn quilts," I pointed out.

"Girl!" Charlie interrupted. "Where did you come up with all of these ideas?"

"Oh, you don't know my daughter," Mom said as she joined the group.

"It would be so much fun," I said, almost pleading. "I see how hard the two of you work, and I don't think you realize what a gold mine you have here."

Rachael and Charlie laughed, and Charlie said, "There's no doubt that we could use the income, but this could be pretty overwhelming." He stood and started pacing.

"I know, I know," I agreed. "I'm offering my services for free, because most of it's going to be getting the word out."

"Claire, you make it sound so easy, but we're so busy as it is," Rachael said with a sigh. "We need to think about this. You are so sweet to think of us."

"Claire has some innovative ideas," Charlie said to Rachael. "We could use a little of that."

"Okay, I know it's a bit much to think about all at once," I admitted. "The event could start small with mostly family and friends, and it could grow from there."

"Now that's more like it," Charlie agreed with a nod. "We'll chew on it."

Chapter 93

"Take your time," I said, trying to sound encouraging. "You would just need a fair amount of time to get the word out. I hear that March is still considered winter around here."

"That's right." Charlie nodded.

"We start to plant by March and April in Missouri," Mom said.

"Our summer is very short," Charlie complained. "If you need any painting or repair work done, the window of opportunity is small."

"That's why I want you to do this in the winter," I said. "There are more than enough locals to make it successful."

"Most locals don't let a little snow bother them," Rachael agreed. "I'm liking this idea a lot, the more I think about it."

"Well, we've kept the two of you long enough, but I'm glad Mom got to meet you guys," I said. "I'm taking her to Al Johnson's for lunch. She's seen the photos of the goats on the roof."

"A must-see in Door County!" Rachael agreed. "Check out their gift shop. It's one of my favorites."

"I'm afraid I already have too much baggage for the plane ride home," Mom confessed.

"Have a safe trip. We're so glad that we got to meet you," Rachael said, giving her a hug.

After we said goodbye, Mom and I walked slowly to the car. I took the opportunity to point out where things could take place during the chili fest.

"Claire, let's get going. I'm starved," Mom pleaded. "It's also beginning to snow again."

I abandoned describing the event any further, got Mom settled in the car, and headed to get some lunch. Inside the restaurant, the atmosphere was warm and friendly. Mom commented about how charming the Swedish uniforms that the waitresses were wearing were. I gave her a brief history of the place and explained that the goats were now toasty warm in a barn some miles away. We ordered vegetable soup and the restaurant's delicious bread tray, which had many varieties of bread to choose from. Mom was tempted to order the Swedish pancakes that Al Johnson's was known for, but decided against it at the last minute.

"I hate the thought of you leaving tomorrow," I said sadly. "Do you think that Michael will come to see you when he returns from Colorado?"

"I really doubt it," Mom said without emotion. "He's so busy, but he'll come when he can."

"I'll bet there are things that you would like him to help you with," I remarked.

"Perhaps, but I'm fine. Mr. Vogel's son has helped me

do some things, and some friends at church are always asking to help me if I need it."

"Why do you always call him Mr. Vogel?"

She chuckled. "He keeps telling me to call him Bill, but I've known him as Mr. Vogel for so many years."

"What do you like best about him, Mom?" I asked, curious.

She looked down. "I know it sounds silly, but when he talks to me, he likes to touch or hold my hand. I miss that personal contact so much. No matter what conversations your Dad and I had, we always used our physical touch to remind us that we were in things together."

I tried to blink back the tears that had unexpectedly sprung to my eyes. "That's beautiful. I miss some of that myself," I admitted.

"As we grow older, we need to comfort each other with our memories and human touch. I know Mr. Vogel – I mean, Bill – misses his late wife very much. He took care of her as long as he could. I think they were a very happy couple."

We took our time finishing lunch. I wished I had a recording of our conversation. I was so lucky to have a good relationship with Mom. The waitress talked us into having some of the warm bread pudding with whipped cream. I wanted that portion of the lunch to last forever!

"I'm so full, Mom. I need to keep my weight off for this long winter," I laughed.

"And for that nice handsome man you'll be dating," Mom teased.

"We'll see about that." I blushed.

I could tell that Mom was fading from the look in her

eyes. It was time for her to have a rest. As I drove along Route 42, there were many places to tell her about. She was pleased when we arrived at home, and I made a fire in the fireplace while she went upstairs for a bit.

Chapter 94

Cher and Ericka came by later to visit us. Part of me was a little jealous that Cher was spending so much time with Ericka instead of with me, but the advantage was having more time with Mom. Cher was playing with Puff, which was fun to watch. Perhaps I could learn a thing or two from her. She also used her phone to show us the furniture she had purchased online for her new condo. I was pleased that she was so excited.

"Are you both going to go to quilt club next month?" Ericka asked.

"No, I'm not going," Cher stated. "Claire is the member who replaced me, but if I do return, they'll have to accept both of us."

"Why would that be such a grave sin?" Ericka teased. "I can't believe that group!"

"We'll cross that bridge when we come to it," I said, hoping to change the subject. "I'm going to make a fundraising quilt for Rachael and Charlie if they agree to have a chili fest."

"Chili fest?' Ericka questioned.

"Yes, I'll explain when the time comes," I said with a sigh. "That's another area where the quilt club could be helpful."

"Good luck with that," Cher laughed wryly.

"What time will you be picking Mom up to go to the airport tomorrow?"

"Around ten," Cher stated. "I can't believe how quickly this visit has gone."

"It's been the best Christmas ever, if you ask me," I boasted. "I can't thank you both enough for coming. I just wish I had finished your painting, Mom."

"Well, it's probably better that I didn't have to take it on the airplane," Mom said.

"I love my painting of Puff!" Cher commented. "You've always been so artistically gifted."

"I have no talent whatsoever," Ericka laughed. "I don't think George has any talent either!" The expressions she made as she said these statements made us giggle.

"Speaking of George, has he gotten any word on Rob?" I asked.

"George thinks he'll remain in jail because of the high bail that was set," Ericka answered.

Cher yawned and said, "Well, ladies, Ericka and I need to get some rest, so I'll see you in the morning. I have to get packed and ready to head back to Missouri. This has been a blast."

We said goodnight to Ericka and Cher, and I went upstairs with Mom to help her pack. How long would it be before I got to see her again? She was tired, so I said goodnight to her and went downstairs to check on the fire. I tried not to think sad thoughts about her leaving. Instead, I chose to concentrate on seeing Grayson the next night. It would be my first date in Door County. What should I wear? The good news was that

Grayson really hadn't seen much of my wardrobe. Did I want to purchase something new for the occasion, though? Perhaps I needed to check out what they had at On Deck again. There might be some after-Christmas sales going on.

The next morning, Mom and I ate breakfast and prepared for Cher's arrival.

"We'll be starting a new year tomorrow," Mom said cheerfully. "I want you to have a wonderful time with Grayson. He seems like such a nice man."

"I will, and you're right about him. We'll see where this goes."

"I'll call you when I get home tonight," Mom promised. "I know you'll be out and about, but I'll want you to know that I got home safely."

"That's good." I saw Cher coming to the door, so we gathered the luggage and headed outside to her car. "Cher Bear, please move back here quickly," I begged as I gave her a hug.

"I will, Claire Bear," she said in return. "It makes me so happy that you like living here. By the way, I want to know every detail about tonight."

"Maybe." I winked, making her smile. I hugged Mom for the last time and then looked up to thank the Almighty for this very special Christmas. Our eyes filled with tears, but that was okay. I watched as Mom and Cher drove away, then took a deep breath and walked back into the house. It dawned on me that Cher had not said goodbye to Puff. "Well, Puff," I said, looking at her curled up under the tree, "I think you're stuck with me. Is that okay?" She purred and went back to sleep.

Chapter 95

I kept busy the rest of the day washing and putting clean sheets on the bed, straightening the kitchen, and cleaning the living room in case Grayson came inside. I planned to take the tree down the next day. It was very dry by now, but I hated to see it go. The live greenery around the cabin had already been removed.

As far as what to wear that night, I decided to go with something I already had in my closet. I chose black knit pants, a turtleneck with a black vest, and boots. The party was casual, but I wasn't up for jeans and a sweater. I pulled my hair up on each side so it would show the silver earrings I had chosen.

As the time got closer, my stomach began to churn. Perhaps it was hunger from not eating all day. I finally got dressed and did my makeup. Grayson seemed like the type of person to be on time, and indeed, at five o'clock sharp, there was a knock at my door.

"Come in!" I greeted him. He smiled, which put me at ease. He looked particularly handsome in crisp dark wash jeans, a white shirt, and a leather jacket. I detected a faint scent of aftershave that was quite nice.

"I always wondered what the inside of this cabin looked like," he said, glancing around.

"I find it rather cozy," I admitted.

"That it is," he agreed. "You look great, by the way."

"Thanks, as do you."

"Are you ready to go?" he asked.

"I'm ready!" I said, lifting my coat from a nearby chair. Grayson held it up so I could slip my arms through the sleeves, and we headed outside. Like a perfect gentleman, he opened the door of his dark gray SUV. It was meticulously clean for the occasion.

Our small talk was a bit awkward at first. Grayson gave me the rundown of who would be at the party. We were going to Liam and Casey's house. His other two friends were John and Brent. He didn't mention if they had wives or girlfriends.

We headed toward Baileys Harbor and arrived at a new residence that resembled a log home or lodge. I wondered if a large family lived here, judging from the size of the house. Grayson was filling me in, telling me that John was unmarried and dating a woman named Judy. We unbuckled and headed to the front door before I got to hear about Brent.

Three couples were gathered around a large stone fireplace when we walked in. Everyone stopped to say hello as Grayson introduced me. I learned that Brent's wife's name was Patty and that they had children. When I complimented Casey on her beautiful home, she said she would be happy to show me around. As she stood to begin the tour, Grayson engaged in conversation with the men.

When we stepped into the second room of the tour,

Casey smiled and asked how long Grayson and I had been seeing one another.

"Well, we aren't really dating," I said slowly. "I guess you could say that this is our first date."

She looked puzzled. "Well, when I heard that Grayson was bringing a date, I was shocked. He's been the fifth wheel in our group for a long time."

I was a little shocked that she would refer to him that way, but I replied, "Yes, he said that he typically comes to social events alone." I began to feel uncomfortable with the direction of the conversation. It felt a bit like a fact-finding mission on Casey's part.

"He's a great guy, and his daughter is a real sweetheart," Casey said.

I successfully got her off the subject by asking questions about the house. Grayson caught up with me, which was a bit of a relief. He told Casey that I lived in a real log cabin in Fish Creek. That got her attention as she expressed her fondness for primitive decor.

We joined the others, who were engaged in friendly conversation. Grayson did his best to be attentive to me, but these were his buddies, and every time they talked, he naturally joined in on their jokes and stories. Casey and Patty tried to include me as much as possible throughout the evening. Judy was the only one who remained rather cool to me, and I couldn't quite figure out why.

The food was amazing and covered the surface of a handmade log table. At one point, Grayson insisted that I sample the olive dip. Determined that I try it, he put some on a chip and lifted it to my mouth. It resulted in a rather awkward but funny moment, since I failed to get the entire amount of food where it was intended to go. Grayson then employed his napkin to wipe some dip off my lip. In an unexpected moment, our laughing subsided. He had leaned close to me, and our eyes met. I inhaled and was keenly aware of his aftershave scent once again. For a magical moment, time slowed, and I felt a spark ignite in me that I hadn't experienced in a long, long time.

Midnight was approaching, so Liam suggested that we go outside to see the annual midnight fireworks from a distant neighbor's house. We grabbed our coats, scarves, and gloves and readied ourselves to stand out in the cold. All of the excitement only served to elevate the anxiety I was beginning to feel about the upcoming countdown. Once outside, the men all stood by their women, and Grayson slipped his arm around me. At the stroke of midnight, Grayson turned me to face him. Gently, he pressed his lips to mine. After giving me a tender kiss, he stepped back. We opened our eyes at the same time, and I held onto his gaze. I had a suspicion that he could do better if he knew more about how I felt. I smiled and raised my lips to his, pulling him just a bit closer and kissing him back. It took him by surprise, but by the expression on his face afterwards, I knew I had made the right decision.

Chapter 96

We walked back inside the house with Grayson's arm still around me. I had really missed this feeling. He quietly asked if I was ready to leave, and I nodded, despite the fact that the jambalaya hadn't even been served yet. We said our goodbyes, and I knew that the room would be buzzing with talk right after we left.

"So, you survived," Grayson teased.

"I did, and I had a nice time. You'll have tongues wagging."

He laughed. "Yes, especially if anyone noticed that I got two New Year's Eve kisses instead of one."

I blushed as I recalled my boldness. "I felt that Judy was purposely standoffish. Do you think it was my imagination?"

"Well, it's probably because before John started dating her, I took her out once. Just once. I had a bad taste in my mouth about dating, especially with someone I wasn't attracted to. It was kind of a setup, you might say. It was a long time before I tried that again."

"Oh, it must have been bad," I said, laughing.

"John always thought she was great, so we all encouraged

him to date her. Don't get me wrong, she's a nice person, and so far, they seem to be hitting it off."

We turned into my driveway, and I asked Grayson if he would like to come in.

"I'd like that very much, but I think I need to get on home. Even though Kelly is at a friend's, I want to get home at a decent hour."

"I understand."

"This evening was much better than I had expected – especially the kissing part," he joked as we walked to the door. "I didn't push my luck for a third one, though."

We laughed, but I moved closer to him to let him know that a third kiss would most definitely be acceptable, taking him by surprise one more time. We once again engaged in a warm, pleasing kiss.

"Happy New Year, Claire," he whispered.

"Happy New Year to you, Mr. Wills," I said with a flirty smile. I went inside feeling happy and drew in a deep breath. When was the last time I'd felt like this? Even in the beginning, I'd never felt this way with Austen. Grayson was very reserved and very careful, and I found that very attractive.

After I got undressed, I crawled into bed and checked my phone for messages. Mom had let me know that she had arrived home safely, and Cher had sent a text to wish me a happy New Year. I would have to call Cher in the morning to report on my evening with Grayson. I went to sleep feeling like I had balance in my life once again. I was indeed ready to see what the coming year had in store for me.

I woke up at four in the morning, as if someone had shaken me awake. I'd truly wanted to sleep in. When I couldn't go back to sleep, I finally got up to get a drink of water, taking a look outside to calm my curiosity. Settling back into bed, I dozed off for a few more hours until I was startled by my phone ringing.

"Claire," the voice said. It sounded like Rachael.

"Rachael, is that you?"

"Yes," she said with a catch in her voice.

"What's wrong?"

"I'm at the Door County Medical Center. Charlie had a slight heart attack around one this morning."

"Oh no!"

"He's fine and is stabilized, so I'm relieved. He hadn't felt good all day, but he insisted on doing some cleanup outside. Finally, late last night, I saw some symptoms that scared me, so I insisted that we have him checked out. I'm so glad we did."

"Are you alone?"

"No. I called Harry right away."

"That's good. What can I do?" Before she could answer, I said, "I could work in the shop!"

"I'm not concerned about the shop," she said. "I'll be fine. I'm not sure if they're going to send him home or not."

"Do you want me to come over there and stay with you?"

"No. Having Harry with me is enough. Do you still have company?"

"No, they went home yesterday."

"Your mother is such a sweetheart."

"I loved having her here. Will you call me if you want to talk or if you know something that I can do for you?"

"I will. Thanks, Claire."

Chapter 97

I got out of bed, entirely awake now and feeling so sad for Charlie and Rachael. This was the last thing they needed in addition to their financial difficulties. I slipped into my robe and went downstairs to get coffee. So much for sleeping in.

I sat at the kitchen table, thinking about how this could prevent the chili fest from moving forward. Charlie would have to get some rest, or he could become worse. I got up and walked around the cabin, assessing what needed to be done that day. Hopefully, Tom would show up to take down my outside lights. How I had enjoyed them throughout the season!

I went upstairs to get dressed and then made a game plan for taking down the tree. Puff knew that something was up, so I decided to wait to remove the quilt from under the tree until the very end. I had very few ornaments, but the garland was quite lengthy. Puff jumped out of the way and thought the unwinding of the garland was a game. She found one end of the string and batted it around and around. It was cute to watch, and I was thankful that she hadn't tried pulling it off the tree. The entire effort made a tremendous mess on the porch, but I decided that someone should have the pleasure of enjoying the process, because I sure wasn't!

I went into the kitchen to refill my coffee cup and thought again about Charlie. I wished I had Harry's phone number so I could call and get an update. On a more pleasant note, I thought about the night before and wondered if I should have heard from Grayson by now. I hoped that he was thinking of me, but he hadn't said he'd call or that he'd ask me out again, so I needed to accept that. I'd had a pleasant New Year's Eve, and I was thankful for that.

I called Cher to check in with her. I gave her a simple description of the party so she wouldn't think I was smitten with Grayson. She wasn't happy to hear about Charlie.

"I'm still going to proceed with making a quilt to raise money for them," I decided. "If the chili fest is off, there will be other opportunities to use the quilt."

"You'll have to handle this carefully, Claire," Cher warned. "You need to start with the quilt club and get their support. That's the key to success."

"Yes, I know. We have our first meeting of the year tomorrow, so I'll have to plead my case."

"Don't get discouraged if Greta balks. You know she doesn't like change, so you'd better hope that you get a little support from someone else."

"You're right."

"I can't help you make the quilt, but what I can do is pay for all of the supplies. Tell that to the club. Some of those gals are penny pinchers. If the materials are already covered, maybe that would be one less hurdle."

"Cher, that's wonderful. Thank you!" I said, touched by

her thoughtfulness. Then I asked, "Do you think Mom had an enjoyable time on the trip?"

"Absolutely! She couldn't stop talking about it. I'll tell her about Charlie. I know she's dying to hear about your New Year's Eve party."

"Thank you again for making my Christmas," I said as we hung up.

I was beginning to formulate an idea as to how to proceed with the fundraising quilt. I checked on Puff, and she was still enjoying the Christmas tree mess all over the floor. I cleaned up what I could, but I knew I would still be finding tree remnants this time next year. As I worked to sweep up the last bits, Tom knocked on the door, and I welcomed him in.

"Tom, you're just the person I was hoping to see!"

"Good morning, Ms. Stewart. Did you have a nice Christmas?"

"I did. How about you?"

"Pretty good. I just finished taking down the lights next door, and I presume that you want me to do the same, correct?"

"Yes, please. I really appreciate it. Tell me, is there a tree pickup service for residents?"

He grinned. "Not unless it's me. I can take it for you."

"That would be great. It's ready to go. Can I get you a cup of coffee?"

"It's pretty cold, so that sounds good."

"Coming right up!" I said, heading to the kitchen. When I returned with the coffee, Puff had returned to her quilt under the tree. Now what? I gave Tom the coffee, and he got started on taking down the outside lights. In the meantime, I started moving the quilt. If looks could kill, Puff had eyes to do it. I picked up the quilt to shake it out as she ran to the safety of her wicker chair. Ten minutes later, Tom came back in to remove the tree. Naturally, it created another mess of tree needles. I admired Tom's strength as he hauled the once-beautiful tree to his truck. I gave him some cash and thanked him immensely, then looked around the room that I had cleaned only minutes ago and heaved a big sigh. I ignored my unhappy cat and proceeded to clean up the porch. Christmas was over!

Chapter 98

The next morning, I decided to get coffee at the Blue Horse in hopes of running into Grayson. I certainly didn't want to appear to be chasing him, but I did want to let him know about Charlie. When I stepped outside, I realized that a light snow had fallen in the night. I wasn't thrilled about having to find the scraper to clean off my car. However, once I got started, I could appreciate how the snow made things clean and quiet with its fresh coat of beauty.

As I looked for a place to park, I didn't see Grayson's SUV anywhere on the street, so I assumed that he wasn't there, but when I got in line to place my order, I spotted him on the other side of the café, where he didn't typically sit. He didn't seem to have noticed me but was instead engrossed in staring at his laptop. I ordered a mocha latte and a cinnamon bagel. When I had those in hand, I headed his way. "Mr. Wills?" I asked, sounding serious and professional.

He looked up. "Oh, Ms. Stewart!" he returned, matching my formality.

We laughed, and I asked, "I know you're busy, but could

I share something with you? It will only take a few minutes."

"Of course. What's going on?" he asked, making room for me at the small table.

I told Grayson what Rachael had said to me about Charlie, and he seemed taken aback by the news. I informed him that I had spoken to Rachael and Charlie about the chili fest prior to Charlie becoming ill.

He listened intently and asked, "How did they react?"

"Well, they were overwhelmed at first, but they seemed okay with the idea. I'm afraid there's little possibility of such an event now due to Charlie's health. Even with Harry's help, I don't see how it can happen."

"Harry?"

"Harry is Charlie's best friend. He's really good about looking for ways to help Charlie," I explained. "I'm just so sad about their situation."

"I can understand that. You have a heart of gold to try to help them out. Don't give up."

"They work so hard to make ends meet," I continued. "I'm planning to make a quilt that can be used as a fundraising tool. That's what we do in Missouri, and it's usually successful. I hope my quilt group will help since Rachael is a member. If the event can be held, I'd still like your help with possible vendors, since you have some of those contacts."

"These things take time and work, plus a..." he started.

I interrupted, saying, "This project needs a driver. Someone who has vision and can develop the vision into reality. I can be that driver."

At that, he raised his eyebrows in surprise and laughed.

"Well, this driver has to be on her way, and I know you're busy, so I'll get going."

"Thanks for informing me about Charlie. I'll think about what you've said."

"Thanks, Grayson," I said. I stood, picked up my things, and stepped back out into the cold. I left feeling proud of myself for not letting the conversation get personal. Grayson hadn't brought up our date, nor had I. On my way home, I stopped to get my mail, which was sparse as usual. I couldn't help but think that Austen could have found me by now if he had really tried. Perhaps I should have accepted that Christmas card he'd sent to me at Mom's house. I'd never know what that was all about.

That afternoon, I concentrated on my quilting. I thought of Charlie's condition as I stitched. My phone rang, and I said a prayer that the news would be good as I answered.

"Claire, it's Harry."

"It's good to hear from you. I've been on pins and needles worrying about Charlie."

"He's not out of woods by any means. They're keeping him now because of his blood pressure."

"How is Rachael doing?"

"She's a trooper, especially around him. She won't leave him, so I'm checking on the farm. They have animals that need to be fed."

"You're a good friend, Harry. I still want to pursue something that will raise some money for them, so I'll need your advice."

"I'm open to ideas. They really need a way to generate some additional income."

"What if I drive out to the farm after quilt club tomorrow? We can talk about some ideas."

"Why don't I take you out to lunch instead? Where's

the meeting?"

"At the library in Fish Creek."

"Okay. How about Gibraltar Grill at noon? My buddy owns that place, and he's about to close for the winter."

"Very well, if you let me treat."

He laughed quietly and said, "You darn women are so independent!"

Chapter 99

I spent a restless night thinking about how to present my idea to the quilt club the next day. I wasn't sure what to expect from them, but I was glad I was going into the situation with the quilt supplies already provided. I had to do this for Rachael and Charlie.

I arrived at the meeting room early in case there would be a chance to visit with anyone. I'd brought Quilted Snow for show and tell. Olivia sat down next to me. I really hadn't gotten to know her; she was always reserved at the meetings. Perhaps we would have an opportunity to get to know one another better at this one. Greta was the last to arrive and came rushing in, looking quite flustered.

"Good morning, ladies," she said as she shuffled her papers. "I hope you celebrated the holidays well. I have a few announcements to make. There's a quilt documentation going on this week at The Clearing. If you have an antique quilt that you'd like to share information about, I encourage you to check into that." She then continued with a litany of civic announcements that had nothing to do with quilting.

After she made a request that we participate in the blood drive at the library, I decided to make my move. "Greta, if I may, I have a request to make as well," I said, pausing for her response.

She turned to look at me, wearing a surprised expression. "Very well," she said reluctantly.

"I'm asking the club to make a fundraising quilt for Rachael. Her husband recently suffered a heart attack, and they were already financially stressed. The two of them are hard workers, and I want to help them in any way I can. If we pitched in to make a quilt top, we could get it quilted. Then, it could be raffled or perhaps auctioned off at some event."

"Claire, what you're trying to do is admirable, but as a club, we do not get involved in others' personal issues," Greta explained. "If we respond to one person's needs, we'll receive an overwhelming number of requests."

Undaunted, I forged ahead. "I already have support from Cher. She can't help make the quilt, but is committed to pay for all of the expenses." At that, I could hear whispers behind me.

Marta was the first to respond. "How nice! That is very generous of Cher. I'm sorry to hear about Rachael's husband." She got a determined look on her face and stated, "I certainly am willing to help."

Greta gave her a stern look.

"How could we ignore one of our members?" Ginger asked. "What can we do? I don't have much time, but I would like to do something to help."

"If you could all just piece one or two blocks, one of us can sew them together," I suggested. "It could be a simple pattern. We have machine quilters in the group."

"Well, we'll think about this, but now it's time to move on," Greta interrupted.

"Greta, I think this request is pretty time-sensitive," I insisted. "Financial obligations don't wait."

"I agree, Claire," Lee said. "Why don't we all just make some simple red-and-white Nine-Patch blocks? They can be arranged in a chain pattern. I did a quilt like that last year, and it went very quickly. Everyone loves a red-and-white quilt!"

"I'll volunteer to set them together," Olivia offered.

Greta could see that she'd lost control and sighed.

"Greta, do you think the library staff would let us meet for a couple of mornings to do this project?" I asked as if we were already moving ahead.

"I have no idea," she said, shaking her head. "I know their calendar is very full."

"I live by the Barn Door Quilt Shop, so I can get everything we need," Olivia said.

"Good idea!" Frances chimed in. "We need to be there for Rachael. She is such a sweetheart."

"I have extra cutters and mats that you can use," Ava said.

"I don't see why we couldn't use this place," Marta stated. "We'll take whatever day and time they give us."

"Well, I guess everyone has expressed their opinions," Greta said. "Do we have a motion and a second?"

"I make a motion that we make a fundraising quilt for Rachael and Charlie," I stated with a smile.

"All those in favor say aye," Greta instructed.

Everyone agreed except Greta, who remained silent.

"The project will move forward," she announced. "I'll check with the library."

Chapter 100

There was no doubt that I had convinced everyone in the room to proceed with the raffle quilt except for Greta. I was certain that she would be ready to have me exit from the group when Cher returned. When we began the show and tell segment of the meeting, my Quilted Snow was a big hit.

After the meeting, I approached Greta to thank her for the club's help. I could tell that she was torn as to how to respond. The good news was that I didn't get a lecture about how the group had never done something like that before. I followed Olivia out to her car to thank her for her support.

"Thank you, Claire!" she said with a smile. "That took a lot of guts. I know someone who works at the Barn Door Quilt Shop, so I'm sure I can get us a discount. I'll get right on that tomorrow."

"Wonderful. This will mean so much to Rachael." I left the parking lot feeling good about the outcome.

When I arrived at the Gibraltar Grill, I was anxious to try their food after hearing so many good things about it. I was also anxious to talk to Harry, but hoping that he didn't get any other ideas.

There he was, waiting for me at a table with a big grin on his face. Of course, he couldn't just say hello, but stood and gave me a giant hug. After asking about his granddaughters, which pleased him, I got into my ideas about having an event and explained the chili fest idea. "I realize that the circumstances have changed and perhaps the timing is bad," I noted. "Charlie needs to rest, and Rachael will be watching out for him while running the business."

"Well, I disagree about the timing," Harry said, surprising me. "We do have to start small, like you suggested, but I think Charlie's recent attack makes the event all the timelier. Why not now?"

"That's music to my ears, Harry, but I doubt whether the two of them will agree to doing this anytime soon."

"You leave that to me, young woman," he said, leaning back in his chair and sporting a broad smile. "Charlie knows me pretty well. He knows that when I set my mind to something, I follow through and get it done."

When I told him about my efforts to make a fundraising quilt, he beamed. He encouraged me to auction it off rather than run around town selling dollar raffle tickets, and I agreed. As far as lunch was concerned, the food was awesome. I had the best chicken quesadilla ever! It wasn't long before the owner visited our table, and Harry introduced me to him.

"We close this weekend, so I'm glad that you got to try our food," the owner said.

"Me too," I said as I suddenly noticed something disturbing out of the corner of my eye. In a side room, Grayson was having lunch with some men. The last thing I wanted was for him to see me with another man. I felt that I needed to leave quickly.

"Harry, I need to go now, but as soon as you hear anything else about Charlie, let me know."

"What's your rush?" he asked, surprised by my sudden need to exit.

"I'm sorry, it's just that I have lots to do. I'll pay the tab, and then we're even!" I said jokingly, patting him on the shoulder. At that, I rushed out of the restaurant to the sounds of Harry calling me sweetie as he was saying goodbye. If Grayson had seen me leave, at least he knew I hadn't come with Harry. In the end, I had high hopes that Harry could convince Charlie to proceed with a fundraising event.

As soon as I got back to the house, I called Cher to give her an update on the quilt meeting. When I finished with my exciting story, there was a pause.

"Good heavens, Claire Bear. I can't believe that you pulled it off! As soon as we hang up, I'll call the quilt shop and give them my credit card number so they can just use it as needed for the quilt. Oh, I can just see Greta's face!"

"Yes, she looked as if she was ready to get rid of me as soon as you get back!"

Cher laughed and said, "Well, maybe I won't want to come back."

"Don't say that! You must! They would blame me forever if you didn't!"

Chapter 101

As I worried about whether Grayson had seen me or not, I tried to convince myself that it didn't matter. We weren't teenagers. He hadn't called after our New Year's date, so that said something. He probably didn't want to get caught up in a relationship at this point in his life.

Late that afternoon, Olivia called and reported that she'd purchased all of the supplies for our red-and-white Nine-Patch quilt for a ten-percent discount. She wondered if we had heard from Greta concerning when we could meet.

"No, and I'm worried that she might drag her feet concerning this. Would you mind calling her and telling her that we're ready to go? I think she's heard enough from me."

"Of course! I'd be happy to. If she hasn't secured a date, we'll find another place."

"But where?"

"The quilt shop has a classroom. Maybe they would let us use it. I'll call Greta first and get back to you."

Harry wasn't the only one who was determined! Once I had an idea, it was hard for me to let go of it. It was turning out that Olivia may have been cut from the same cloth!

Since I'd had a filling lunch, I nibbled on fruit and cheese in front of the fire that evening. Every time I peeked out the window, there was more snow on the ground. I was glad I was home. Puff was restless, missing her nest under the tree.

My phone rang at around eight. I thought it would be Olivia getting back to me, but it was Grayson!

"Claire, it's Grayson."

"Hey! How are you?"

"I'm good." He cleared his throat and continued. "When I saw you having lunch today, I said to myself, 'I'd like to spend a little more time with that woman.'"

I smiled. "Well, that's nice to hear, because this woman was thinking the same thing about you. I did see you at the restaurant. I was having lunch with Harry about the chili fest idea."

"I figured as much. I do remember Harry now from seeing him around. What did he think?"

"He loved the idea and wants to move forward if Charlie and Rachael agree. He's got the time to help with it and can finance it as well. Do you know how much property he owns?"

"No, not really."

"A lot. However, he's so down-to-earth that no one would suspect how wealthy he is."

"Let's get back to why I'm calling you, Ms. Stewart. The chamber is having a business-after-hours gathering at Joe Jo's Pizza in Ephraim tomorrow. I wondered if you'd like to go together and then have dinner afterwards."

"I did see that in the newsletter. I'm curious about the place since the owners are both quilters."

"Yes, they have really nice quilts hanging on the walls. If

you're free, would five o'clock work for you?"

"Absolutely!"

"We have a date."

I chuckled. "A second date it is," I confirmed with delight. I hung up and wanted to pinch myself. Maybe Grayson seeing me with another man hadn't been a bad thing! I agreed with taking things slow. We both had every reason to be cautious. Grayson was handsome and had a respectable job. He could possibly be the most desirable single man in Door County. Honestly, he could probably get a date with any woman he wanted. I was eager to get to know him better and smiled at the thought of having dinner with him. I thought of Mom and how thrilled she would be, so I gave her a call.

"Claire, I was just thinking of you as I was getting ready for bed. Is everything okay?"

"It is! Grayson just asked me out on date number two, so I couldn't wait to tell you."

"Oh, then things are going well. I'm so happy. He seems like such a nice man. I just heard from Cher that Charlie had a heart attack. How is he doing?"

"I think okay, but I haven't had a recent update. I'll check with Rachael tomorrow. What's new there? Have you seen Mr. Vogel lately?"

She paused before saying, "When I got back from my trip, he brought me yellow roses, which are my favorite. Imagine that. Yellow roses!"

"He's got your number, Mom," I teased.

"I think he missed me, especially since it was the holidays and all. He wanted to get me a Christmas present, but was at a loss. Neither one of us need anything."

"Flowers are always appreciated."

It felt good to end the day talking with Mom, and I would have guessed that she felt the same way. Once in bed, I thanked the Almighty for my many blessings. I was going to be having date number two with Grayson, my quilt for Charlie and Rachael was going to become a reality, Harry was helping me with an event, and Mom had gotten flowers from Mr. Vogel. Life was as good as it could get.

Chapter 102

Around noon the next day, Olivia called to say that Greta had gotten permission to use the library from seven to nine in the morning before it opened. Olivia and I both moaned at the early hours, but it was better than nothing.

"Between me and Ginger, we should have everything we need. How does tomorrow morning suit you?" Olivia asked.

"I can do it!"

"Okay. I'll call the rest of the group and see who can make it."

"Olivia, you're such a trooper to take the project on in the way you have. I can't tell you how much I appreciate it."

"It's the first exciting thing our club has done since I've been a member."

"Fantastic! I'll see you in the morning." I put the quilt out of my mind and concentrated on my big date with Grayson. The chamber always recommended business casual dress for gatherings like this, but I wanted to look especially nice for dinner afterwards. I tried to remember the outfits Grayson had seen me in before. I couldn't ignore the fact that there was snow on the ground, so I had to wear boots. I auditioned many combinations of outfits on my bed and finally decided that I was safe with black and white.

Knowing Grayson, he would be on time, so I was ready a half hour in advance. I made sure that the downstairs was straightened up and that the kitchen was clean. I couldn't remember ever being this excited about a date with Austen.

I jumped when I heard the knock on the door. Grayson was wearing an overcoat over his suit. I hadn't put my coat on and appreciated that he assisted me after I retrieved it from the closet.

"Your outfit suits you, Claire," he said, smiling. "I like it very much."

"Thank you," I responded, amused at how we always seemed to be so formal with one another when we first got together. I looked forward to the part of the date when we both loosened up and felt more comfortable. On the way to Joe Jo's, I filled Grayson in on the club's plans to make a quilt for Rachael and Charlie. He wasn't surprised when I told him that the club hadn't done anything like that before.

"It's so kind of you to try to help Rachael and Charlie, Ms. Stewart," he said as we pulled into the parking lot. "Before you fill up on pizza at this event, I need to tell you that I've made reservations for us at The English Inn for dinner."

"You did? I've heard that it's wonderful. Thank you."

Joe Jo's owners, Kathy and Dick Luther, greeted us as we entered. Behind them was a charming Door County quilt that certainly got my attention.

"I love this quilt!" I exclaimed. "Which one of you made it?"

They smiled. "We have to say both of us because it contains fabric from both of our stashes," Kathy shared.

"Stashes?" Grayson asked, looking confused.

"It's where you keep all of your personal fabric to make your quilts," Dick explained. "Please come in and make yourself at home."

"There's plenty of food, so help yourself," Kathy said as she pointed in the direction of the pizza.

"Kathy, a little bird told me that you belong to a quilt club that meets in Sister Bay," I said.

"I am," she responded happily. "Are you interested?"

"I might be." I nodded. "I'll be in contact with you."

The restaurant had plenty of space. The tall ceilings made it feel even larger. Gorgeous quilts made by the owners provided the decor. I was impressed. I stayed with Grayson, who began engaging with chamber friends from all over the county. Eventually, we ran into Judy and John. I was curious to see how Judy would be in this setting, but John guided her in another direction after our initial greetings.

I was getting hungry. Since we were going to dinner soon, I chose not to have anything to eat, but the pizza smelled delicious. Grayson had a small slice and insisted that I take a bite. The crust was cracker-thin, and it served as the perfect appetizer. There was no doubt that I would be returning soon for more than just a single bite.

Chapter 103

After a half hour of socializing, we exchanged looks, quietly left the reception, and headed to The English Inn. Grayson was in a good mood from the chamber event. I was sure that I would enjoy those gatherings more as I got to know people better.

At The English Inn, we walked into a very darkly lit atmosphere. The lighting and heavy furnishings gave it the feel of a fancy supper club. As we followed the receptionist into the dining room, I noticed that the pristine white tablecloths were a stunning accent against the dark woods.

"There are so many dining areas," I marveled.

"I've never had a bad meal here," Grayson assured me. "I thought you would like it. It's nice to be able to hear yourself talk to the person you're sitting with."

After the chamber reception, I had to agree. It was relaxing to sit down and look forward to an evening of good company and tasty food without feeling rushed. After we ordered, I asked about Kelly. Grayson's face lit up.

"She won a spelling bee this week, but she really shines

as an artist. All she wants to do is paint and draw. I'm afraid I can see the writing on the wall for her future."

"Hey! Being an artist isn't so bad," I laughed. "My father couldn't quite accept that his daughter and son chose to pursue the arts. He was concerned about us getting 'real' jobs. Michael, my brother, is a great writer. He surprised me with his first published book at Christmas."

"Wow, that's pretty cool. I didn't mean to downplay being an artist," he assured me. "I'm envious of your having a brother. I was an only child. I would think that your parents would be enormously proud of you."

"We were never sure about my dad, but he left us a nest egg so we could pursue our dreams. That must have meant that he trusted us, so we've always wanted to make him proud."

Our dinner arrived, and it looked amazing. It had been a long time since I'd had a filet. It melted in my mouth. As we talked and ate, I couldn't help but see snippets of the little boy Grayson had once been. I found it innocent and charming. We took our time enjoying every bite.

"I think I'd like to order dessert tonight!" Grayson suddenly announced.

I was shocked, because I'd seen him put away a great deal of food.

"Seriously?" I laughed.

"I happen to know that they make a wonderful bananas Foster," he said enthusiastically. "I think you should share one with me."

I laughed while giving him a frown that indicated I might be less than sold on his big idea. "Okay, a bite or two," I agreed.

We ordered coffee as we continued to engage in

wonderful conversation. Little by little, the customers around us thinned out. The waitress kept coming by to see if we needed anything, which was a hint for us to leave, I was sure. Grayson mentioned Kelly a couple of times, which was my clue that he was ready to leave as well.

"Does Kelly know that you're out on a date tonight?"

He grinned. "Oh, yes! I tried to downplay it, but she wouldn't have any of it. She felt the need to approve of what I wore – even down to my choice of tie."

"I was just going to tell you how much I like it." I winked.

"Thanks! Kelly has subtly tried to encourage me to date, but at the same time, she's very protective of me."

"As she should be."

He smiled. "By the way, she remembers you from when we ran into you at the deli counter at the market."

"Really?"

We continued enjoying small talk as we left the restaurant and returned to my home. When we arrived at the cabin, I asked Grayson if he wanted to come in.

"It's pretty late, Claire. Maybe for only a few minutes."

"At least it's warm and cozy in here instead of being out in the cold. Why don't you build a fire?" Puff saw us and immediately ran up the stairs, thinking I had finally come home and was going to bed.

"How are you doing with your adopted cat?" Grayson said as he watched her scamper upstairs.

"I'm afraid that I have permanent custody," I said, shaking my head.

"Kelly keeps pestering me for a cat, but I've held off so far."

"What's the problem?"

He sighed. "Kelly doesn't have the best history with pets,

and I don't have the time or interest to bail her out all the time." Grayson started the fire and settled back on the sofa, content with his accomplishment.

Chapter 104

I joined him on the couch, and we smiled at one another.

"You know, this dating thing isn't as bad as I thought," Grayson said rather matter-of-factly.

I burst into laughter. "And what did you expect?"

"I thought it would be really awkward, and I'd have to pretend to be having a good time. I've worried about how I'd be able to read the other person. I was happily married, and things were natural between us."

"Not to bring up something that may be uncomfortable for you, but how long has it been since your wife died?"

"Marsha will have been gone five years in June," he said, looking at the floor.

"I'm so sorry. Was she ill?"

He put his hand on his forehead and shook his head.

"I'm sorry. It's none of my business."

"It's alright. It's a very normal question to ask. She died in a boating accident."

He didn't readily offer any more information, and I swallowed hard, taken by surprise. "Oh, Grayson, how awful.

I'm so sorry that I brought it up."

"Don't feel sorry for me. I have Kelly, and I worry about what goes through her head. I have to be there for her."

"Of course you do, and you're doing an excellent job."

"Well, Ms. Stewart, I just gave you a lot to digest, so why don't you tell me more about yourself? Why were you so eager to leave Missouri and move into Cher's cabin when she left?"

"Fair question. I moved out of a small town to leave a man I was living with for five years. I needed to start over, and when Cher offered me her cabin, I felt it was meant to be."

Grayson looked puzzled. "Were you in danger?"

"No. I was just done. It was going nowhere, and I actually think I did him a favor. I gave up a beautiful home with a studio to die for, but I was alone. You can be very lonely when you're with someone, did you know that?"

He nodded.

"I talked myself into staying many times and watched the years pass by. When I left, I felt so free, became more creative than ever, and even felt better physically. Honestly, God helped me get through it. Isn't that crazy?"

"Not at all. I think sometimes we lose ourselves. I'm glad that you mentioned God. My spiritual strength certainly got me through the worst of my grief."

"I don't know how people function without faith."

"Did you break this man's heart?"

"Evidently not. I moved out when he was out of town so he couldn't talk me out of it. The saddest part of it is that he didn't call or try to contact me. I think he drew in a breath of fresh air and was relieved."

"That's hard for me to imagine. You must have really hurt his ego."

"He does have quite an ego. He's a pediatrician and has an image to uphold in that community. He wouldn't have wanted a scene or any bad gossip about him or his personal affairs."

"Your hurt is such a different kind than mine."

I nodded. "Absolutely! However, I'm fine, and I'm very content with my decision."

He grinned and nodded. "I'm happy for you. I can tell that you're a strong woman, and I'm pleased to know you."

"That's very sweet," I said, patting his hand. "After going through this, I know that I can be happy with or without someone."

"That's what I told myself as well. Kelly is a teenager now and is growing a little bit further away from me each day. Watching her grow up is wonderful, and yet difficult."

"She'll always need you, Grayson, no matter her age. There's something about a father and a daughter's bond that's always special. The relationship you have will affect how she reacts to the men her life."

"You're just full of wise information," Grayson said as he turned his body to face me. He leaned close to me and surprised me by whispering, "I think I want to kiss you right in the middle of this conversation."

"A kiss might be just be the thing to shut me up," I answered. At that moment, a gentle and loving kiss came my way. Grayson's arms circled around me in a brief hug that warmed me inside. As we wordlessly settled back in our places, I knew that I had made Grayson more comfortable now that I'd told him a bit about my past. We said nothing as we stared at the fire. Now that I knew about his wife's tragic death, it explained a lot of things – like why he was too busy to do any boating.

Chapter 105

Grayson ended up staying until midnight. Every now and then, he would look at his watch in disbelief that he was spending as much time with me as he was.

"I had a great time tonight," he said, getting ready to leave.

"So did I, Grayson. Unfortunately, you're an extremely easy person to talk to," I joked.

He chuckled. "I think that's a compliment. By the way, I'd like to have a follow-up committee meeting again very soon, so I hope you can make it."

"I wouldn't miss it. After all, I'd get to see you again."

At that, he then pulled me into his arms for a final kiss. "A wonderful way to end the evening," he said, smiling. "I must go. Take care now."

I watched as he drove away. What had happened here this night? I felt so much closer to him after telling him about my past with Austen, but I knew I had to keep my guard up and not get hurt. Grayson was fully committed to Kelly. In that sense, he didn't have the freedom that I enjoyed.

I went upstairs to join Puff. She wasn't totally asleep and

was busy trying out different positions on the Log Cabin quilt, looking for what felt just right. I hoped that my dreams would be about Grayson. It was exciting to have something so new to think about. I turned the memories of the evening over and over in my mind until I finally fell asleep.

The next morning, I was awakened by an early phone call from Harry. "Harry, I'm not quite awake, but I was going to give you a call later. How's Charlie?"

"He's back in the hospital. We got him home but had a bad scare with him experiencing shortness of breath. Luckily, I was still there and got him back to the emergency room. They're keeping him for observation now."

"How's Rachael holding up?"

"She's a mess. She's supposed to work at the Bayside tonight. She wanted to cancel, but I told her to go. I think it will help her to get away from all of this for a while. Charlie is in good hands."

"Did you convince her?"

"I think so."

"Did you get to bring up the chili fest?"

"No, the timing wasn't good. I think I need to talk to Charlie first. Rachael doesn't know the extent of their debt. If he settles down, I think he'll trust what I have to say."

"Okay. I'll leave it to you, Harry. We're going to get busy on the fundraising quilt today."

"Great! You take care," he said, hanging up.

I hurried to be on time at the library. I hoped that Olivia had good luck getting everyone to come. I brought coffee from home and had to wait outside until someone from the library came to let me in.

"Good morning!" Olivia said cheerfully.

I couldn't believe my eyes! There were Ginger, Lee, Frances, and Marta, seated around the table.

"Good to see you all!" I said with excitement.

"Ava's got a bad cold. She wanted to come," Olivia reported. "I haven't heard from Greta."

"Okay, Olivia, what's my job?" I asked as I saw others getting started on their assignments.

"That empty cutting mat is for you," she informed me. "We need 2½-inch strips cut for the white part. Ginger brought her machine, so she'll be doing most of the piecing. We don't have much time to be here, so we need to work quickly."

"Okay, I'm on it!" I responded.

It had been a while since I'd done much cutting. I knew how dangerous the rotary cutter blades could be, and blood would not look good on the white fabric! Everyone stayed focused, eager to make quick progress. Greta showed up fifteen minutes before we were to leave, and we were quite surprised to see her.

"Greta! Welcome," I said to her.

"Well, I thought I'd better show up and make sure you gals were out of here by nine," she announced.

"We're making great progress!" Olivia reported.

"I see that!" Greta said, looking around the room. "It appears that you'll need a machine quilter soon at this rate, so give me a call when the top is done."

We stopped what we were doing and looked at her in disbelief.

"Greta, that would be wonderful," I responded. "Thank you so very much!"

She didn't know what to say, and I could tell that she was a little embarrassed. I knew how much courage and pride it took for her to agree to someone else's idea.

Chapter 106

We all worked diligently until our time was up. Olivia and Ginger took work home with them to do on their machines, but we had indeed made great progress. Olivia told Greta that she would bring her the top as soon as it was finished. Olivia deserved so much credit, but to see all the quilters beam with pride at their accomplishments was very gratifying. Rachael would be delighted if she knew.

I was exhausted when I got home. I checked my phone and saw that I had missed a call from Carl at the gallery. I thought that maybe he had good news, so I anxiously called him back.

"I'm glad you called, Claire. I have a commission job for you if you're interested."

"Of course!"

"It's for a particularly good customer here at the gallery who wants to remain anonymous. He's really big into lighthouses, and there's a particular one that he wants done in watercolors. I thought of you right away. He admired a lighthouse painting of yours on your website."

"That's the South Haven Lighthouse in Michigan."

"When can you come by? I'll be here for another hour or so."

"I'll come right over!" I couldn't believe this was happening! If I could land one good, happy client, I could stay busy with my work. I was brimming with excitement when I walked into Carl's gallery. He smiled as he handed me the photograph from the client. I hadn't been expecting what I saw.

"You look puzzled. Have you seen this lighthouse?"

"No, I haven't. It sure doesn't look like your average lighthouse," I said, studying it carefully.

"Well, it's quite a landmark and is located in Sturgeon Bay. You'll probably want to take a look at it in person."

"Does the client have a deadline?"

Carl shook his head and referred back to the picture. "It's the Sturgeon Bay Ship Canal North Pierhead Light. Really, you need to go see it for yourself."

"The red is so striking!"

"Yes, and against the water and sky, it gets your attention. Odd shape, too! There's a tall lighthouse nearby called the Sturgeon Bay Ship Canal Light."

"This will be a challenge, but I'm excited."

"He'd like something around 23" by 20" because of a particular frame he wants to use. I have that here."

"Oh, let me see that. The frame is usually the last choice I make, but I'll make sure it's appropriate."

"Good. Now, don't forget, I could use more Quilted Snow pieces when you have some."

I smiled and nodded, excited by this surprising turn of events. I left the gallery feeling completely elated. I wanted to go right home and get started, but I needed to get ready to see Rachael at the Bayside. I knew she'd appreciate me stopping by. I thought about calling Ericka and asking her to come with me, but time got away from me as I busied myself getting some things done around the cabin. I put on a pair of jeans and a sweater, looking forward to having a good hamburger.

Arriving early at the tavern was a good decision. It felt a lot more pleasant, and there were lots of empty seats at the bar.

"Hey, Claire! What a surprise," Rachael said from behind the bar.

"How are you doing? How's Charlie?" I asked.

She looked so serious. "I shouldn't be here."

"Hey, stop that," I scolded her. "Charlie is in a good place, and you need some distraction. I was thrilled when Harry said you might go ahead and work tonight."

"Okay, my friend," she said as she tried to force a smile. "Are you here for a delicious hamburger?"

I laughed and placed my order. After Rachael had put it into the computer, she came back for a visit. I couldn't wait to tell her about my new commissioned piece. She got excited about it as well, especially when I told her about the photograph.

"I've walked all the way out to that light," Rachael claimed. "It's pretty cool. You do need to see it in person."

"I can't wait!"

My food arrived, as did more customers, and Rachael got busier. When she finally got back to me, I had finished eating, so I paid the bill and prepared to move on. "Please keep your spirits up and let me know how Charlie is doing," I said before I left.

She nodded and blew me a kiss.

Chapter 107

The next day, I got busy arranging my easel and paints to begin sketching and painting. When Cher called around ten, I told her about my commissioned piece. I was still so excited that I felt nearly ready to explode! To acquire a local client was a big step toward succeeding artistically in a new community.

"Well, my news isn't quite as exciting as yours, but I'll be driving to Egg Harbor next week, so be prepared."

"What? Cher, I'm so happy and excited."

"I think I've signed enough papers. The moving van won't get there until a day later, but that's okay. I really have mixed feelings about all of this and wonder what will bring me back to Missouri now that Mom is gone."

"Not to worry. Time will tell. Is there anything I can do to help?"

"You're a much better decorator than me, so you can advise me in that department. I have a contract on the house, but I'm worried that it will fall through."

"Keep your spirits up. Did you tell my mom?"

"Yes, and she's sad. I think it's a lonely time for her. My moving is another big change."

"She wants your happiness, though, Cher Bear. Tell Linda and Carole that they have to visit us soon."

"They said they would. We had a little going-away party this week."

"That must have been fun. I know that Puff will be glad to see you again."

"As soon as I'm settled, I may get a cat of my own. Our cats can be buds like we are."

I had to chuckle at the idea. "Good thought. I'm so glad that you brought those balls of yarn. It's Puff's daily pastime."

Cher paused and then said, "I saw Austen at Rozier's a few days ago."

"Did you say hello?"

"Are you crazy? I practically jumped from aisle to aisle to avoid him."

"Good idea! Keep me posted on your plans," I requested before we hung up. When I walked back to the porch, I saw Brenda coming towards my door.

"What are you doing here?"

"Just came from work. I thought I'd stop by to tell you that hygge is tomorrow. Would you like to go together?"

"Oh, Brenda, I'm so sorry that I still haven't gotten there. Now I have a commissioned piece to do, so I'm really busy. I'll get there someday. Are you doing okay?"

"It's just the winter blues, I guess. Sometimes they get to me. Hey, how are things going with you and Grayson?"

"Very well. We're taking things slow. Do you want to come in?"

"No, I need to go," she said, then said goodbye.

I had a feeling that I hadn't cheered her up, but I had to get back to work. My sketching skills were a bit rusty, but I got better the longer I stayed with it. An hour later, I took a break to make myself some tea, and a call came in from Grayson.

I was eager to share my exciting news with him. In the end, he offered to drive me out to the light, and I quickly took him up on that. I told him that I was working from a specific photograph that looked as if it had been taken in the spring.

"How's the quilt coming along?"

"Great! Greta surprised us by offering to quilt it for us, so everything worked out, and the group seems extremely excited. The bad news is that Charlie's back in the hospital. Rachael is a wreck worrying about him. Because of all of that, Harry hasn't been able to bring up the possibility of having any kind of event."

"I'm sorry to hear that. Just so you know, the chamber has various events where we auction off things, so don't worry about a venue for that quilt."

"Really?"

"Of course. Let me know when it's done. Can I do anything to help Rachael and Charlie through this?"

"Getting money from this quilt is the main focus now. Thank goodness they have Harry. Rachael really depends on him. I did visit with Rachael last night when she was working her shift at the Bayside."

"You should have called me. I love their hamburgers."

"Well, would a delicious hamburger have been the main reason you would have shown up if I'd asked you?" He laughed quietly, but I think my bold teasing took him a little by surprise. "I've been doing all of the talking. Did you have a reason for calling?"

"Yeah, I'm having a breakfast committee meeting tomorrow morning at Pelletier's. Do you think you can come?"

"I suppose, but I really need to get busy on this painting."

"I promise that it's only going to be one hour – and you have to eat breakfast," he teased.

"Okay, Mr. Wills. I'll be there."

Chapter 108

The next morning, I turned on the local news while feeding Puff and cleaning the kitchen. I was shocked to see a photo of Rob, but I'd missed the first part of the news story. I did hear them say the trial would be in May in Montgomery, Alabama, at the request of Rob's lawyer, who didn't think that Rob could get a fair trial back in Wisconsin.

I called Ericka right away, but it went to her voicemail, which meant that she was at work. I couldn't help but wonder if George would go to Alabama for the trial.

I barely got to the restaurant in time for Grayson's meeting. His smile when I walked in made me glad that I'd made the effort. We helped ourselves to the breakfast buffet, and then Grayson very quickly got to the business at hand. He said the chamber president had been pleased with the results of the previous meeting.

"Just as a reminder, we have our Honors Dinner coming up in early spring," he announced. "We have an auction to raise money for the scholarship fund and any additional charities that we want to add." Grayson turned to me and said, "I think we could fit in the quilt for Charlie and Rachael if need be. I would want to get their permission before we do so, however."

"If you think it would work, I'd very much like to keep that in mind," I replied, touched by his thoughtfulness.

"They're good chamber members, and we certainly want them to be able to keep their business."

After that, we discussed a couple of changes to the bylaws that were going to be presented at the next meeting, and then someone made a motion to adjourn.

The others left, and Grayson asked me to stay a bit and enjoy my coffee.

"I really appreciate you coming, Claire."

"I think that getting this opportunity to auction off the club's quilt is another good reason to have contact with the business community and the chamber of commerce. Thanks for bringing it up."

"I promise to bid on it myself! I can always use another quilt."

I smiled.

"By the way, I got a lot of questions from Kelly after our last date."

"You did? Is that good?"

"Well, she suggested that you might want to come for dinner one night. She offered to fix spaghetti! I took that as a good sign."

We chuckled.

Grayson joked, "I didn't respond right away to her suggestion. If she thinks I'm too excited, she may feel the opposite!"

We refilled our coffee cups, and I told Grayson about the news report saying that Rob was being held in Alabama. He hadn't seen it, but also thought it was a good idea to keep Rob there. He thought that the publicity would be bad for the tourist trade.

"What's the latest on Charlie?"

"I'd bet that Harry will try bringing him home today or tomorrow. I'd better get back to my painting now. I'm glad that I came, and especially glad that we got to talk."

"Me too," he said as we walked out together.

Back on the porch, I made more progress on the painting. I started painting the sky, which would be such a sharp contrast to the red lighthouse. I took time for a bit of lunch around noon, and my phone rang. I saw Harry's name. He was probably calling to give me a report on Charlie. I picked it up, hopeful that Charlie had been released from the hospital once again.

"Claire?" His voice sounded different.

"Yes, Harry. What is it?"

"It's about Charlie."

"Did he come home?"

"He did come home, but we couldn't save him."

"Save him! What...?"

I could hear Harry take a deep breath. "I picked Charlie and Rachael up from the hospital. When we got to their property, Charlie insisted on stopping at the barn before driving up to the house, so I stopped the car. He wanted to get out, which I discouraged, but he insisted. Rachael and I sort of guided him because he wasn't steady on his feet."

"So what happened?"

"He made it about ten steps towards the barn and collapsed. We thought he was just weak or had stumbled, but he dropped to the ground. His hand went to his chest like he was in pain. I knew it was serious. Rachael called 911 right away, but when I helped adjust his head to make him more comfortable, I knew he was gone. I couldn't do a damn thing!" He began to sob heavily into the phone.

"Oh no! Charlie is gone? I'm just so shocked – and so sorry for you! How is Rachael?"

"She's definitely shocked. It was horrible," he recalled. "She ran around screaming like a chicken with her head chopped off until the ambulance came. They gave her something to calm her down."

I started crying. "Rachael, poor Rachael. Where is she now?"

"She's at home. I called her sister in Green Bay, and she came right away."

"Tell her that I'm on my way." I hung up the phone, grabbed my coat, and flew out the door.

Chapter 109

I looked at the clock in the car. It was three in the afternoon. I was driving much faster than I should, and there was still snow on most of the roads. I couldn't believe that Charlie was dead, and I couldn't imagine what Rachael was going through. What a horrible, horrible experience.

There were several cars parked in front of Rachael's house. I entered without knocking. There sat Rachael, surrounded by three women. When she saw me, she jumped out of her chair and ran into my arms. I couldn't understand a word she was saying between her sobs.

"Rachael, Rachael," I consoled her. "I am so, so sorry. You're exhausted. Let's sit down."

I held her shaking hand as we found a place to sit. Her two sisters then introduced themselves, and the other woman said she was a neighbor who had heard all of the commotion and come over to help. Rachael could hardly talk, which I guessed might be from the medication. One sister suggested that Rachael take a rest. Numbly, she agreed to try to take a nap. Just as that was decided, Harry came inside. Seeing that

Rachael was heading to the bedroom, he suggested that we go outside to talk.

"How could things get worse?" I said, frustrated. Harry shook his head. I could tell that he had been crying.

"Charlie was like the brother I never had," Harry shared. "I think I meant the same to him." He leaned against the porch post and rubbed his forehead as if it were throbbing.

"I can't stop thinking about Rachael," I said.

"I'll do everything I can. I just hope she doesn't make any rash decisions."

"I sense that you know their financial situation better than anyone at this point. Did Charlie have any insurance that Rachael will receive?"

He paused. "Yes, but I also know he borrowed against a policy to stay afloat. You need not worry. I'll get Rachael through this. In fact, you should get on home. There isn't much to do here right now. Rachael is close to her sister Ruth, and I think Ruth plans to stay here with her."

"That's good to hear. I hope she can get some rest. Please remind her that I'm here for her, and thanks for all you're doing, Harry." I gave him a big hug and headed to my car.

I drove home feeling like it was all a nightmare. I remembered Charlie's laugh and how he never met a stranger. His energy. His exuberance for life. How could it be that he was gone? My mind didn't want to believe the information that it had received.

When I got home, I wondered who else should know about Charlie's death. The quilt club would have to know. I went upstairs and dressed for bed even though it was still early in the evening. Dusk really mirrored my feelings at this point. I decided that I really needed to talk to my best friend.

I gave Cher a call, and the phone rang and rang. When she finally answered, I rushed through the sequence of events. She listened intently and immediately asked about Rachael.

"She's exhausted and resting. I have no idea how she really is. What should I do about the club?"

"You need to call Greta first thing in the morning. How is the quilt coming along?"

"Greta will be the last one to work on it, so I hope she doesn't let us down."

"I still can't believe that she offered to quilt it."

"Grayson said that if all else fails, we can auction the quilt off at a dinner that the chamber hosts."

"Oh, now you're talking! That will be a better audience. Folks like to show off and outbid each other at that event."

"Oh, I can't wait until you get here, Cher. I'm so, so sad."

"I know. I'll be there very soon. Please give Rachael a hug for me, and keep me posted, okay?"

"I will. Love you, Cher Bear."

"The same, Claire Bear."

Puff was sound asleep at the end of the bed. I put on my robe and went downstairs. The cabin was chilly with no fire in the fireplace. I went into the kitchen, made myself a glass of wine, and took it to the couch. Rachael. Poor Rachael. I got lost in my thoughts, and quietly, time just passed as I sat in the peaceful cabin.

I saw a light shine across the driveway that stirred me into awareness. Was someone turning around? I looked at the clock. It was eleven, much later than I would have guessed. I heard a car door slam. I got up from the couch and walked onto the porch. Who would be here at this hour? A chill came over me. This day had already offered too many surprises. Then there was a knock. Should I turn on the porch light or pretend not to be home? Given that the lights were on inside and that my car was in the driveway, they'd already know that I was home, so I felt that I had to answer the door. I turned on the porch light and couldn't believe my eyes. Was I dreaming?

"Austen! What are you doing here?"

WHITE GULL INN'S DOOR COUNTY CHERRY PIE

Crust:
2½ cups flour
1 tablespoon flour
1 cup vegetable shortening (Crisco)
4-5 tablespoons ice water

Filling:
4 cups pitted fresh or frozen tart Montmorency cherries*
¼ teaspoon almond extract
1¼ cup sugar
1½ tablespoons cornstarch
Preheat oven to 425 degrees.

Combine flour in a large bowl. Cut in shortening with a pastry blender until dough begins to stick together. Add ice water, one tablespoon at a time, and toss with a fork until all flour is moistened and pastry forms a slightly sticky ball. Divide dough in half and pat into 2 rounds. On a lightly floured surface, roll dough 2 inches larger than an inverted 9-inch pie plate. Place 1 round in the bottom of a pie plate.

To make filling, combine cherries and almond extract in a medium bowl. In a separate bowl, stir together sugar and cornstarch. Gently toss sugar mixture into cherries to combine. Pour filling into prepared pie crust. Cover with the remaining round of crust. Pinch edges and seal; trim excess dough. Cut several slits in top crust to allow steam to escape. Bake 35-40 minutes or until crust is golden brown and filling is bubbly.

*If using frozen cherries, drain and reserve ¼ cup juice. Combine cherries and reserved juice.

Frozen Montmorency cherries are available in some supermarkets and specialty food stores and can also be purchased directly from several Door County orchards. For more information on where Montmorency cherries are sold near you, please contact Seaquist Orchards in Ellison Bay, Wisconsin by emailing Robin Seaquist at robin@seaquistorchards.com.

Cozy up with more quilting mysteries from Ann Hazelwood...

WINE COUNTRY QUILT SERIES

After quitting her boring editing job, aspiring writer Lily Rosenthal isn't sure what to do next. Her two biggest joys in life are collecting antique quilts and frequenting the area's beautiful wine country. The murder of a friend results in Lily acquiring the inventory of a local antique store. Murder, quilts, and vineyards serve as the inspiration as Lily embarks on a journey filled with laughs, loss, and red-and-white quilts.

THE DOOR COUNTY QUILT SERIES

Meet Claire Stewart, a new resident of Door County, Wisconsin. Claire is a watercolor quilt artist and joins a prestigious small quilting club when her best friend moves away. As she grows more comfortable after escaping a bad relationship, new ideas and surprises abound as friendships, quilting, and her love life all change for the better.

Want more? Visit us online at ctpub.com